A Day at

Georgie and Armand's Place

By

Ian Brazee-Cannon

Based on

Characters and Concept

Created by

Bryan Hineser

A Day at Georgie and Armand's Place

Printed in the United States of America
First Printing, 2019

ISBN 9781696449199

Edited by Virginalee Berger

Cover Art By Chaz Kemp:
https://www.chazkemp.com/

Follow the author at:
https://www.facebook.com/IBCauthor/

Follow Georgie and Armand at:
https://www.facebook.com/gandaplace

Ian Brazee-Cannon

This book is dedicated

First and foremost to my boys, Quinn and Hayden.

Everything I do is dedicated to them,

As they play a huge part in inspiring me to

Create and be my best.

I hope I inspire them as well.

This book is also dedicated to

The vast crowd of creative people in my life.

As this book praises diversity,

I am privileged to have such

Diverse people around me,

Giving me inspiration by getting to experience

Their diverse forms of art and creativity

A Day at Georgie and Armand's Place

Characters:

Georgie (Hax'georget'krestdawn)- Dragon Master Mage. Long-time lover of Armand. Co-creator/co-owner of Georgie and Armand's Place.

Armand- Dragon Master Mage. Long-time lover of Georgie. Co-creator/co-owner of Georgie and Armand's Place.

Sna- Master Mage who serves as a Sacred Gatekeeper for Georgie and Armand.

Mmm'ddeliommm - Master Mage who serves as a Sacred Gatekeeper for Georgie and Armand.

Pods – An expert of steampunk technology who serves as a Sacred Gatekeeper for Georgie and Armand.

Myts- An expert of computer-based technology who serves as a Sacred Gatekeeper for Georgie and Armand.

Lonna - Pods' apprentice.

Stephan Riley- Accountant from Earth.

Alejandra- A freelance Spirit Guide/mage/bounty hunter.

Kwando - Alejandra's spirit advisor/assistant

Orr'koor'lon- Aquatic freelance computers/high technology expert

Shea Blossk- Androgynous crime lord.

Kra- A flying messenger in the Hotel.

A Day at Georgie and Armand's Place

Fringe- An extremely religious warrior

White-Star- Freelance soldier for hire.

Gateway- White-Star's son. A powerful Master Mage.

Han'Gra - Warrior woman. Worshipper of the great god Rya'Je, overseer of existence.

Conrad Pendragon- Former politician turned dimensional traveling Pop Star. A favorite entertainer for Georgie and Armand's Place.

Novick - Manager of the Bonita Lobby, a subterranean lobby of the Hotel.

Liemen – Head Librarian of the Grimm Hall Library in the Hotel.

The Nine Masters of the Realms:

Archmage Lionope - Member of a short, four-armed, orange-skinned species.

The Coulder – A large bald humanoid mage with black stripes all over his body.

Klacki'Nicoo – A plump, little green-skinned imp mage who prefers to float around instead of walking.

Master Joh – Appears as only a blurred face and silver cloak.

Dwar Kwando – A blue-skinned spirit guide.

Magus Ebright – A soft spoken, elven lady.

The Enchantress Allidy – Appears as an attractive female version of the species of the person looking at her.

L'Jerdak – A raven-haired mage.

Royal Chatwell – A fur-covered, quadruped with long orange hair and large black eyes.

Their apprentices:

Hax'georget'krestdawn - Archmage Lionope's apprentice.

Armand - The Coulder's apprentice.

Sna - Klacki'Nicoo's apprentice.

Mmm'ddeliommm - Master Joh 's apprentice.

Jesillip – L'Jerdak's apprentice.

Je'Garramone – Magus Ebright's apprentice.

Rodfire – Royal Chatwell's apprentice.

Schilt – Dwar Kwando's apprentice.

A Day at Georgie and Armand's Place

Pronouns-

Masculine -	Feminine -	Neutral-
He	She	Ze
Him	Her	Zir
His	Hers	Zirs
Mr.	Ms, Miss, Mrs	Mx.
Master	Mistress	Honored One

A Day at Georgie and Armand's Place

The Day Begins

Georgie shook off the fuzzy cloud of sleep as he lifted his head off of his love's comforting black scales. It was a rare morning for him to awaken and find the slumbering form of Armand still asleep in their nest of pillows. He gently brushed one of his ivory talons along Armand's neck. The day before had been a long one of negotiations with a tribe of mystic, sentient water plants. They wished to use one of the landlocked ballrooms for their ceremonies in which they would need to flood the space and allow for a special species of algae to fully mature, in a two-year ritual. None of which would have been that hard to accommodate, except they had no form of acceptable payment to cover such an expensive undertaking. The whole experience had left Armand grumpy, so Georgie had turned off the wakeup alarm to get some extra rest.

With a flick of his tail, Georgie knocked a block of lavender-scented essence into the

A Day at Georgie and Armand's Place

chamber's smoke pit. Soon, the room filled with the light scent.

Georgie took a few moments to watch the love of his life sleep. He was mesmerized by Armand's dark black scales shifting with every breath. He let his claw barely touch Armand's cool scales. The attractive contrast of Georgie's brilliant red scales against the darkness of Armand's always comforted him.

Trying to move as little as possible, Georgie gathered up the various pillows they had pushed out of their nest during the night. He had always been puzzled by the desire of other dragons to sleep on piles of gold and jewels. Such things were meant to be used as adornments and decorations, not bedding. He and Armand had collected thousands of pillows, from thousands of worlds, and rotated through them on a weekly basis. Georgie was quite proud of his pillow closet, which was larger than most of the other rooms in the Hotel, although to be fair, every chamber in Georgie and Armand's residence were spectacular. It was one of the perks of owning an interdimensional hotel. While their sleep chambers were simple, generally a large pit for pillows in the center with their smoke pit for warmth and atmosphere, their other personal rooms were much more elaborate.

Above the bed, built into the chamber's ceiling, was Armand's personal clock. Only Georgie and Armand knew how to read it. Various shapes moved by via intricate clockwork across the ever-changing background of their 'secret' world's horizon, which they based the Hotel's clocks upon. Both Armand and Georgie could look up at it and know the time and date on over a hundred different worlds relative to the Hotel.

The symbol they called the Forever Star was crossing the line known as the Prosperity Tree, which was nearly an hour after Armand had set the alarm for. Georgie knew he would be cross when he woke, but the silly, overworked boy needed his sleep. The Sign of Order appeared above the Prosperity Tree and Georgie realized that Armand must have set up a second alarm.

The deep ringing of a series of large bells echoed through the chamber.

Armand's black spear of a head lifted from his coiled form. He opened his eyes. A couple blinks cleared the crud from his deep yellow orbs.

A Day at Georgie and Armand's Place

"Awake already?" Armand asked, followed by a massive yawn that displayed his impressive teeth. It was a sight that many creatures would cower in fear from.

"Actually my dear, you've slept in," Georgie replied.

Armand came fully awake. He twisted his head to look up at the dome ceiling.

"Is that the time?" Armand slithered out of the nest. He arched his back, stretching out his arms, legs and his massive bat-like wings. "You should have woken me for first shift."

"You needed the sleep, silly. The Hotel will run just fine without you there to micromanage it all."

"We must function beyond such luxuries. We have a business to run." Armand rose on his back legs and stretched. "You need to be focused on that."

"And you need to relax more."

"We do not have time for rehashing old arguments," The dark form of Armand shrunk down. Where the great black dragon had stood was now a solidly-built, dark-skinned man.

"One that has never been settled," Georgie replied. He, too, had shifted into human form.

Now his skin was light with a mild red tint to it and a wild seeding of dark red hair covered his head.

Both of them could assume any form they desired, but they found the human form to be their favorite. It was the most common basic body style that they had run across in their explorations of the dimensions, which meant it was the most comfortable for the greatest amount of beings to deal with. It also was a highly practical form that worked well enough in a large variety of environments. Then there was the fashion issue. While many beings wore clothing of various types and many had embraced the concept of fashion, none so much as the humanoids, and while it may have been considered something of a perversion among most dragons to wear clothes for anything, outside of being polite to other species, Georgie and Armand loved their fashions.

Armand wasted no time. He moved into their clothing chamber to pick out his suit for the day. Georgie followed, sifting through more colorful clothing.

"Will you make it to the show this afternoon?" Georgie asked.

A Day at Georgie and Armand's Place

"As always, I shall try, but no promises" Armand answered. "Which stage are you using today?"

"The Peachy Pegasus, of course. Conrad is going to perform."

Georgie walked out onto their balcony. The portal view was set on the Groatyan Gardens, part of one of the methane-breathing wings. The tall orange spikes of the Dysetti bushes always fascinated Georgie. He loved their smooth outer layers, and how the secretions of the plant were both poisonous and medicinal, depending on the species and preparation methods. They were beautiful to look at, but their spines were strong and sharp, able to pierce the skin of most creatures. It was a plant of contradictions that normally did not do well away from Groat. Georgie had personally taken on the project and by working with the greatest gardeners across all realities, they had created a setup where the Dysetti thrived.

Georgie took the controls and browsed through the Hotel. From their balcony one could focus on any public areas of the Hotels and, if deemed necessary the private areas as well. They knew enough to respect their customers' privacy and kept the settings to the public spaces as a default.

"Did we get caught up with the Bloof'Kins?" Georgie asked.

"Yes," Armand replied. "We worked it out, and they agreed to only release their ink in their own chambers, not the open water."

"Good. I don't feel like going aquatic today."

"You do look cute with gills, though."

"You think I look cute in all my forms."

"Of course you do."

"After all these centuries, you still find me appealing?"

"You have only grown more attractive with age," Armand said as he came up behind Georgie and gave him a kiss, before returning to finish dressing.

"Now," Armand stated. "I expect Alejandra will be sending me a formal request for access to that unsubstantiated world for the Neewoll'ah Imperium. I will take care of investigating the odd reports concerning the Grimm Hall Library and Rebellious Soul. Liemen claims a 'black spot' has been moving from book to book. Lee Ball is claiming part of his shop

A Day at Georgie and Armand's Place

keeps shuddering. I have three detailed audits scheduled for today. So I need you to do a standard audit of the group 3435 lobbies. We're a little behind with them. Start wherever you want, but let's get that done this morning, before your show. Shouldn't take more than a couple of hours."

"Oh, that sounds like a pleasant start to the day," Georgie replied, looking through a rack of blouses. "It's been a few weeks since I was on that side of the Hotel. I can start with Nona'He Mountain. It's one of my favorite lobbies."

"Every lobby is one of your favorites."

"We just know how to create beautiful lobbies together. I should be able to get away with looking festive there. A little playful blouse feels right for today. Have you seen the one Suked gave me?"

"Most likely in that stack of boxes over there," Armand gestured. "Do we need to expand your side again? It's getting crowded."

Georgie looked up at the three levels of walkways that made up their closet, lined with filled to overflowing clothing racks.

"I'm always willing to expand my wardrobe space, dear."

Ian Brazee-Cannon

A quick browse through the stack of garment boxes waiting to be shorted revealed the teal blouse Georgie had been looking for. He raised it up to the light and looked at the elaborately embroidered purple unicorn design. The dazzling beads that had been used for the mane and horn sparkled in the lantern light.

"A little tacky isn't it?" Armand remarked.

"Well, I like it."

Armand, now fully clothed, walked over to Georgie. Georgie reached out and straightened Armand's light purple tie. He looked sharp in his dark blue suit with silver dragons embroidered on each lapel, with a small handkerchief in the breast pocket that matched the tie.

"As handsome as always," Georgie said.

"I'm starting my day already behind schedule. I should be mad at you, you know."

"And yet, you'll forgive me." Georgie moved in and embraced Armand.

Armand gave Georgie a kiss on the forehead. "You need to get going as well. We have a hotel to run."

"I know. It'll be just a few more minutes."

A Day at Georgie and Armand's Place

"You never get ready that fast," Armand said, then set the controls and disappeared through the opening.

Georgie spent twenty minutes choosing the rest of his first outfit for the day. He sat at the make-up desk for another twenty putting his face on. While he could use magic for the same effect, he much preferred the ritual of make-up. Nothing fancy at this point, just foundation, light mascara and eyeshadow, and a little blush. He would save the heavier makeup for the show.

It took Georgie little time to pin his hair back, yet he spent nearly half an hour trying on wigs before he was satisfied with his look for the morning. He had settled for a subdued light brown loose wave style.

When he was finally satisfied, Georgie left through the balcony exit. He paused at the railing and looked down into the Hotel.

For most, the view Georgie had would be overwhelming and confusing. Multiple levels of walkways were criss-crossed through a vast expanse. Each walkway was modeled in the architectural style that fit with the theme/dimensional needs of its floor. This was only one of the countless such sections of the

Hotel that the private residence could be set to overlook. Only Georgie, Armand and a handful of truly trusted individuals ever got to see this view.

Georgie turned the wheel so that the image of two dragons, one red, one black, both atop a mountain, was at the top. He shifted the focus to a busy lobby with a colorful variety of beings moving around it. He placed his hand on a globe next to the wheel and pushed down on it. The gate opened, revealing a passageway floating in space. Georgie stepped casually into the opening.

Georgie walked through the opening into the lobby, waving it closed once he was clear. Where the opening had been were now rocky walls, indistinguishable from the rest of the lobby. There was a healthy flow of creatures hustling about on whatever tasks they were caught up in. The staff was busy at their stations, as this section of the Hotel always seemed to be popular.

Behind one of the counters stood a silver-skinned humanoid with a red inner glow, ready to help customers.

"Good morning, Nirron."

"Morning sir," Nirron replied. "Are you working the lobby?"

A Day at Georgie and Armand's Place

"Just here for a quick audit and maybe sneak in some mingling."

A familiar sense of comfort filled Georgie as he stepped behind the counter. He loved the lobbies. They were where you got to meet the grand variety of beings that passed through. There was nothing more exciting to Georgie than meeting new people.

Ian Brazee-Cannon

Accountant Out of Water

In the smoky light of dawn Stephan woke up,
looked to his right and smiled. The young lady
who was fast asleep next to him was beautiful. He
had just met Alejandra a few days before, but the
two of them had hit it off and soon found
themselves lovers.

Their relationship had developed more
quickly than any he had been in before, but
Stephan had no complaints.

He got up and took care of his bathroom
needs and then headed for his kitchen nook to
make breakfast. It felt good to have someone to
cook for besides himself.

"Is that the time?" Came a shout from
Stephan's bedroom.

A Day at Georgie and Armand's Place

Several seconds later a young half-dressed woman with messed red hair rushed out of the bedroom and into the bathroom.

"Damn it," came a shout from the bathroom. "Stupid, stupid, stupid, stupid."

"Alex? What's wrong?" Asked Stephan.

A chorus of incoherent grumbling answered.

"Alex?"

The redhead rushed out of the bathroom. Her hair was now back in a rushed ponytail. She pulled on her blouse followed by her vest and searched the area around the sofa.

"By the damned spirits where are my shoes?"

"I think they ended up over by the TV," Stephan replied.

"Thanks."

Stephan stood watching Alejandra while holding a plate filled with freshly cooked breakfast goodies.

Alejandra stood up and worked at smoothing out the wrinkles in her clothes.

"Lost souls. I guess this will have to do," She said to herself.

"Is everything okay?"

Alejandra turned to face Stephan with an apologetic smile on her face.

"Wow, that smells really good," Alejandra said as she noticed the food. "And I really wish I could stay and enjoy, but I have a… Prior work-related appointment I have to get to."

"Okay…"

"I really got to get going now. I… well I'm not sure when I'll be in this area again. This little vacation is over. My work takes my all over and often I have no control of where I end up."

There was silence as Stephan stood holding the plate with a blank look on his face.

Alejandra gave Stephan a kiss and took a piece of toast off the plate.

"You've been great," she said as she hustled across the room. "I really do wish we could have more time together."

As Alejandra headed out the door, she turned and blew Stephan a kiss, not quite closing the door behind her.

Stephan absently put the plate down and walked over to close the door.

"Yes, I know I'm running late," Alejandra's voice could be heard coming from down the hall. "The desk staff knows to just send the client up to my room and make sure he's comfortable until I show up for our session.

"No, I don't think this is going to be too demanding. Should be a standard quick job. He forwarded what he wanted and there was nothing out of the ordinary to it."

"Is she a? No way. I'm misunderstanding something here," Stephan thought.

"He'll get the services he's willing to pay for, and with my reputation, he already knows it'll be discreet and worth the money. I'll be at the Hotel shortly."

"Okay, I did not hook up with a prostitute," Stephan mumbled to himself. "No way. I'm just misreading this..."

Stephan grabbed his shoes and pulled them on as he climbed out the window. He rushed down the fire escape and around the corner. He caught Alejandra crossing the street and was able to keep her in sight while keeping his distance.

He followed her through the city. There were not too many twists and turns in her path. The whole time Alejandra was having a somewhat aggressive conversation. There was no phone in her hand and Stephan didn't remember her having a Bluetooth. As Stephan thought about it, he realized he never saw her with a phone and she never gave him her number.

After about twenty minutes Alejandra entered a doorway that Stephan had not noticed before. In fact, he was sure that he would have looked right past the nondescript building without a second thought on any other day.

Outside the building Stephan paused and gave it a once over. He could find no clue as to just what the building housed. No signs were present to reveal the name of the place. There were no windows or architectural adornments present. It was just a door resting within a plain brick wall, in an area people continuously walked by without noticing it.

"What kind of a hotel is this?" Stephan pushed open the door and walked through.

*****

A wave of dizziness washed over Stephan as he emerged into the lobby. His vision was blurred. He took a moment to blink. The Hotel came into focus around him.

A deep red carpet covered the floors, merging with the wood paneled walls, while

A Day at Georgie and Armand's Place

evenly spaced traditional chandeliers illuminated the lobby and the furniture was simple, yet comfortable looking. Something about the setup was familiar to Stephan, but he couldn't put his finger on it.

Not far away Alejandra leaned on a counter talking to a stout effeminate man who was clearly wearing a wig, dressed in a light blue flowery blouse that had a purple unicorn embroidered on it.

"He should be up in the room waiting for you," the man was saying. "He was a rather unpleasant sort, though. You are talented enough that I don't see why you do not hold out for a better quality of client."

"A girl's gotta make money somehow," Alejandra replied. "Besides Georgie, Kwando's the one who finds our clients. I'm just the talent in all this."

"Is he with you?" Georgie asked, noticing Stephan for the first time.

Alejandra turned. "What in the void are you doing here?"

With his presence now known, Stephan walked straight over to Alejandra. He knew it was now or never. While he hated confrontation, he pushed through his doubts and jumped right into it while he was still worked up enough to say everything he wanted to with an uncharacteristic sense of aggression to give his words strength.

"I know we only met a few days ago, but there was clearly something between us. And while I don't really know you that well, I can tell that you're an incredible woman. You don't need to sell yourself. I may be just an accountant, but I can help you start over…"

"Wait a moment, what do you think I do?" Alejandra asked.

"Personally, I find this all so romantic," Georgie said, a silly smile overwhelming his face.

"I don't want to hear anything from you, mister girlie man,' Stephan replied. "You're clearly just an enabler in all this."

"What did you call me?"

"Stephan, this really is not the right time or place," Alejandra said, attempting to lead Stephan away.

"You're going to let this sissy intimidate you? What does he have over you?"

"Okay, that's enough!" Georgie roared.

The response that Stephan was preparing vanished wherever unspoken words go, as a large shadow fell on him. His nature quickly returned to a more passive level.

Where the effeminate form of Georgie had been, there now stood a twenty-foot-tall winged, serpentine creature. Stephan barely noticed the brilliant red scales as his focus was drawn straight to the massive mouth filled with sharp teeth that were part of the head just inches from his face.

"You will show me respect when in my hotel. Is that understood?"

Standing stiller than Stephan had ever known possible, he slowly nodded his head. The massive creature shrunk down and once more the unassuming human form of Georgie stood before him.

"Now let us try to talk like civilized beings," Georgie said as he readjusted his wig.

"I think it might be better if I take it from here Georgie." Alejandra led Stephan into a cavernous hallway, which Stephan had not noticed before. "I think you need a little rest now."

"That was a…a…a…dragon?"

"Yes, Georgie is a dragon. That's why it's best not to upset him."

Stephan halted and looked around. The hallways did not look right. In fact, nothing

around him looked like a hotel any more. He
turned to glance back at the lobby and saw that it
was nothing at all like what he remembered.
Instead of the single door he came through, that
wall now housed doors stretching out in all
directions, hundreds of them. What he had seen as
red carpet was now intricate stone work,
impregnated with precious stones to create a mural
depicting two dragons, one black, one red,
standing atop a mountain, which glimmered as the
light hit it. The walls were carved stone, that
reminded Stephan of something out of a horror
movie, yet the comfortable lighting countered any
horrific effects.

"Had your skin always been blue?"
Stephan asked looking back at Alejandra.

"Georgie's outburst shattered the illusion
spells for you. We've a lot to talk about, but first I
have a meeting I'm late for."

It felt as though Stephan was seeing
clearer than ever, while what he was seeing made
no sense at all to him. Moving in all directions
through the oddly crisscrossing passageways of a
multitude of architectural styles, hinting at a
structure far more massive than should have been
possible with what he had seen from outside, were

A Day at Georgie and Armand's Place

countless creatures, many of which defied description.

Stephan found comfort in looking at Alejandra as they walked. He had quickly gotten used to her blue skin, which he found more attractive than he would have thought. Her eyes were now a deep violet, which Stephan found pleasing. With all the insanity that was going on around him, Alejandra somehow felt reasonable.

Alejandra stopped at an ivory door, opened it and entered the chamber beyond.

"Kwando, I need you to keep an eye on my friend here while I talk with the client," Alejandra said as she disappeared into the room.

Stephan froze right inside the door. Instead of a bed, mini fridge, dresser or television as Stephan expected to find in a hotel room, he found himself standing on a cobblestone path that led around a massive four-tiered fountain, with a base large enough to swim in. The room was carpeted in a soft orange grass, flowering vines draped the walls, with large cushions as the only pieces of furniture to be found. The smell of vanilla/nutmeg dominated.

Alejandra vanished into a side room.

Stephan tried to follow her only to find his way blocked by a transparent man with no legs.

"Funny, Alejandra is not one to pick up pathetic strays," the ghost remarked. "Have a seat and behave yourself until she's done with the client."

Stephan stumbled back and found a cushion to collapse into. He silently watched the floating figure, his eyes wide.

"What's with you now?"

"You're a…a ghost."

"Ah, we have a bright one here," Kwando said with a smug expression. "What did you think you would find in the employ of a Spirit Guide?"

"A what?" Stephan replied.

"Oh, this is going to make for an interesting conversation. I shall let Alejandra deal with it. Just stay there and be a good simple-minded creature."

Stephan tried to relax and gather his thoughts. He tried more than once to close his eyes and wake up from the dream he was obviously trapped in, failing with each attempt.

He opened his eyes at the wrong time and saw an eight-foot-tall black skeleton wearing a red blouse with a cream colored skirt walk by.

A Day at Georgie and Armand's Place

Alejandra led her client to the door as casually as ever.

Alejandra turned as she closed the door. "That's dealt with. Time for a bath."

Alejandra stripped off her clothes and made her way to the fountain.

"Would you like to join me?"

Stephan awkwardly climbed out of the cushion and begun to remove his clothes. Out of the corner of his eye he caught Kwando moving towards the fountain and ceased his disrobing.

"I'm good," Stephan said. He found himself trying to look at something other than Alejandra's naked body.

"Are you doing okay?" Alejandra asked as she lowered herself into the cool water. "I understand this place might be a little overwhelming for someone new to it all."

"A little bit."

"You seem nervous. We've been intimate. There's nothing to be shy about."

Stephan eyed Kwando then looked back at Alejandra, "I'm good, really."

"Is Kwando making you uncomfortable? Relax, once you cross over you're no longer driven by the desires of the flesh."

Kwando gave Stephan an innocent smile.

"I'll be fine," Stephan replied.

"At least sit over here so we can talk," Alejandra said as she raised herself out of the water and patted the edge of the fountain.

Stephan found a seat on the fountain with his back to Alejandra. He looked around to find something comforting to look at.

"You followed me here remember. If you want to be part of my life you're going to need to relax," Alejandra said as she swam up behind him and started to rub his back.

"Dragons… ghosts… walking black skeletons… Spirit guide… An impossible hotel…" Stephan started to rub his forehead. "I've yet to find something here that allows me to relax."

"I guess it's time for an explanation of it all," Alejandra started.

"This is Georgie and Armand's Place. It is an interdimensional hotel. Georgie and Armand are dragons and high-level master mages. They may be the only ones who know just how many worlds the Hotel is connected to, but most estimate it to be over a hundred thousand. So the first thing you'll need to get used to is encountering beings that are very much not human.

"I am a Spirit Guide, which is a highly skilled position on my world."

"So... you're not even human?" Stephan turned to examine Alejandra.

"Interestingly enough, my world is an alternate version of yours," Alejandra said with a smile. "It's just that at some point mystic energies were what shaped my world while yours ended up going the tech route. Unlike your world, on mine we live in harmony with the spirits. Guides like myself have a strong bond with them and are able to sense spiritual energy and to some degree manipulate it. Spirits like Kwando search us out in order to keep from fully crossing over. If they can present a strong enough case to justify our intervention, we help to stabilize them between worlds."

There was a moment of silence.

"Do you have any questions?"

Stephan turned and looked into Alejandra's violet eyes. He had found the one thing that did relax him

"What is a Spirit Guide doing in this place?"

"I do freelance work. You'd be surprised at how useful my skills are for a variety of services. Like Mr. Zoon'kilk, who has hired me to confirm that a world is truly lifeless in order to lay a claim to said world."

"That makes as much sense as anything around here."

"Georgie and Armand's Place makes a lot of sense really," Alejadndra replied. "If you understand the concept of multiple realities. It's a place where people from all manner of words can meet up, intermingle and be part of a community where you can find something new every day just by taking a walk."

"Sounds to me like a good way to ensure chaos."

"Not really. It's easy to get along with each other by simply following the basic rules. You're free to do just about anything you wish, as long as you don't violate other individuals' freedoms. So no stealing, fighting or killing allowed in the Hotel. Respect privacy. Oh, and no teleportation or time travel on hotel grounds."

Stephan gave a doubtful look and said,"Time travel? Really?"

A Day at Georgie and Armand's Place

"There are several time travelers who are regulars here. I generally avoid them as their conversations can get confusing. I find the whole wibbly-wobbly mess of time travel to be a bit much."

"You'd think it'd be hard to enforce any security in a place this massive," Stephan remarked.

"You've seen Georgie in his natural form," Alejandra said with a mild laugh. "That serves as a fairly big deterrent to misbehaving. Besides, they have a good amount of spells in place to keep everyone from being able to break the rules."

"This day has just been too much."

"I think I can help you relax." Alejandra smiled, lifted herself up to Stephan and gave him a deep kiss. She motioned Kwando to leave, as she took to the task of unbuttoning Stephan's shirt. Stephan put up no fight as he was stripped and pulled into the soothing waters of the fountain.

*****

"This is not your best thought out plan," Kwando said. He was impatiently floating in a circle around Alejandra and Stephan.

"He either joins me for the job or hangs out here with you."

Kwando and Stephan looked each other in the eyes. Stephan gave a smug smile.

"Fine, just don't get too emotional on me when he meets a gruesome fate," Kwando remarked.

"I can take care of myself just fine."

"I wish I were going along to see you try to live up to those words."

"Enough you two," Alejandra moved between the two of them. She was now dressed in a tan top that showed off her midriff, with black pants of some light fabric and a dagger strapped to her right thigh. She referred to these are her work clothes. "We need to get going. I've already got Orr'koor'lon on retainer. Best not to keep him waiting."

Once again Stephan was led through the Hotel. He stayed close to Alejandra, still unsure about everything around him.

A Day at Georgie and Armand's Place

The hallways soon turned to cold, sterile metal, lit by strong artificial light. Stephan felt as if they had entered a secret military base.

"These tech sections are so ugly," Alejandra commented. "I'll never understand how anything can live in such an environment."

"I find technology comforting myself."

"Just wait."

Alejandra knocked on a door. The door slid open.

"Yes, yes, come in girl. I am almost ready," came an artificial voice from inside.

Alejandra gestured for Stephan to enter first. He quickly realized there was to be no end to the surprises still waiting for him.

Stephan found himself standing before the oddest aquarium he had ever seen. He walked into the small area of the room outside of the aquarium and moved up to the glass.

Inside the water instead of fake coral or colorful rocks, there were a series of chambers connected via tubes. Inside each chamber were various platforms he could only guess as to their use. One chamber had a set of video screens with control panels for them.

In the water swam an octopus or not an octopus. At least it was something close, very octopus-like. It moved head first through the tubing, its various legs pushing it smoothly through the water. Stephan had a hard time figuring out why he knew this was not just a regular old octopus like he had often seen at the local aquarium. There were some differences in its shape and movements- the head seemed noticeably larger in proportion to the body and not as spongy. Stephan also noticed that half the tentacles ended in double appendages.

The creature swam to the glass and looked down at Stephan.

"Not really an impressive specimen, even for a biped," came the mechanical voice.

"Excuse me?"

"Don't play into it. Orr'koor'lon thinks we're clumsy creatures that evolution was unkind to."

"Well, you are, my dear. Although, you can be good company at times."

"Orr'koor'lon is an octopus?"

"A what?" The artificial voice asked.

"They're invertebrates that live in the seas of Earth... My world"

A Day at Georgie and Armand's Place

"It is not uncommon to see similar evolutionary paths across the various worlds," Alejandra replied. "There are some forms, such as ours, that can be found repeated in many realities."

Orr'koor'lon swam over to a section of the aquarium containing what looked to be a smaller aquarium on an odd metal table which Stephan for a moment thought was some kind of gaming/entertainment system until he realized the controls were inside the small aquarium.

Orr'koor'lon lifted the smaller aquarium up, which was apparently attached by hinges to the table. He then entered the aquarium and closed it behind him while a section of the larger aquarium wall opened up, revealing a shimmering green field in the opening. The 'table' took several steps and moved through the green field. Only a little water leaked out as Orr'koor'lon emerged in his exosuit.

"Okay, now that is cool," Stephan remarked.

Orr'koor'lon looked up at Stephan from inside his exosuit. "Odd. The temperature is pleasant enough. Why is that a concern of yours?"

"Uh, it's just an expression."

Orr'koor'lon stared at Stephan with eyes that were far more focused than any octopus he had ever seen. The two stood giving each other a full once over. Stephan became more aware of all the non-octopus like aspects of Orr'koor'lon. Outside of the noticeably sturdier outer shell, each of his front four arms split off at the ends into two appendages, which he was using to manipulate the controls of his suit. Stephan had also never seen a green and grey striped octopus, but he could not say such a thing did not exist on his world.

"Okay boys, let's head over to the Peachy Pegasus and do the preliminary work," Alejandra said.

*****

Walking down the halls with a blue skinned woman and a not-an-octopus in an exosuit felt odd to Stephan. It made him feel even more out of place to realize that none of the passing creatures took a second look at them. For everyone else in the Hotel, such a group was nothing special.

"Just like comic con, only a whole lot weirder," Stephan mumbled.

A Day at Georgie and Armand's Place

He found himself being led into a place that finally felt familiar to him. There were tables with groups of chairs around them, with a big stage dominating one wall. Various creatures were moving around, preparing the place for the day's business. Outside of the decor that consisted of a great many paintings that Stephan decided were based off some other world mythology, and the vast collection of species, this was a restaurant. It even had what was clearly a bar.

A large pink teddy bear with purple antennae walked onto the stage. The place had not opened yet, but Alejandra had friends working there, who let her do her business outside of serving hours.

"Okay staff of the Peachy Pegasus, you're in for a treat today. The one and only Conrad Pendragon is going to do his warm up session for the show now. So keep working and get this place ready for the real show, while you enjoy the live music."

The gathered staff cheered as the teddy bear left the stage to be replaced by a very handsome looking human male. Stephan eased himself into a chair, seeing more aspects of what he considered normalcy.

"I just spent some time on a little world called Derovial," Pendragon said once the crowd had quieted down enough. "I learned a lot about music and the power of sound from their chanting skills. Be ready for a deep experience."

Stephan found Pendragon's voice to be pleasant and comforting. He found himself excited about hearing this performer he never knew existed before.

The series of squeaks and chirps that followed caused Stephan to grimace in discomfort.

"What the hell is that noise?" Stephan asked.

"That spawn of a mutant," Alejandra relied. "Pendragon actually learned Derovian Chanting. And damned souls, he's good at it. I'm already feeling aroused."

"Actually I find this to be far better than the man's usual fair of nonsense," Orr'koor'lon remarked. "Sounds almost like a mating song, though."

"It is. It's the mating song of the Derovians. A strong one." Alejandra put her hands to her ears and recited an incantation. She removed her hands and let out of sigh of relief. "Okay, that blocks it out. Now we can get to business, although we may have to stop back at my room before heading out."

Alejandra's hand fell to Stephan's thigh and gripped down.

"Did you forget something there?" Orr'koor'lon asked.

"Let's just get on to business."

Alejandra produced a crystal and moved her hand over it. The image of a landscape appeared above the crystal.

"This is Plot 243, a world recently discovered by the Neewoll'ah Imperium. It is an 'unsubstantiated' world. I have asked Loy to get authority from Armand for us to journey there. The Hotel will, of course, want a full exploration report and the Neewall'ah are interested in gaining exportation and naming rights. There are no signs of civilization, so it should be a simple confirmation job."

"Confirming what?" Asked Stephan.

"That there are not indigenous sentients with a claim to the world. I will do a check on spiritual energies and Orr'koor'lon will do a tech check. It's fairly routine. Should only take a few hours."

"You two are going to check out a whole world in just a few hours?"

"Beings with skills like ours know how to be efficient and thorough. With the right technology and spells, it takes little effort to confirm an entire planet is void of sentients."

Stephan was about to reply when a creature flew down and landed in front of him. He jumped back and raised his hand preparing to swat the pest away.

"What's her problem?" the creature asked.

"Actually Loy, Stephan is male."

"Whatever. You all smell alike to me," Loy replied.

Stephan watched as the winged creature, who looked like an orange, four-inch-long, lizard standing on its hind legs, stared back at him.

"Is there something wrong with him?"

"His first day at the Hotel. Are we good to go?"

"The big guy said he'll have someone there in an hour to open it up for you."

"Good, that gives us time." Alejandra got up and pulled Stephan to his feet. "We'll meet back at the unassigned portal in an hour."

A Day at Georgie and Armand's Place

Stephan followed Alejandra obediently.

Back at her room Alejandra threw open the doors and yelled, "Kwando, stay the void out of here."

Stephan allowed himself to be stripped and thrown onto the floor.

"I like this aggressive side to you," Stephan remarked.

"You can thank Pendragon for that. Those chants are powerful things," Alejandra said as she stripped off her clothes. "Now just shut up and enjoy."

*****

Fifty minutes later Alejandra led an out of breath Stephan, sporting a huge smile on his face, through the maze of hallways.

"I am so going to destroy Pendragon," Alejandra mumbled. "Derovian Chanting should be outlawed."

Orr'koor'lon was waiting with a tall, solidly built, dark skinned man wearing a suit that Stephan found impressive, even though he was at a loss as to why he did so. Next to them floated a purple ball with a row of three black horns on its top, and what looked like nostrils on the front. Four tentacles, two on each side, emerged from the ball. Moss like material hung down from its bottom in a rough beard.

"So this is the one who upset Georgie," the well-dressed man said, his voice as stiff as his demeanor.

"Yes," Alejandra replied. "Stephan, this is Armand. He is Georgie's partner in both business and life."

Stephan stumbled as he backed away in reflex.

"He's a…"

"Yes, I am a dragon," Armand said. "Now if we can conclude with the trivialities, I do have other matters to attend to."

"If all is approved," came a voice from the floating ball.

"Alejandra, do you agree to the terms?"

"Yes, I agree to the standard exploration terms of the Hotels."

"Approval granted. Sna, go ahead and open the portal."

The tentacles of the floating ball stiffened out from its body forming an 'X'. The ball began to spin like a saw blade. A doorway took form in the wall behind them.

The ball stopped spinning. Its tentacles gestured towards the door, which opened.

"When you are ready to return, just knock and call my name."

"Time to earn our pay people," Alejandra said as she and Orr'koor'lon led Stephan through the door.

*****

"What just happened?" Stephan asked.

"You mean back there with Sna?"

"The talking ball."

"Yes, that was Sna," Alejandra explained. "One of the Sacred Gatekeepers of the Hotel. They're mages, or masters of tech and such, depending on the area they oversee, entrusted by Georgie and Armand to help with the overall security of the Hotel."

Stephan nodded his head slightly in understanding, then remarked, "It was a floating ball,."

"I get the impression Georgie and Armand went out of their way to find the most unique mages they could for the Gatekeepers. I've only met a few as far as I am aware of. Each of them unique though."

Stephan paused and looked around. They had emerged from a doorway that was standing all alone in the middle of a rocky wasteland. The soil and rocks had an orange tint to them, but otherwise felt normal to Stephan. What little vegetation there was seemed limited to small, twiggy bushes with brown needles and patches of blue moss. There were no signs of animal life.

"At least this place feels Earth-like," Stephan reflected.

"This world is disgustingly dry," Orr'koor'lon replied. "I will be greatly relaxed with a quick return."

"Let's get this over with," Alejandra said. "Let's get to a higher elevation and begin."

The three of them made their way to the top of a nearby hill. Stephan was surprised at the mobility of Orr'koor'lon's suit and how it had no issues traversing the rocky terrain.

The view from the top of the hill was both breathtaking and depressing. You could easily see for miles around, as there was little in the way of obstacles. The land was mostly flat and barren

A Day at Georgie and Armand's Place

with the orange tint everywhere, giving little definition to the landscape.

The red sky was mostly empty. There were a few small clouds off in the distance. The world's sun could be seen, but something in the atmosphere distorted the light, weakening the impact and distorting the size and shape.

Alejandra stood with her arms raised and was reciting an incantation while Orr'koor'lon busied himself with controls in his suit. Stephan found he had little to do other than scan the landscape. His attention was drawn to a hill not too far away that seemed out of place to him.

"The Neewoll'ah Imperium will be disappointed, I have found working satellites in orbit," Orr'koor'lon stated. "Although there are no signs of activity on the surface and the signals from the satellite seem to be…unfocused."

"The spiritual energies here are…odd," Alejandra said. "There is something here, yet it does not flow as it should."

"Why don't we go and check out that building over there?" Stephan added.

"What building?"

"The one entirely covered in dirt and bushes, just down there."

Both Orr'koor'lon and Alejandra followed Stephan's gesture.

"Are you sure that's a building?" Alejandra asked.

"All the angles on that thing are too perfect,' Stephan explained. "I'm fairly sure I can make out several doorways even."

"Best we investigate," Orr'koor'lon replied.

As they neared the structure, it became clearer that it was not a natural formation. While it blended in well with the rest of the landscape, the shape was just too exact.

Stephan reached out and wiped away a thick layer of orange dust to reveal a metal structure underneath.

"Fill up my sample container with some of that dust," Orr'koor'lon said as a transparent tube opened up on his suit. Once that was done, Orr'koor'lon instructed "Stand back". A nozzle unfolded from Orr'koor'lon's suit and a jet of air sent the dust on that area of the wall flying. Stephan noticed that it did not drift like the dust he was used to, but flew off in solid lumps.

It was not long before they had cleared off a doorway and the surrounding frame.

A Day at Georgie and Armand's Place

"Should we knock?" Stephan asked.

The three of them stood for a moment contemplating the question. Finally Alejandra took the initiative and rapped her knuckle on the door. A hollow clang echoed from beyond the door. A panel, hidden in the dust lit up next to the door.

"Okay Orr'koor'lon, this is your area," Alejandra said.

Orr'koor'lon moved in front of the panel and after some trial and error, was able to find a way to interact with it. It was not long until the door opened for them.

The dark hallways came to life with lights that had not been powered up for some time.

The three of them entered the sterile, cold building where Orr'koor'lon's metal footsteps echoed loudly through the passageways.

"I've seen enough horror movies to know this is not going to end well," Stephan remarked. "Any moment now, some crazed killer alien will jump out and rip us apart."

"Technically we're the aliens here," Alejandra replied. "And unless you plan to do something real stupid, I doubt anything hostile is going to jump us. There is a lot of spiritual energy in here, but it's in a strange state. Nothing active though."

"These 'horror movies' you refer to sound like some destructive propaganda," Orr'koor'lon added. "I am curious about the level of xenophobia your world must suffer from. How many alien races have your people had contact with?"

"None."

"Considering the hateful propaganda, that is not surprising."

The hallway had no doors or turns. They followed it straight as it went into a large open room.

The room was massive and stretched deep down below them. The walls were lined with panels filled with various readouts.

"Why does it feel like we're inside a giant computer?" Stephan remarked.

"While not fully accurate, there is a sense of truth in that," Orr'koor'lon stated.

Alejandra walked over to the railing and looked down as Orr'koor'lon made his way to a panel and attempted to interface with it.

Stephan was at a loss as to what he could do. He found a chair and sat down. His hands fell onto the globes on the arm rests. Without warning, the chair came to life with activity. A screen formed up from the floor, activating once it was at his eye level.

A translucent, purple face appeared on the screen. The being's features had fish like qualities to them. The face seemed to look at him and then it started speaking in a language far from being anything humans could reproduce.

"What's going on here" Alejandra asked approaching Stephan.

"I think I activated a recording, but I don't understand what it's saying."

As Alejandra neared the sounds suddenly changed and Stephan heard in English, "…we are a peaceful race. I ask for mercy for my people in our vulnerable state."

"That's odd. It's English now?"

"No, it's just my aura of translation being back in range with you. What is it saying?"

"Talking about the people being vulnerable."

"Yes, we really are," said the face on the screen.

"What?"

"If you could tell me your intentions here, I am authorized to negotiate for my race as a whole."

"Hi?" Stephan asked with a confused frown.

"Hello."

"I'm sorry, I didn't realize this was a video phone."

"A what?"

"Never mind. Are you the guy in charge here?"

"I am Droven, the elected Chancellor for our rebirth. As you are not one of us, it would seem something has gone wrong. Are you here to conquer our world while we are stored?"

"Stored?"

"You do not appear to be armed nor is there anything militaristic about you. Are you just an explorer then?"

"Maybe, I'll have my girlfriend take over from here, I'm just an accountant who is way out of my element."

Stephan got out of the seat and made room for Alejandra.

"Did you just call me your girlfriend?" Alejandra asked as she took the seat.

A Day at Georgie and Armand's Place

"I think so," Stephan answered, scrunching up his face.

"Not sure if we're there yet. We'll talk."

Alejandra took the seat and took over talking with Droven.

*****

It did not take long to learn the history of the planet.

Some time ago, the actual time frame could not be determined, the planet was going to pass through a deadly cosmic storm that would last for generations. All signs pointed to the end of all life on the planet and the destruction of everything they had built. All the countries got together to work out a plan. They were able to develop their technology to a point where they could transfer all of their societies into digital information, to be saved until their world was through the storm. Near-indestructible facilities were built to house the massive computers that would hold the whole of their world. Once the planet was safety through the storms, the systems would wake up and they could restart everything. From the perspective of the people, no time would have passed and within reason, their world would be just as it had been. Droven had been chosen by all the countries to be in charge of the reforming of their world. The computer was supposed to pull his consciousness up every so often to check if conditions were stable enough for them to return. If things were working right, he would be able to begin the process through the video screen.

Something had happened. The system had not awakened him for some time. He would need to get out and do a thorough inspection to see just what state his planet was in.

With Droven's help, Orr'koor'lon was able to figure out how to work the system and they were able to pull him out of storage and give him a body again.

The two of them got to talking about how to best go about reviving the world.

Alejandra realized that there was nothing she could do there. The feeling of souls that were stored in a computer was off putting as well. After a reasonable time, she grabbed Stephan and they made their way back to the Hotel.

"While I am not going to get my bonus on this one," Alejandra said, taking in the landscape with a new understanding of what she was looking

A Day at Georgie and Armand's Place

at. "Learning what souls that are neither alive nor dead feels like useful knowledge. I hope I never have to feel it again though."

"You could try to renegotiate with the big black skeleton," Stephan suggested. "I mean if his people want to get to this world's resources, they might be able to strike a deal with Droven to help get their world back on track."

"That might happen, but I don't see how that involves me."

"Make it involve you," Stephan replied in a strong voice. "You already have an in with Droven. Sell yourself as important to the negotiations to big black and creepy. Get him to agree to a bonus if a deal is made"

"Seems like you're already adapting to my life. We might be able to make this whole thing work."

"Maybe. Although, with a thousand, thousand worlds going through the Hotel, I'm betting accounting there can be a little much. I don't know if I could grasp how the exchange rate works with all the currencies that have to be traded."

Alejandra looked at Stephan with a curious smile. "You can always go back to your world and your life there."

"Why? You're here."

"Trying to be romantic?"

"So what do we do now?"

"I believe Pendragon should be on stage by now. We could catch the end of his performance."

"Why?"

"I thought you liked the results of Derovian Chanting on me. This time I won't try to block it out."

A smile of realization came to Stephan's face. "We could give that a try."

The Cost of Doing Business

A ray of sun light broke through the gloom of Shea Blossk's bedroom. Ze had gotten a suite with a window that faced out into a world that was on a close day/night cycle to zir homeworld. Ze had been a resident here in Georgie and Armand's place for some time but preferred to keep with the sleep cycles ze was raised with. Blossk made it a priority to not allow others any more control over zir life than possible. If Blossk was one thing, ze was a realist, but that did not mean ze just blindly accepted everything as it is.

With an almost mechanical essence, Blossk rose out of zir bed, stretched in a clear routine, ensuring each limb and muscle group got the needed attention. Ze went to the facilities and got a glass of water. Ze gargled some water, spit, and then drank the rest.

The shower that followed consisted of a precise routine, ensuring every part got the needed attention.

"Schedule," Blossk proclaimed to a blank screen as ze reentered the bedroom. A series of times and appointments soon filled the screen. "Delete all meeting requests by Doolig, Nog'alli and Millson Graff or their representatives. Not dealing with their nonsense today."

Over half the entries vanished.

"Good." Blossk looked at the first entry on zir list. "Breakfast with Moannit. Promising start for the day."

Ze found zirself a tan, form fitting suit that showed zir fit build in a flattering manner.

Half an hour was spent on fine grooming and makeup before Blossk was ready.

"Transfer schedule to Colby," Blossk stated as ze opened the door to the rest of the suite.

As soon as Blossk stepped out of the room, two large creatures fell in behind zir. One was covered head to hoof in dark brown fur, enough so that when it stood motionless it all blurred together, hiding its actual form. The other

A Day at Georgie and Armand's Place

was a higher alert-looking, bald being, with dull red skin, standing at over two meters tall.

From off a perch, a ball of swirled brown and white fur with twig-like legs jumped onto zir shoulder. A wormy tongue flicked out of its beak like mouth to lick Blossk's cheek.

Ze pulled a small piece of dried meat out of zir pocket and feed it to the creature.

"And how is Prags doing today?"

The creature gave a pleasant chirp as Blossk scratched its top.

"Now I get to go have my morning meal," Blossk said as ze placed Prags back on its perch.

*****

Moannit waited in his portable tub of mercury heavy water. It was a specially built craft that allowed him to sit up, with his lower half, not much more than a thick tail, fully submerged while his upper portions, a compact, purple, scaly, humanoid body, could poke out through the rubber orifice to conduct business with land beings. At times when he felt too dry, he could pull himself into a ball and fit his whole body under the water to moisturize. The setup had a built-in computer system that only responded to his touch as well as a variety of security and self-defense devices, some more obvious than others.

The Infinite Consumables, a name which apparently was more poetic in the language of its original owner, had the most diverse menu in Georgie and Armand's Place. In the two centuries since it opened it had expanded its menu regularly, now serving meals that meet the needs and tastes of thousands of beings, with several hundred kitchens at the ready. Ordering could get complicated at times, but for those who knew the system, there is always something enjoyable to try, no matter the digestive system.

Blossk enjoyed eating there because it added to the mystery of zir home world.

"How is business going today?" Blossk asked, taking a seat.

"For you or me Mx. Blossk?" Moannit replied.

"Your business is your business and none of mine, as long as it doesn't interfere with mine."

"Your business is doing well today,' Moannit stated. "Surprisingly you were right about the Murt family. Completely clueless. Sent a team to 'negotiate' and they gave in without thinking

A Day at Georgie and Armand's Place

about the agreement. They will back down on their operations on Aerok, while you have agreed to look into suspending your activities on the Rewol Peninsula."

"Of course," Blossk replied. "Despite all his boisterous talk, the man has no idea how to make a real deal. He inherited his power and money without being taught how to actually succeed. A spoiled child of a man. Easy pickings really."

"With that deal signed, you look to quadruple profits as well and influence there. The Murt's basically put themselves out of business with this."

"Let's start approaching some of their higher ups," Blossk suggested. "Non-family members of course, with opportunities if they wish to get off the sinking ship."

"Of course."

"Are we caught up on the payments from the Bows River group?"

"Let us see."

As Moannit's long purple fingers went to work on his keyboard to find the needed reports, a small, chubby, green skinned man with crazed dark blackish hair came over to the table and took a chair.

"Colby, I was wondering where you were," Blossk remarked.

"Sorry Honored One," Colby said with a slight bow. "I needed to deal with the backlash from you once more canceling all the appointments with the Graffs. They are highly agitated today, more so than usual."

"Unless they have something of value to offer for once, I really have no desire to deal with them. There is no profit to be made there."

"I know, but they are truly stubborn. I would recommend meeting with at least one of them."

"I'll think about it."

"There was also a last-minute request that I originally would have just ignored," Colby added. "But the offer was one I could not see you refusing."

"You have my attention," Blossk replied.

Colby pulled out his communique screen and handed it to Blossk. Blossk did not hide zir interest as ze read the exchanges.

"That is quit the prize just for one meeting," Blossk remarked.

A Day at Georgie and Armand's Place

"I am aware."

"Do you think he will deliver?"

"It would be a risky play for a simple con-job or joke of some kind," Colby said. "I do believe he is sincere."

"I shall take the meeting then. Let's do it at the Peachy Pegasus, during the big show today."

Colby nodded as he took back his screen and got to work on replying.

"Now, where were we?" Blossk remarked.

"I was pulling up the payment information regarding the Bows River Group," Moannit answered.

"Right, so where are we with them?"

*****

The rest of the breakfast meeting went smoothly, if a little routine. Blossk didn't mind. It meant all zir dealings were on track, no complications.

Running what in most societies would be viewed as a criminal organization, which operated on several dozen worlds at once, could get a little heavy on the day-to-day details. Blossk had long ago figured out effective ways to balance it. Ze only allowed the best and most loyal to zir upper circle, setting up a system where a handful of chosen beings were able to maintain an organization better run than most governments.

As Blossk and zir two associates made their way through a low-traffic public hallway of the Hotel, Blossk froze when ze caught a familiar scent.

One of Blossk's most useful tools was being able to smell pheromones. Some beings had truly unique pheromones, and for one who had a sensitivity to them, accurately reproducing them for certain species, could give influence over individuals, making all the difference in an encounter. The Ki'Jongun were one such species, and the Graffs broadcasted their pheromones with unbridled abandonment. Blossk suspected this was related to their species' gender roles, where the females were never seen in public once they were claimed by a male and made to be part of his harem.

As the scent grew stronger, Blossk knew ze had no way of avoiding Nog'alli, the oldest of the two brothers, the one who the father, Doolig,

A Day at Georgie and Armand's Place

had recently given full authority to, even as he still played his role in the family business.

Instead Blossk picked up the pace and turned the corner, charging right into Nog'alli and his entourage of large, muscular beings.

Blossk, who knew ze was not considered by them to be of impressive build, had hunched over to reinforce that image. Ze found zirself looking up at Nog'alli's neck. The batch of large beings around him had to rearrange themselves in an awkward dance as Blossk refused to back up. Nog'alli himself backed up a few steps once there was a space cleared behind him.

"Nog'alli, what a surprise," Blossk remarked, zir face showing no emotion. Ze did release a pheromone mimicking that of a female Ki'Jongun as ze altered zir skin tone to the feminine light grey. "You seem to be about some business, I will let you get to it."

As Blossk ducked away to move past Nog'alli, the Ki'Jongun reached out with his thick grey arm, blocking Blossk.

"Not so fast, androgynous one," Nog'alli said in his gruff voice. "You will attend to meeting with me. I will not tolerate any more delays. There is business that needs to be discussed."

"I do apologize for having to cancel on you and your family once again," Blossk replied, making motions considered feminine by the Ki'Jongun. "I have been so behind in my own affairs that I have had to postpone many meetings lately. In fact, right now I am running late to meet with representatives from the Murt family, who have been working with me for several months for a meeting."

Nog'alli shook his head and paused, making it clear that the pheromones and the act were having the desired effect.

"No, too many times now you have delayed this," Nog'alli stated, as he moved to grip Blossk's wrist. "I shall not be played any longer. You will come with me."

Blossk quickly grabbed Nog'alli's wrist before he could grip zirs. Ze then stood up to zir full height, zir skin turning to a noticeably darker grey and released a strong burst of mimicked Ki'Jongun masculine pheromone.

"No I won't," Blossk said as ze tightened zir grip. "You do not give me orders, ever."

Nog'alli's men shifted their stance, as did Blossk's.

A Day at Georgie and Armand's Place

"I don't think any of us want things to turn violent here," Blossk remarked. "Understand, no one pushes me around. I may have bodyguards with me, but they are more for show than anything else. I can easily handle the likes of you and your flunkies here."

Nog'alli was now shaking and instinctively taking a submissive stance. The confusion on his face was clear.

"You will back away and let me pass," Blossk commanded. "Feel free to once more petition for a meeting and if I feel like being generous, I may accept it."

There was silence as Nog'alli fell to his knees and Blossk walked around him.

The laugher from Nog'alli's goon squad soon followed Blossk down the hall, making zir smile.

*****

Blossk and zir group had taken a table with a good view of the stage to watch Georgie's big show. The first act had ended and it was time for Conrad Pendragon to perform. Blossk admired Pendragon's abilities. His voice had an effect on a wide range of beings of all sexes. He was one of the few beings of any gender that could arouse Blossk spontaneously. It was a secret kink of Blossk's to listen to his music and let that voice fill zir with pleasure. Zir would never admit it openly, but ze did think about seducing Pendragon and seeing if the human was really into the manner of perversion his reputation suggested. It had been so long since ze had shared the joys of the flesh with someone else.

Conrad had just begun his first song when Colby showed up with the mysterious individual.

The being was clearly humanoid: he had a darkness to him that made it hard to look directly at him or remember any of his features. Blossk was unable to get a smell of pheromone from him or a read on anything about him.

"Hello, I am Shea Blossk and you are?"

"No need for a name," the dark stranger said. He pulled out a small box and set it on the table. "Here is your reward for meeting with me."

Blossk took the box and opened it. Inside was a small red crystal, placed in a silver frame with an inscription carved into it, in a language from a world long destroyed. Blossk closed the box and moved it over to Colby.

A Day at Georgie and Armand's Place

"It looks like the real thing," Blossk remarked. "Colby, please verify."

"Of course, Honored One," Colby said as he opened the box. He froze for a moment admiring the piece before he pulled out his equipment.

"Now what is it you wish to discuss?"

"I am of the understanding that you know a great deal about this hotel," the dark stranger commented in a soft, controlled voice. "There is information concerning the Hotel I am looking for."

"That can be a dangerous thing to ask for. What is it you are wanting exactly?"

"It is a structure unlike any other across all of the realities. There are a great amount of hidden halls and passages to link these worlds. I wish to understand it, if there were maps of the Hotel that one could use to see the greatness of its set up, it would be such a spiritual experience to view them."

"I'm afraid you're out of luck there, no such maps exist," Blossk replied. Ze wasn't comfortable with the clearly misleading manner in which the question had been asked. There was undeniably much more going on than what he was revealing. "Georgie and Armand are the only ones who know the full arrangement of this place and how to navigate it all."

"What of those who are trusted by the Dragons? Do they not know the halls as well?"

"You're talking about the Sacred Gatekeepers?" Seha now had no doubt the stranger was playing a much bigger game than ze wanted to be involved in. "I wouldn't mess with them. They're as powerful in their arts as the Dragons. And they're fully loyal. Rumor has it, a few of them were apprentices with the Dragons way back when."

"How interesting. Surely there must be someone who knows the inner workings of this place and is not loyal to the Dragons."

"I can't see the Dragons allowing any beings they don't trust to walk around with that kind of information. Your best bet would be to find a powerful enough location spell that can pierce dimensional barriers, and not be affected by tech worlds. Although, with what you just gave me, my guess is you're good at finding rare magic."

"So you believe it is a hopeless quest I am on?"

A Day at Georgie and Armand's Place

"Maybe, although we did get word today of a batch of real ancient mage scrolls having been uncovered on a mid-level tech world where we have influence. No idea what's on the scrolls really, but the report has it being one of the Forgotten Higher Languages. There might be something in them along that level of power. Why don't you come back in a few days, after my mages have had a chance to look them over, and we can see if there's a bigger deal we can work on."

"That seems like a fair offer. I shall take my leave then."

"Not sure if it matters though, as any powerful spells being used in the Hotel are going to attract the Dragons."

"If that is where my path takes me, I shall deal with what comes of it."

The dark stranger got up and took his leave.

Blossk turned to look at Colby, "That was a strange meeting to say the least. Did it pay off though?"

Colby was practically overflowing with laughter, "I am positive that this is the real thing.

We are now is possession of one of the Sacred Hearts of the Gods."

Blossk peeked in the box and looked at the piece of jewelry that was the most powerful artifact ze had ever taken possession of. Ze closed the box and held it close to zir chest.

"There is a bigger game being played here," ze commented. "No one would give up such a powerful artifact so easily, especially when in the end I was of little help to them, unless it was a small move to a bigger prize. And there is no idea he was misleading us with his motives."

"What should we do?"

"I shall keep the heart with me. Call in our mages and have them meet me at my office. I wish to see just what we can do with this and prepare for when this person begins his final game. My money is on it concerning the Hotel itself, and if someone is preparing to challenge Georgie and Armand, then woe be to anyone caught in the crossfire unprepared."

Colby's joy turned to solemn contemplation.

"Come along," Blossk commanded. "We have much to do."

A Day at Georgie and Armand's Place

Blossk pulled zirself away from Pendragon's performance with great regret.

*****

Blossk's group hurried down the hallways in rushed silence. Blossk clutched the heart close to zir body. Zir mind was drifting over the possible outcomes as they rounded a corner just down the hall from Blossk's chambers.

Nog'alli and Millson Graff stood there with their thick grey arms crossed, holding intimidating stances.

"You will be talking with us now," Nog'alli stated.

Blossk made note that both of them were now wearing nose plugs and smiled at the knowledge that they feared zir abilities.

"I have no time for your nonsense now," Blossk explained. "There is something far bigger than your petty little attempts at becoming a criminal empire."

"There is nothing petty about our family."

The sounds of movement from behind them made it clear that this was not just a simple confrontation. The Graffs had brought along a lot of friends this time.

"I am through with playing games," Blossk remarked. Ze was tempted to pull out the heart and let loose, but ze knew better than to attempt something like that in Georgie and Armand's Place. "It is time to end this. If it's a battle you want, then fine by me. Let's see if your little army is powerful enough to take out the four of us."

Colby folded into a ball as Blossk and zir two shadows took up a defensive stance.

The Graffs smiled and moved towards Blossk with fists ready.

"Oh, this is going to be fun," Nog'alli said as he closed in.

Blossk stood with zir eyes focused on the Graff brothers as they prepared to let loose with their fists. Zir two bodyguards had turned to face the ones coming from behind.

Right before Nog'alli's punch would have made contact, the hallway filled with a shimmering blue light. The Graff brothers and their men all spasmed, as they fell to the floor.

"You idiots," Blossk remarked as ze stepped over their prone forms. "This is Georgie

A Day at Georgie and Armand's Place

and Armand's Place. While you can get away with some minor fisticuffs, quick spontaneous, heat-of-the-moment fights. There are spells in place to keep the clientele from being viciously attacked. Now there really is something far more important going on that I must see to."

Blossk and zir entourage made haste into zir chambers and waited for the mages to arrive.

Ian Brazee-Cannon

The Courtship of

Georgie and Armand

Part 1:
The Meeting of the Nine

"Hax'georget' come, we must make haste. You will transform and attend now," Archmage Lionope commanded. He crossed his two sets of skinny arms and stood impatiently outside the large doorway to his apprentice's chambers. "It does not do you well to make your own Master, let alone the gathered Masters of the Realms, wait for you to attend."

A Day at Georgie and Armand's Place

"Sorry Master Lionope," came the soft reply. A moment later the door began to open and then stopped. "Whoops, almost forgot."

A young man in a simple tunic entered the chamber. At first glance there was nothing impressive or outstanding about Hax'georget'. The short dull red hairs on his head seemed unfamiliar with the concept of being combed. The awkward, bony body would not stop shaking as his head refused to look up.

"Still uncomfortable with this form I see," Lionope stated.

"Yes master."

"We should not be at the library long. It will be good practice to see how well you hold the form."

"Yes master."

"Now head up, you need to see where you're walking."

"Yes master."

They came to an open doorway that held nothing but blackness on its other side. Master Lionope raised his upper hands and gave a brief incantation. A whirl of light filled the doorway, revealing an active small town beyond.

"I have a question master," Hax'georget' said.

"Yes?"

"Why do you not set up a series of doorways, each with its own portal, preset to a different realm for quicker access?"

"Um, I never thought about that. I'm old and set in my ways I guess. Although such a set up would need a lot of room and a continual source of magic to maintain them..." Lionope paused to examine the doorway in contemplation. "We can see what is feasible when we return. It might make for a good learning experience, for both of us."

Lionope stepped through the doorway and Hax'georget' followed.

They emerged from the doorway of an old stable that was presently not being used, as the stable's roof had collapsed several years before. No one had felt the need to repair it. A simple charm by Lionope kept anyone from showing interest in the structure.

They made good time as it was still early enough in the morning that the street had yet to become packed. Hax'georget' fought the urge to stop and look at the wares as the merchants set up

A Day at Georgie and Armand's Place

their stands. He knew that there was no time for frivolity this day.

The Great Library of Dela CoErwine had stood for over a thousand years, expanding over the centuries to engulf several universities, two observatories, a morgue and four theaters. It now housed chapels for 33 different faiths, from a dozen different realms. There was no greater gathering place for knowledge and the pursuit of truth to be found in any realm. What once had been the little unknown village of Eli Craig, was now a thriving crossroads of commerce for beings from countless realms.

Lionope and Hax'georget' entered the library through the Great Philosopher Nixiefae's archway. The fragile stone face of Nixiefae looked down at them with the pleasant, carefree smile she had been known for.

Lionope clearly knew where he was headed, making no hesitation as they navigated through the maze of halls and chambers. The grey stone walls were covered with tapestries telling the histories of numerous worlds in stunning detail. Hax'georget' always regretted not having the time to give them his full attention.

"Leave it up to Chatwell to reserve an oversized lecture hall for what should be a simple gathering," Lionope mumbled. "It was a mistake to let him give our group a name to begin with. He better have a good reason for calling this meeting."

Hax'georget' said nothing, knowing this was his master's way of venting.

Beings of all kind rushed by them as they made their way. It was a rare moment for the halls to be without activity, as the library was always in use by someone.

"Here we are," Lionope said as they approached the lecture hall.

The doors to the chamber were open and the two of them walked right in. Six figures were waiting on the stage.

"Lionope has now joined us," the short, dark green, imp who floated several feet above the floor remarked. "Waiting on The Coulder and not surprisingly Chatwell."

"I'm surprised you are here on time Klacki'Nicoo," Lionope replied.

"Miracles happen."

"As it turns out, he has been here for several days," a silver face without a body

A Day at Georgie and Armand's Place

commented. "He seems to think he is close to a breakthrough."

"He is always close to a breakthrough Master Joh," chimed a raven-haired woman in a functional soft-blue dress, that gave her a scholarly aura. "With all the buildup he has given us through the ages, it should be a truly impressive reveal any moment now."

Klacki'Nicoo stuck out his long purple tongue in jest and said, "Soon my dear L'Jerdak, soon."

"It is good to see that Hax'georget' is getting the hang of keeping his form." the blue-skinned man remarked. "The other apprentices have gathered on the balcony. Best for him to join them."

"Thank you Dwar Kwando, I shall, with Master Lionope's leave."

"Yes, of course."

Hax'georget' gave a polite bow before rushing off.

*****

It was not difficult to locate the other apprentices. They were the only ones on the balcony. Even then, this group would find it hard to blend in with most crowds. There was a tall humanoid covered in light black scales, whose body clearly would have been more at home in the water, sitting next to a small, female being with light pink skin and transparent sky-blue wings talking to a floating round purple creature with two tentacles on either side of its body as a furry being with a long nose, whose body resembled a giant brain rested nearby with its four long, twig-like legs tucked beneath its body.

"...Master Klacki'Nicoo is so close to a breakthrough. Today we figured out-Hax'georget', glad you're joining us," the floating purple ball remarked.

"Hello Sna, good to see you again" Hax'georget' replied. "And you Je'Garramone," he nodded to the small pink female.

"Thank you."

"Jesillip, you are looking well," He said to the tall humanoid.

"I just finished a swim. Some of the larger fountains here are perfect for a quick, relaxing dunk."

"Hello Mmm'ddeliommm," he said to the furry one.

A Day at Georgie and Armand's Place

"Greetingsss back to you."

"You've not yet met Kwando's new student," Sna remarked. "Ze doesn't like to sit still."

"Life is about being active," came a clattering voice.

Hax'georget' turned to find a being with a large dark red carapace coming up over its head where two large, dark eyes made up most of its face with a set of strong pinchers extruding from beneath them. Ze stood slightly shorter than Hax'georget', but zirs armored body made zir feel much larger. Ze stood on two large legs and had four upper appendages that looked as though they could be used as either arms or legs as needed.

"I am Schilt," ze said, giving a bow.

"It is a pleasure to meet you."

"So, you're a dragon?"

"Yes, I am."

"There are no dragons on my world," Schilt remarked. Ze was clearly taking zir time examining Hax'georget'. "Yet stories of them are common."

"That is a regular occurrence actually," Hax'georget' replied. "My understanding is that at one time dragons roamed through all the realities freely. My ancestors left their marks on countless worlds I guess."

"And now very few of us roam the worlds like they did," came an emotionless reply.

The group turned to find a dark-haired young man dressed in a well-fitting leather jerkin with golden embroidered highlights. The stern look on his face and his crisp posture emphasized a no-nonsense aura about him.

"Hello Armand," Je'Garramone said. "The Coulder must be here now."

"At last I get to meet the other dragon apprentice of the Nine," Hax'georget' said, holding his hand out with a smile on his face. "It is so nice to finally meet you. I've heard a lot about you, but our masters seem to rarely end up together."

"You must be Hax'georget'," Armand replied, ignoring the offered hand. "Interesting."

"Why do you say that?"

"It is always interesting to meet another dragon and see how they hold themselves."

"I find all new beings I get to meet to be interesting."

"You're a social creature?"

"I guess."

A Day at Georgie and Armand's Place

"Very interesting," Armand stated, his voice cold and formal.

"How so?" Hax'georget' asked, a sense of annoyance creeping into his voice.

"Being social is not a description most would use for dragons."

"Well…I guess I'm just unique ."

"That is a reasonable word for it."

"You know, just because you're cute and look good in those clothes, does not justify you being so ill mannered."

"I apologize if my honesty has come off as being rude. I find it best to be direct in my communications." Armand paused. "You think this outfit looks good on me? Appreciation of fine clothes? Another abnormal trait for a dragon. One that some might call perverted even."

"Well… I… It's just…" The frustration clear on Hax'georget's face.

"Might want to step back now," Sna said, floating in front of Armand. "He's getting upset and will need some space."

"Rather sensitive for a dragon," Armand remarked.

Hax'georget's clothes filled out as he began his transformation. He pulled off his tunic and ran out of the lecture hall.

He shoved past the tall man with four eyes, covered in white fur with brown stripes and let out a, "Sorry Rodfire," before continuing down the hall.

*****

The Wilchael Gardens had been maintained by the Library of Dela CoErwine for centuries. While new plants were introduced every once in a while, there was a balance of colors, scents and sizes that were taken into account to maintain the original esthetics that had made the gardens a treasure of botany worthy of study and admiration across the realms.

Hax'georget' was in his natural form, flying in circles above the gardens as part of his calming routine. Watching how the patterns of flowers flowed as he flew, he had convinced himself Wilchael must have been a flying being with anxiety issues to have created such a perfectly relaxing pattern when seen from the sky.

A Day at Georgie and Armand's Place

"I see meeting Armand was not fun for you," Rodfire said as he entered the gardens.

"He is arrogant and harsh," Hax'georget' replied. "He would fit in perfectly with my family."

"All I know is you have the right idea in coming out here." Rodfire fell to his hands and knees, let out a growl and quickly transformed to three times the size. Two tusks and a trunk emerged from his face as his hands and feet became clawed with a long tail appearing. "I hate spending so much time in that unnatural form."

"I find the human form has its uses and attractiveness," Hax'georget' remarked, landing in a large patch of grass. "Although it would help to decorate my body with something more interesting than those boring tunics."

"I think Master Chatwell just enjoys torturing me" Rodfire remarked. "He rarely changes his form but makes me be humanoid most of the time."

"Think about it. You are noticeably larger than him in your natural form," Hax'georget' observed. "Also, most hallways and buildings were not designed for creatures of our sizes. It's rare to find any structure built with more than one species in mind. I always found that to show a lack of understanding about the nature of sentient beings."

"You certainly do not think like a dragon," the dull voice of Armand flowed from one of the balconies.

"I have nothing to say to you," Hax'georget' said, turning his back to Armand.

"You stormed out rather hastily there. I figured you might want this back." Armand put the folded tunic on the railing of the balcony. "It seemed a bit ill-fitting for you, so I took a moment and did some alterations. It should be a better fit now and more flattering to your form."

"You're a tailor?" Hax'georget's face filled with interest as he turned to face Armand.

"It is a skill I have that I find useful."

"And you're fast with it."

Armand explained, "Considering what simple clothes I had to work with, it took little time for such basic alterations."

"Was that supposed to be an insult?"

"Not at all. I was just stating fact. And I do apologize if anything I said before came off harsh. If the appreciation of clothes is a perversion, it is clearly one I embrace as well. You

A Day at Georgie and Armand's Place

should try it on and see how much better a fit it is."

Hax'georget' leaped onto the balcony, switching form, landing as human next to Armand. He plucked up the tunic and got dressed.

Standing there looking at his reflection in a window Hax'georget' ran his fingers over the altered tunic, smiling at what he saw.

"I am impressed," he remarked.

"Now if you would hold still for a moment," Armand said approaching Hax'georget'. "I was off with my measurements, as I had not been able to get a good look at your full form."

Hax'georget' held still as Armand pulled and folded the fabric, made a few quick motions as needle and thread appeared. As he worked, Hax'georget' felt Armand's hands brushing against his body despite the layer of fabric, sending shivers through him. Holding back his feelings of embarrassment, Hax'georget' closed his eyes and tried not to think about it.

"There, finished."

Hax'georget' once more looked at his reflection in the window and was unable to hide his surprise. What had been a dumpy piece of clothing, that always looked more like an old grain sack than proper clothes, was now a form fitting garment that looked and felt as if it belonged on his body.

"I find it hard to believe this is the same tunic I wore here," Hax'georget' commented.

"I find it rather chaotic that too many beings roam around wearing clothing not adjusted for them,' Armand replied. "It is just sloppy laziness."

"I can see that… Although you do understand that some of us have no choice but to settle for whatever we get our hands on."

"I am sure you could find better quality clothes if you tried. Just because our kind has poorly conceived notions about clothing, does not mean we have to limit ourselves by those ideas."

"That… Makes a lot of sense. I…" Hax'georget' flashed Armand a friendly smile. "I never met a dragon with such… Non-traditional views before."

"My bloodline would never make the claim of being traditional."

"Mine holds to traditions strongly," Hax'georget' replied with a solemn voice. "I always thought that an odd mentality considering how solitary most of them live."

A Day at Georgie and Armand's Place

"We are an odd race, but most species seem to have various levels of such hypocrisy in their habits."

Hax'georget' turned to look out at the gardens. The rest of the apprentices had followed and were resting in the grass socializing. Schilt had challenged Mmm'ddeliommm to a friendly duel and the two of them were preparing as Sna took on the role of referee. It was a simple contest with each mage using non-destructive spells to try to push the other one out of their marked dueling circle. All the apprentices were familiar with the basic rules, as this was a common teaching method for certain spells as well as a way to teach how to combine spells and be quick with one's summoning and thinking.

Armand stood with perfect posture as Hax'georget' rested on the railing, leaning over to watch the match.

Mmm'ddeliommm was clearly not ready for Schilt's aggressiveness, losing the duel quickly. A quick flash of light to blind, followed by several blasts of air was all it took. Mmm'ddeliommm wanted a rematch, which lasted longer with Schlit finding zirself face first on the ground dazed.

This led to several other duels and soon all eight of the apprentices found themselves taking turns facing off against each other.

Armand had been challenged three times and won all three matches. In his last match a blast tore through the stitching in his jerkin. He sat bare chested working on repairing the damage. Hax'georget', who had only fought one match, was doing all he could to not stare at Armand.

"Do you think you can take him?" Rodfire asked.

"I don't know," Hax'georget' replied. "I'm not really that good."

"Nonsense, you won your match against Jesillip."

"He was not really trying, not seeming to care about winning. I don't think Armand would give me a chance. It'd be over quickly."

"I've seen you run through practice drills, and you're good. Far better than you give yourself credit. That pompous fool could use a lesson in humility."

"I really couldn't…"

"You won't know unless you give it a try."

"Well.. maybe…"

A Day at Georgie and Armand's Place

"Okay," Rodfire said. He turned and raised his voice. "Hax'georget' wants to challenge Armand."

"I didn't…" Hax'georget' said quietly. No one seemed to hear him as the others were cheering him on.

"This should be interesting," Armand said, putting down the unrepaired jerkin, he found his place on the grassy area and conjured his circle. "Whenever you are ready."

Hax'georget' took his place across from Armand and created his circle. He nervously stood there, trying not to focus on Armand's bare chest.

Sna rose between the two of them and awaited their signals of readiness. Once both sides were prepared he started the countdown.

Armand let loose the first attack with a simple push spell, which was deflected by Hax'georget'. Next came a series of various disorienting spells, all of which Hax'georget' countered. Armand upped his aggressiveness with a round of quick pushes and pulls, aimed mostly at Hax'georget's legs and while Hax'georget' countered them, he tried to sneak in a push to Hax'georget's head, which was deflected.

The aggressive, strategic strikes of Armand's, which had allowed him quick victories before, seemed to be ineffective against Hax'georget's quick reflexive nature. And while Hax'georget' kept with defensive spells, he held his stance, with Armand having to adjust to keep his balance.

The earlier matches had attracted their share of curious passersby creating an unplanned audience, the new match, which was lasting much longer, was attracting a much larger crowd.

No matter how Armand adjusted his attacks, Hax'georget' seemed lost in a trance, producing a perfect counter spell by pure instinct. Several of Armand's stronger blast were deflected back at him causing him to have to dispel his own work.

The other apprentices found themselves stuck with the task of shielding the audience and buildings from unintended spillover of forces as the match intensified.

No one was keeping track of time, but the sweat accumulating on Armand became an indicator of the intensity of the match. Hax'georget' on the other hand, appeared unfazed

A Day at Georgie and Armand's Place

by the effort. No matter the attack, he was able to counter it with defensive spells.

No one noticed that the Nine Masters of the Realms had made their way to the front of the crowd and were all watching the match intensely.

The frustration was clearly getting to Armand. While he maintained his grim, emotionless visage, his movements showed clear signs of stress. His arms no longer moved with the practiced ease that had given him the air of a disciplined mage. Now his motions were filled with wild desperation, unleashing whatever spells he could as quickly as possible in hopes of overwhelming Hax'georget'. Yet nothing broke through.

The crackling in the air as Armand pulled forth electrical energy into him caused those who understood what was about to happen to gasp, as it looked as if Armand might cross the line and use a potentially dangerous spell.

Several of the Masters exchanged quick looks and gestures, but all seemed to silently agree to let it happen and see what resulted.

From Armand's hand a bolt of electricity shot out in a controlled arc, striking at Hax'georget' from above. With a quick motion of his hands, Hax'georget' stopped the energy just inches away from his head and then guided it to launch straight back at Armand.

Having been so focused on being the aggressor in the match, Armand was not prepared to be on the defensive. The blast struck him, picked him off his feet and sent him flying several yards, slamming him into a fruit tree. Several white fruits with blue spots fell loose, landing on the lap of Armand's now dazed form.

The loud cheers from the crowd echoed through the halls of the library and the open grounds of the gardens.

*****

Lionope and L'Jerdak rushed over to Hax'georget', who was still standing in position ready for another attack.

"Hax'georget', stand down," Lionope commanded. "The match has ended."

Hax'georget' shook his head, clearly coming out of a trance.

"Mmmm... Master Lionope... I... I... I don't feel good," Hax'georget' said in a weak voice. He stumbled back, but was kept from

A Day at Georgie and Armand's Place

falling by those gathered around him. They led him to a nearby bench.

"That was a truly impressive display for an apprentice," L'Jerdak remarked as she sat on one side of Hax'georget' helping to hold him stable.

Hax'georget' turned to her with glazed over eyes and said, "Armand is highly skilled I guess."

"She was talking about you," Lionope replied.

"Me? What did... I ... Armand... His spell got me. It disoriented me... Must have been a quick match."

Lionope exchanged glances with L'Jerdak.

"You really don't remember anything about the match?" Lionope asked.

Hax'georget' blinked his eyes a few times to try to clear his mind. "I was standing there... Looking at Armand's bare chest... I went over all the basic defensive spells in my head... Sna finished the countdown... Armand began with a push, easy enough to deflect... Then a batch of disorientation spells... And then you were there saying the match was over."

Lionope once more looked over to L'Jerdak. A glance around confirmed that only the two of them were close enough to hear what had just been said. They exchanged a round of silent gestures, agreeing to keep Hax'georget's revelation between them.

"I am thinking Armand's last attack must have dazed you, as you redirected and won the match," Lionope said.

"I... Won the match?"

"Yes, and it was undeniably impressive," L'Jerdak replied. "It clearly took its toll on you."

Armand approached the bench. At his side was The Coulder, a large hairless man with light green skin accented by a series of black stripes that ran horizontally around his body. He wore a simple, sleeveless top.

"You showed a high level of skill out there," The Coulder stated.

"Thank you Master The Coulder," Hax'georget' replied. He had always found The Coulder to be the most intimidating of the Nine on the few encounters they had had in the past. He realized The Coulder might be the only person he had ever met that expressed less emotions than Armand.

A Day at Georgie and Armand's Place

"Yes, congratulations. I was not expecting such a display," Armand said, holding out his hand.

Hax'georget' took the offered hand and replied, "It seems I surprised myself as well."

"As with any defeat, I will be reviewing what happened and learn from it," Armand explained. "If we ever go up against each other again, I will be better prepared."

"Okay…"

Armand gave a bow before he and The Coulder took their leave.

The noise of the audience drew Hax'georget' attention. He looked up to see the gathered crowd. When they saw that he was looking at them, they gave out a powerful cheer.

"Oh, this is a little… much."

"Right," Lionope said. "Let's get you inside and find a quiet place to recover."

*****

Back inside the lecture hall Hax'georget' found a seat and collapsed into it.

A fur covered, quadruped with long orange hair and large black eyes came up and said,

"You really knocked that gloomy wiseass a good one there."

"Thank you Master Chatwell," Hax'georget' replied. "It was Rodfire who encouraged me to take him on."

"My student's got a good head for figuring out how powerful people are. He also has never liked Armand. I'm betting there might have been a little manipulation on his part with that."

"He was still very encouraging."

"And hey, if you're ever up for a new Master who knows what he's doing," Chatwell said in a joking tone. "I could see if old Lionope would go for a trade."

"Thank you, but I am happy with Master Lionope's teachings."

"Trying to recruit my apprentice now?" Lionope said with humored mockery. "Not sure if I have been offended or complimented."

"That's how people feel after most conversations I have with them," Chatwell replied.

"I doubt you have ever felt offended."

"True, offense only works if you let it."

"Here Hax'georget', have some water," Lionope said handing Hax'georget' a cup.

"Thank you Master."

A Day at Georgie and Armand's Place

"Get some rest now, we will be leaving soon."

Lionope went and joined L'Jerdak, Master Joh and The Enchantress Allidy, who Hax'georget' saw as a blurry female dragon. His understanding was that the Enchantress appeared to each individual as the most attractive female version of their species. He had often speculated on the reasoning as to why he was unable to see her clearly, but never was willing to ask her directly.

The other Masters and their apprentices came by with congratulations for Hax'georget' as they took their leave of the Library.

Jesillip and Mmm'ddeliommm joined Hax'georget' as they waited for their Masters to finish up.

"We all need to be taking lessons from you," Jesillip commented. "The speed and precision out there. I don't think any of the Masters could have done better."

"I agree with Jesssillip. That wasss a sssurprisssing disssplay by you."

"Thank you both. But I just…" Hax'georget' started to say.

"Enough of that now," Master Joh said as zir silver face floated up to them. "Let him get some rest. His aura is clearly stressed. Come along Mmm'ddeliommm, we need to get back."

"Yes Master Joh."

The others soon left as well, leaving Hax'georget' and his Master alone in the lecture hall.

"You've had quite the day," Lionope remarked with a comforting smile.

"I didn't mean to do anything wrong."

"You are always so ready to admit error where there is none. Today I saw evidence that you have natural abilities far beyond what I thought. You will never reach your full potential if you keep holding yourself down with self-doubt."

"I know, it's just…" Hax'georget' took in a deep breath in an attempt to calm himself.

"No excuses now," Lionope said putting a reassuring hand on Hax'georget's shoulder. "And let's not cause you any more stress by talking about it. Are you up for the walk home?"

"Yes Master, I believe I am rested enough for that."

A Day at Georgie and Armand's Place

The two of them made their way back through the maze of hallways and out through Nixiefae's archway.

"Is that a new tunic?' Lionope asked.

"No, it's the old one. It's just been modified to fit me better."

"You really should pick up a few better fitting outfits. I know it does not fit with dragon culture, but you always seem fascinated with clothing. It might help you relax and better tap into your skills."

"I like that idea. Thank you Master." Hax'georget' let out a quiet laugh as he started to calm down.

Ian Brazee-Cannon

The World With-In

Kra hung from his station, wings tucked in, but ready to go if needed. He kept an eye on the reception desk but let his gaze wander around the lobby. It had been a slow morning, so he was finding himself watching the crowds a great deal to keep himself alert. There had been some excitement when Georgie got upset with some bipedal being and morphed into his natural form, shocking most of those who were in the lobby. Kra found a dragon to be one of the sexiest creatures ever. He never understood why Georgie and Armand spent so much time in those grotesque bipedal forms. He had been told it had something to do with their interest in 'fashion', which was a bizarre concept for Kra. The idea of

A Day at Georgie and Armand's Place

putting on extra layers of false skins, that could only serve to weigh one down. Why would anyone take part in such counterproductive undertakings?

Being a messenger for the Hotel was a unique job, to say the least. As the Hotel runs through countless dimensions, most of the regular methods of internal communications are out of the question. Electrical systems are useless when they pass through certain magical areas, and mystic methods are unable to be received in the strong tech sections. The interference that comes from so many differing dimensional energies, while there are safeguards in place to keep it from getting to dangerous levels, ensures complications with communications. Although lobbies and public areas are connected to each other as much as possible, it was realized early on that most of the Hotel would have to rely on messengers to get information from one area of the Hotel to another. Small fliers such as Kra were perfect for the job. There were thousands of messengers of all variety of species working for the Hotel. Often on a busy day, the passages were full of them coming in and out of their service ways. A Hotel messenger had to keep up with all the shortcuts in the ever-growing facility.

Nirron held up his silver hand and signaled for a messenger. Kra let go his perch, unfolded his wings and sailed smoothly over to the messenger platform on the desk and picked up the pouch that was waiting for him. It had been shrunken on this end and upon delivery, at which point it would grow to the appropriate size for the recipient.

"Got a request for the Peachy Pegasus concerning this afternoon's show. This is obviously a rush run," Nirron said.

Kra nodded his understanding and kicked himself off into the air. He soared smoothly through the hallway, above the unknowing heads of the guests. He took a sharp left into an opening that most who passed below were never aware of. The tunnel Kra entered was large enough that he could flap his wings and even move out of the way if another messenger needed to pass. These were known as the messenger routes, and they crisscrossed the Hotel. Kra turned as needed through the small maze of tunnels without any real thought to his path. The Peachy Pegasus was a fairly regular delivery location, he knew the route well.

A Day at Georgie and Armand's Place

It was a nice, easy trek, with one optional use of an accelerator, which Kra always enjoyed. He tucked his wings in and allowed the push from the accelerator to fling him through a significant straightaway. He popped out and landed on a resting platform, before taking flight once more.

He soon returned to the larger hallways in the proper commerce area of the Hotel where The Peachy Pegasus was located. He made an unneeded spiral as part of his final approach to the club, flew through the messenger port and landed at the side of the greeting podium.

Groat was currently manning the station, swaying slightly to a rhythm in her head. Her species were semi-transparent, boneless creatures with four short limbs, used for legs, and two longer limbs, each with three manipulators on the ends, used for arms. They kept their shapes through a variety of bladders that emptied and filled as they moved. Her resting color was a light blue, but certain sounds could change her color and music could give a shimmering effect with the colors changing with the rhythm. During concerts, she often offered a pleasantly distracting display.

Groat finished up the superficial task she had been engaged in and reached two of her manipulators to take the courier pouch Kra was holding out to her. She waited patiently for the pouch to fully enlarge so she could pull forth the parchment from inside and read it.

"Of course," Groat remarked. "Everyone wants a front row seat for Pendragon. I have told them countless times we only take requests for reserved seating on the days before hand, not the day of. If they have a guest who does not understand the club's policies, that is not our problem."

Groat got to work writing down her reply.

Kra glanced above him at The Peachy Pegasus greeting area for guests his size, which was built into the wall at a height above head level for most of the Hotel's average sized beings. Few of the larger creatures were aware of the existence of the smaller clubs in the upper areas of the gathering places around the Hotel. This one had its own bar and restaurant and even its own stage, although it also had seating that looked out at the bigger stage on the main floor. As with any restaurant in the Hotel, the seating was highly adaptable for a large variety of beings.

The greeting area was presently staffed by Ta'bith. She was of a reptilian species like Kra,

A Day at Georgie and Armand's Place

just not winged. She had lovely purple scales with red and blue edges, forming a mesmerizing pattern that Kra could always lose himself in. He would often let his mind wander with the idea of wrapping tails with her and how pleasant that would be.

"Here you go," Groat said, handing the pouch back to Kra, which shrunk to size once Kra touched it.

Kra broke from his trance, took the pouch and strapped it on. He took the chance for a quick flight up to see Ta'bith.

"Hello colorful," Kra said.

"Kra," Ta'bith replied. The two of them touched tongues in greeting. "How are you?"

"I am good. And you?"

"Getting ready for a busy afternoon," Ta'bith replied. "Georgie has his show, with Pendragon doing a set for it. We are expecting the place to be packed."

"Sounds like you'll be busy. I was thinking of stopping in after my shift, if the place is not too crowded."

"I can hold a place for you."

"And what will that cost me," Kra said, his tail raising up, showing his excitement.

"Actually," Ta'bith said with a suggestive bugling of her eyes. "If you could do me a small favor, that would help."

"Sure, anything for you colorful."

"There was a fairy couple in here this morning and they lost a charm bag. It just turned up. If you could run it to their room…"

"No problem," Kra said, his tail stretching past his head now. Ta'bith moved her tail playfully with its tip just beyond touching his.

Ta'bith handed Kra the small leather pouch, as with all such fairy effects, it was magically sealed, with only the owners able to gain access. Kra quickly recognized this one, as this was not the first time it had been misplaced around the Hotel.

"Soc and Naw again I see," Kre remarked. "It's a quick stop on my way back."

"Thank you," Ta'bith said, touching his tail tip with hers, just slightly.

Kra let out a soft hiss of pleasure.

He took off, full of delight, with the enthusiastic belief his evening was going to be highly enjoyable.

*****

A Day at Georgie and Armand's Place

Over the centuries, Georgie and Armand's Place had added additions to the Hotel to accommodate all manner of beings. Not surprisingly there had been many sections added to accommodate the smaller creatures. These were built into the construction as they added areas to the larger hotel, often blending them into the walls, escaping notice to anyone not aware of them. There were hundreds of sections, referred to as the Hotel With-in, matching up to the various needs of the smaller species. Just like with the larger hotel, there were sections for magic and tech, along with differing atmospheres, gravities or whatever the requirements. The Hotel With-in stayed busy and active with its own flow of life alongside the larger areas. The larger hallways of the Hotel With-in sometimes worked as part of the messenger routes, when there was enough room.

Kra exited a messenger route into the Tuath Dé lobby, one of the strongest magical sections of the Hotel With-in. It was an area often filled with incorporeal beings and creatures only alive through the use of enchantments.

Colliven, a chubby, black furred rodent, was at the reception desk. He sat with his paws crossed on his belly. Even though he was much larger than Kra's natural prey, there was a clear resemblance.

"Looking nice and tasty today, Colliven," Kra remarked.

"And what can I help you with?" Colliven replied, with an indifferent tone.

"Soc and Naw left their pouch at the Peachy Pegasus."

"I've not seen them come back through, so they should be in their room at present. Why don't you be a good messenger and deliver it."

"No problem buddy. Just remember, you still have an open invite to join me for dinner whenever you want," Kra said, heading down the hall.

Colliven made no reply, turning his attention back to observing the various patrons in his lobby.

Kra hissed in amusement at his brilliant joke. It was too bad that beings like Colliven just didn't understand real humor.

An odd breeze blew past Kra. There was something to it that sent an uncomfortable shiver through his body. He turned the corner and froze.

A Day at Georgie and Armand's Place

He blinked a few times as he tried to understand what he was seeing.

"Colliven! Come here Colliven!"

"I'm not in the mood for your games," the rodent replied.

"Seriously, this is not a joke."

"I'm coming."

Colliven took his time trudging down the hall.

"What is it?" Colliven turned and found himself in the same state of puzzlement as Kra. "Where is the hallway?"

The two of them were looking into a cloud of swirling darkness.

"What did you do?" Colliven snapped.

"Nothing," Kra replied. "You're the one who is supposed to be aware of what's going on here."

The cloud shifted, moving closer to them.

"We need to send for a Gatekeeper."

"Agreed." Kra stood there for a moment silently as Colliven looked at him. "Oh right, that's my job."

Kra turned and headed for the Messenger routes, only to find himself too disoriented to move. He looked around and saw Colliven losing his balance before falling into the ever-encroaching black cloud and disappearing.

"Klog guts," Kra exclaimed. He closed his eyes and tried to focus. He forced his body to move in the direction of the lobby. Step by step he made his way down the hall with his eyes closed tight. He could feel his pace picking up as he put distance between himself and the cloud.

Once he felt the reception desk, Kra opened his eyes. There was a crowd gathered near the desk.

"You work here?" A stone skinned creature asked.

"Yeah," replied Kra.

"We need to get out."

"Yes, that sounds like a good plan."

"Ok, then can you open the doors?"

Kra stood in puzzled silence, not sure that he was having the same conversation as the being in front of him.

"Just use the exit doors," Kra remarked questioningly. "Best to evacuate the Hotel right now."

"Evacuate? What doors do you think I'm talking about? I have business on several worlds today and the exits won't open."

A Day at Georgie and Armand's Place

"What? That can't be right."

Kra rushed over to the closest exit door and noticed that it was no longer three dimensional. He pressed his front claws against the surface. It was flat, with nothing to grab on to.

A loud scream came from behind Kra. He turned to see the cloud had finally reached the lobby and the guests there had finally become aware of it.

"Okay beings, please remain calm," Kra stated. "Things are a little weird right now. Let's move away from the ominous dark cloud thing."

Kra leaped over the guests and raised his tail into the air. "Follow me."

He led the group down the largest of the hallways, that led to several restaurants. It also had a low entrance to the messenger routes, that all of them should be able to reach. Kra wasn't sure if all of them would be able to make it through the maze of passages in the route, but he knew he'd feel safer inside those passages.

"Once inside the messenger routes, keep moving. It can get a little confusing in there, but I know every turn of them. Just keep your eyes on me the whole time."

The crowd mumbled and complained as they mindlessly followed Kra. He blocked out their noise as he focused on getting back to the safety of the route.

Kra reached the place for the turn off into the Messenger Route. Instead of an opening there was just solid walls on both sides of the hallway.

"Grubby, stinking klog guts," Kra cursed. He jumped onto the wall, right where the opening had always been before, and dug his claws as deep as possible into the stone. It was undeniably solid.

"You lost boy?" The stone skinned creature asked with a smug grin.

"Oh shut up," Kra replied. "There's something wrong here. All ways out of this section have been removed. That shouldn't be possible."

"I don't have to put up with that kid. I'm a paying customer and you better show me some respect if you…"

"You are a true buthan's rear end," Kra said, giving a rude crinkle to his mouth. "Now shut up and let me think.."

"That's it. What's your name?"

"I said shut up." Kra smacked the creature with his tail and started off down the hallway towards the restaurants. He hoped that somehow at

A Day at Georgie and Armand's Place

least one of their back passages would still be accessible. His tail was hurting from the smack, the creature's skin was hard as rock. As Kra wasn't about to let the customer know he was in pain, he played it tough and moved on.

With a new level of determination Kra once more led the group down the hall.

Their march came to an unexpected halt, as a group of beings were rushing towards them from the restaurants

"This can't be good," Kra mumbled.

"Run you fools," yelled a gnome in a chef's outfit.

Kra looked past the mob and saw the swirling dark cloud making its way towards them from the area of the restaurants.

"You're not going to escape it that way," Kra replied. Kra did a quick reorientation in his head and realized without the messenger routes, there were now no other ways out of the hall.

As the various beings took on various panicked actions, some running in whatever direction they thought safest, while other just froze, and lots of them yelling pointlessly, Kra separated himself from the crowd and curled himself into a disk.

"Klog guts, I was so looking forward to this evening."

Kra closed his eyes, took in a deep breath and relaxed.

It was not long before he felt the disorientation of the dark cloud followed by a sensation of being pulled into free fall. He opened his eyes and saw nothing but swirling darkness as he floated with no sense of up or down.

"I see you were unable to do your job," Colliven's voice came from behind him, somewhere in the chaos.

Kra said nothing as he closed his eyes and returned to his state of relaxing, letting himself drift aimlessly.

The Endless Cleansing

All the poor lost souls.

      The Pendragon boy once more squeals out his corruptive tones. There is nothing of value in the nonsense that emerges from his mouth. He is sinful and wicked. His lust for carnal pleasures is well known. I find it sickening at how the masses gather to watch his insulting performances. He tempts them, and many allow themselves to get lost in his deceptive display.

      I dare not concern myself with this gathering of sinners. Yes, they are wicked, but it is a personal damnation they create. I have found that warning them serves little purpose as they are not wont to listen to such truths. They present a great danger mostly to themselves.

While the Pendragon is a corrupter, I find he mostly draws the already-wicked to his side. I have not seen him actually pursue an innocent soul, although such beings are a rarity in this cursed place. This dwelling of the foul dragons is a testimony to depravity, a repellent to all things pure.

In a den of sinners, one needs to be selective in choosing the greater powers to combat or one will find oneself quickly overwhelmed in their duty to cleanse. No matter how noble the soul, there is none able to destroy all the sinners. Best to pick targets of higher potential corruption.

I have spent a great many hours in this den of wickedness studying them. I have learned all I need about the hierarchy that rules here.

I watched as the androgynous one known as Shea Blossk entered with its standard entourage of the lesser wicked hoping to gain favor with the great seducer. Here in the Temple of the Dragons, Shea Blossk is not the highest of the evil, but it ranks in the higher circles with open ambition to achieve that top position, using its omni-sexual ways to gain control over others. Shea Blossk does

A Day at Georgie and Armand's Place

not leave the Hotel proper; it is one of those who dwell eternally in this foul hole. It knows it is safe as the dragons have proclaimed no killing within their realm. For while these monstrous beasts encourage debauchery of all manner, if their guests openly slaughtered one another their profits would soon be in decline.

Those like Shea Blossk, who have acquired a great number of enemies, know to hide in holes where they are untouchable. It is a cowardly action. They sit back and have others commit the sins for them in their name. They are the greater demons here, yet I am limited in my actions towards them.

Shea Blossk's group always congregates in the darkness, hiding as deep as they can in the shadows where they belong. If only they possessed some level of decency and remained there.

I shall not hide. I walk through their territory with unflinching determination. They all know I am there.

"Can I help ya, ya grey freak," one of the lesser of them spits out in an attempt to intimidate me.

I gaze into his eyes, allowing my righteous light to pierce into the emptiness of his soul.

He backs away.

Shea Blossk grins at me. It takes on this face when it is attempting to be unafraid. I know better.

"Hello Fringe. I'm guessing you have no actual business with me, as usual. I've often wondered if you get off on harassing us poor legitimate business folk. Don't even know if your species *can* get off."

It looks at me hoping for a reply. I am aware that my gaze has no effect on it, as it is already too much of a corrupted soul for the light to affect. Yet I am also aware that my presence unsettles it.

"I am expecting someone of real importance, so if you could please remove your creepy little self, we can avoid a problem."

I take my leave of it. Not because its threat worries me. I do not fear those such as it. They can do no true harm to me.

I find a new area from which I can witness this meeting of corrupted souls. There is

A Day at Georgie and Armand's Place

anticipation of the emergence of an accessible beast deserved of being cleansed.

I blend into the crowd as is my talent. I go unnoticed in the shadows, motionless, watching all.

I wait. I have learned to be patient. My task is great and deserving of restraint. The opportunity will come.

Shea Blossk's pawns come and go. I know many of them. I have debated in the past if they need to be cleansed and someday they will be. They are my regular targets when there is no greater evil that needs to be cleansed. Today, I let them go. The aura from the corruptors is that something greater is in the air this day.

I did not notice this new creature enter. He moved casually. If he had not gone to Shea Blossk's table, I might never have taken notice of him. Yet there he is. An unassuming being that like me knows how to go unnoticed.

I know not who it is and might never once think it to be a greater demon if our paths crossed at a different point. Here it is associating with Shea Blossk with no fear, no nervousness, as an equal or maybe even a better.

This is a being best kept track of.

I am able to catch some of their conversation over the mindless chatter that flows around us.

"…no such maps exist. Georgie and Armand are the only ones who know the full arrangement of this place and how to navigate it all."

"…The Sacred Gatekeepers? I wouldn't mess with them…"

All I am hearing is Shea Blossk's words. Nothing this newcomer says reaches me. He knows how to be heard only by those he chooses. He is clearly skilled and more cautious than those he deals with. Talk of the Gatekeepers is troublesome. As I do not believe this creature to be suicidal or foolish, he must be confident in his abilities to contemplate confrontational interaction with them.

They do not talk long. I get the impression that a lot is discussed in the short time. This creature is very much business oriented, not one to waste time. He is soon on the move. I do not allow him to vanish from my sight.

He moves through the corridors with the casual ease of one free of all worry. It is clear he is

A Day at Georgie and Armand's Place

at home here. The foulness of this place seems to empower him.

No one takes notice of him. If I were not focused on him, he would have already faded into the crowd, even in these lightly traveled hallways. He is highly skilled. I find myself in both awe and apprehension.

This being slips through the lobby, moving with ease around those coming and going. He makes no pause, with no one pausing for him. Even I have a hard time moving that flawlessly.

He exits. I follow.

The world I find myself in is a tech based one. Low level. Unremarkable. It will be easy for me to do my work here. I shall catch this creature and remove it from life for the better of all. Best to end it before we have to deal with his full potential.

I gain on him quickly. The crowds here matter none to me. I shall return to the dragons' den before any local authority can arrive.

It is time. I give my prayer. I allow the righteous energies to overtake me. I take the leap, dagger in hand.

I find myself landing awkwardly.

He is not there. I had not taken my eyes off him.

A quick look around and I see a form entering a doorway. I waste no time.

Through the doorway I find myself entering a large room. There are people gathered here. In my haste I have allowed myself to be seen. None of them look happy to see me.

The smell of sin fills this place. It does not take a trained eye to see the signs of corruption. A table covered with weapons. Another overflowing with currency. There are many items I cannot identify, although I am sure some are narcotics. In the mix of technological components I spot a bundle of scrolls that are clearly out of place.

"Okay now little grey dude, best not to do anything stupid."

"What the hell is that thing?"

"Looks like some undead monkey."

"Yeah, some kind of orangutan in a gasmask and a hoodie."

"What's the call, boss?"

The man who is clearly in charge looks me over. He is not the creature I followed here, but he is clearly a powerful corrupter. I make a prayer. I am empowered to make a clearly needed

A Day at Georgie and Armand's Place

cleansing here. I take in the location of all thirty-three individuals in the chamber with me.

"Kill it and get back to work."

I am at their table of weapons before they are able to respond to their master. My daggers have already flown into four of their throats. I leap from the table with projectile weapons in both hands.

As I discharge their weapons upon them, they scatter. They know fear now. Those who have not been lucky enough to meet their ends already, will be filled with fear before they get released.

The weapons are empty. Nine more have been cleansed.

I take a leap and let loose a barrage of my special darts. I need only pierce their skin to deliver them into the cold embrace. Three are hit.

I pull out my razor cord. I hold still, allowing these puppets to gather around, believing they have me surrounded.

The cord flies out of my hand. I direct it around in a wide circle. Limbs go flying. Seven more fall to the ground. Three of them release panicked screams that soon fade.

I snatch up the weapons they had prepared to use on me. I quickly deal with those who are fleeing. Six more fall.

The boss is making for a transport with three of his sheep discharging their weapons at me. Three daggers fly from my hands, each one finding its target.

The boss is left alone with me. An effortless leap brings me face to face with him.

"What the hell are you?"

I give no reply. I reach out. I take the man's head in my hands and I twist. The snap signals that my work here is done.

I go to gather my gear back up. I am alone with the cleansed.

"Now that was quite the show."

The voice is soft and controlled. I am left clueless as to the direction it comes from. I know it must be the creature who led me here.

I scan the tables and take note that the scrolls are missing.

"I thank you for your help here. I wonder if our paths will meet again, although it will be best if you do not attempt to make that happen any sooner than needed."

A Day at Georgie and Armand's Place

I dislike being used. This being has left me unbalanced. It is not an enjoyable feeling.

It is time to return to the dragon's establishment. There is more cleansing to do.

Now there is a new force of corruption out there that I need to watch out for. I know not what it has planned. All I am sure of at this point is that there is activity in motion that will give the advantage to the sinners.

Ian Brazee-Cannon

It's Complicated

The five short rosy-skinned creatures danced in
circles around each other in time to the upbeat
music that could barely be heard over the noise of
the gathered crowd. They lined up, kicking their
stubby legs into the air, raising their frilly skirts,
performing an overly ridiculous rendition of the
can-can. Laughter erupted as one of them flirted
with one of the more humanoid audience members
of the audience.

White-Star sat in his faded military
fatigues, devoid of the patches that once were
worn proudly, nursing his drink and playing with
the compass circle on his watch, as he watched the
show. He did not know the world the bitter bluish
green liquor came from, but there was a taste to it

A Day at Georgie and Armand's Place

that attracted him. It was called 'Latchen' and was served at all the bars in the Hotel, or, at least all the ones that served carbon based, oxygen breathers that he knew of. White-Star had been a long-time resident of Georgie and Armand's place, but even he had not yet made it to all corners of the inter-dimensional hotel.

"This is not your normal hangout old man," came a control voice from behind White-Star

White-Star turned to face the owner of the voice and froze when he saw the slender young man that was standing there. He wore a simple leather vest covered in beads and charms, along with a pair of loose trousers being held up by a leather belt, with various pouches hanging off it. He also carried a satchel and a hefty staff.

White-Star got to his feet and put his arms around the young man. The hug was returned.

"It's great to see you Gateway. What brings you to this part of the Hotel?"

"Well father, I was actually looking for you. For some reason you were not at the Peachy Pegasus."

"Pendragon was scheduled to perform as part of Georgie's big show today and he's going through some damn phase where he sounds like a bag of drowning chipmunks."

With an understanding nod Gateway replied, "That would be his Derovian Chanting."

"Whatever it is, I don't wanna be around it," White-Star replied with a dismissive wave.

"During mating season the Derovian males use their chanting to attract females,' Gateway explained. "Interestingly, there appears to be some crossover as females from a fair amount of humanoid species can become highly sexually aroused by the chanting. While the chanting only enhances the feeling a female already has, those females would be more likely to act upon any attraction they might have been denying. My guess is that Pendragon will find his groupies more susceptible to his charms."

"Wait, you're saying the girls back at the Peachy Pegasus will be…"

"Most likely."

"Well, maybe I ought to head back over there and learn to appreciate the contributions of other cultures."

"Actually, father, I ask that you put your womanizing ways aside for a little bit. I have need of your skills."

A Day at Georgie and Armand's Place

Silence fell between the two of them.

"You want to hire me?" There was clear doubt in White-Star's face.

"Yes."

"You have no problem with actually working with me?"

Gateway gave an understanding bob to his head. "When you are sober and refrain from chasing after everything female, your company is not unpleasant."

"But what can an old merc do that a grandmaster sorcerer of a million disciplines cannot? You looking to give me a little charity now?"

"I am only master of twenty-four disciplines and a mere student of two hundred and seventeen others," Gateway replied. "Yet, even with all my mystic knowledge, there are times when more traditional skills, like those of a military nature, prove to be essential for a given situation. And, while, if I put effort into looking, I am sure I would be able to find someone of greater skill, I do believe you are a good choice and as my father it seems like a reasonable way to help you out and do something together. I believe that has been one of our requests of me after all. "

Again, there was silence.

White-Star looked his son in the eyes. There was no hiding the awkwardness he felt, but he knew his son wasn't going to pick up on it. He couldn't deny that he wanted to spend time with Gateway, even if the bizarreness of his life has left the son being older than the father.

"Well, take the lead, boy. You can tell me the details on the way."

*****

Gateway never once paused as he traversed the twisting passageways of Georgie and Armand's place despite the hallways and bridges being confusing to even some of the more established inhabitants. As they were moving mostly through the magical zones of the Hotels, White-Star found himself in unfamiliar territory.

"A short while ago I was supposed to meet up with a Cralton mage, a regular associate of mine. He wanted me to assist in an exploration that he claimed would 'open new doors' for us," Gateway explained as they walked. "I was curious enough to agree to hear the details. For unknown reasons, he never made the meeting. I attempted to

A Day at Georgie and Armand's Place

communicate with him to learn why, but there was no reply.

"Normally I would not have pursued the issue, just assumed something had changed and that he would contact me at some point to clarify. However, during my time at the meeting place, others came looking for him. These others were known to me to not be interested in what I consider fruitful ends for others with their endeavors. If they were interested in the discovery, then I needed to ensure their failure."

Gateway left the regular hallways and entered a side passage that was clearly enchanted to not be noticed.

"Where are we going?" White-Star asked.

"Our destination is not one of the more regularly traveled worlds. We will be using one of the lesser known lobbies to get there. It is a highly technological world, with weak magic."

White-Star was getting uncomfortable with the ever narrowing and darkening corridors they were traveling. If it were not for his son's undeterred pace he might have turned back.

"In my further investigation, I discovered that my associate may have discovered the secret to a legendary artifact from that world. In his overly secretive nature, he left no clues as to just what he had discovered. After several days I had gained little knowledge and it felt as though there were pieces missing. It was clear I was overlooking something. Then, today, I received confirmation that the others who were looking for my associate were headed for that world. I knew I needed to act, even without a complete picture.

"As your training as a ranger is all about looking at such situations with a unique perspective," Gateway explained. "It was clear to me that you possessed the skills that could help me put the pieces together."

They emerged into a cool, dark chamber. Across the chamber was a solid wall of grey rock. A black, monolithic podium rested in front of the wall.

"This is a dead-end..." White-Star remarked.

"Not for us," Gateway replied. "It is a special access-only world. No open travel is allowed from it."

"What do we do now?"

"She'll be her shortly."

A black spot appeared on a segment of the grey stone behind the podium. It quickly expanded

A Day at Georgie and Armand's Place

like an aperture of a camera. It stopped with a two-foot diameter. Two brown twigs emerged from the darkness and elongated to form a pair of spider-like legs, followed by a rat-like head missing the nose, attached to a circular, furry brain-shaped body, with a second pair of spider legs finishing off the creature. The spider/rat/brain took perch on the top of the podium.

"Mmm'ddeliommm, I hope all is well."

"Yessss Massster Gateway," Mmm'ddeliommm replied. "Thisss mussst be you sssire."

"Father, this is Mmm'ddeliommm. She is one of the Hotel's sacred gatekeepers. Mmm'ddeliommm this is my father White-Star."

"Hisss accessss hasss been approved."

"Uhh, thank you," White-Star replied.

"Are you sssure he isss you sssire? He doesss not project even a fraction of your grandioussss."

White-Star gave Mmm'ddeliommm a cold look and said, "What's that supposed to mean?"

"I assure you he is my father," Gateway said, placing a calming hand on White-Star. "Best we get on our way."

"Of courssse."

Mmm'ddeliommm bobbed up and down a few times. Shadows danced over the walls, though White-Star could make out no source for the light. Mmm'ddeliommm froze with her legs fully stretched, then slowly returned to her original position.

White-Star was so caught up in watching Mmm'ddeliommm that he stumbled in surprise when he noticed there was now an open doorway in the stone wall.

"I wisssh you sssuccessss in your quessst."

"Thank you Mmm'ddeliommm."

"Uh yeah, thanks."

*****

The world on the other side of the doorway had clearly seen better days. White-Star found himself in the wreckage of what must have, at one time, been a truly magnificent city. The gleaming silver of the buildings was still obvious through the overgrowth of vines and the crumbling of the structures.

"What the fuck happened here?" White-Star asked.

A Day at Georgie and Armand's Place

"No one knows for sure," Gateway replied.

"Do you think this magical doohickey we're after had anything to do with it?"

"No. I can sense that there was nothing mystical about what happened here. There clearly was a war, but the weapons that could have caused this, wiping out a population without destroying everything, are cause for caution. It is why this world is sealed off from regular travel."

"Why do you need to use the Hotel's doors? Can't you just poof yourself here?"

"The magic on this world is so weak," Gateway explained. "Creating my own portal here could drain me with no way to recharge and leave us stranded."

"Nice to know my kid has some limits and ain't the all-powerful demi-god the stories make him sound like."

"There are stories about me?" Gateway inquired in a surprised tone.

"Seriously?" White-Star replied. "Come on, you're a legend at the Hotel. The tales of you often talk about your father having carried and birthed you with the help of an actual goddess, yet somehow never mention me by name. According to these stories your father was a warrior from a distant land and pretty much ends it there."

"That has accuracy to it."

"I try to fill in the blanks when I can, as that is about all they tell of my story."

Gateway gaze his father a quizzical look. "Would you like them to include how my mother was a drunken one-night stand in the Hotel, that you have never seen again? Or that you are not even sure what species she was, just that we are sure she was not human?"

White-Star let out a frustrated breath. "How about how me and my team were caught up in a battle of gods across multiple dimensions? Or how I slayed a crazed Darkening Beast with you strapped to my back because the goddess put me on a quest to secure your destiny? Or any of the deadly adventures I was caught up in with you as an infant?"

"They really mention none of your adventures in their stories of me?"

"Not a one," White-Star said with a shake of his head. "They barely talk about anything before your birth, then they jump four years to when Merlin showed up and convinced me to let him take you for training."

A Day at Georgie and Armand's Place

"Interesting."

"That's all you have to say about it?"

"Well, it is not like I have control over the stories people tell of me."

"Let's just get this over with. Where we headed?"

"Out of the city towards those mountains," Gateway replied, gesturing towards the not too distanced peaks. "There should be a mining facility not too far out, where the workers uncovered an ancient temple with the artifact. My associate was reported to have been traveling there when he disappeared."

*****

The trek through the city was uneventful. Outside of various rodents, insects and birds that kept their distance, there was nothing alive beyond the abundant plant life that was slowly covering over the once-great city. White-Star made note that there were no signs of any larger creatures.

Past the buildings a young forest was reclaiming the land, breaking through the roads and artificial structures that clearly had dominated at one time.

"I'm getting a faint sense of something magical," Gateway said. "Hard to pinpoint though."

"I'd say not too far off to the right from here."

"What is the reasoning for your claim?"

"Look at the trees here," White-Star said motioning with his head to their right.

Gateway turned and looked up at the trees.

"What am I looking for?"

"Look at the very tops."

"I see a lot of broken branches," Gateway replied.

"Right."

"Which means?"

"Looking at the branches, you can see patterns. It's a clear grouping of them, with the ones further to our left having the highest branches broken, while the ones to our right go lower. And if you look even farther along, you see broken branches at even lower spots the farther right we look."

"I see. That would suggest a descending craft of some manner having passed over this area."

A Day at Georgie and Armand's Place

White-Star turned face-to-face with his son. "And since this planet seems to be empty of its native advanced lifeforms, chances are your friends are already here."

"That is not a beneficial turn of events," gateway remarked.

"Do you really think these guys are going to be dangerous if they get this thing?"

"I have no doubt they would use the artifact for purposes that will be harmful to others."

"Then let's get moving and hope they haven't left yet."

"Right," Gateway said, tapping his staff on the ground. The staff glowed and reconfigured its form so that Gateway's right arm and shoulder were now covered in a wooden armor that contained the same inscription the staff had. "This will make it easier for me to move stealthily."

White-Star nodded in agreement and the two of them ducked into the canopy of trees to follow the path that ship had taken.

*****

Father and son emerged at a clearing and took cover behind a long-abandoned piece of loading equipment. Many such vehicles were left deteriorating around the crumbling mining site. A beat-up, but clearly functional shuttle craft rested on the open ground across the site from them.

"Looks like they're still here," White-Star said in a whisper. "Can you sense your magic thingy?"

"The source of magical energy is in there," Gateway replied with equal quiet. "But it is far weaker than it should be for a talisman of the expected level."

"You sure it's worth the effort?"

"I cannot say. My associate could have overstated its value. While at the same time it could be encased in some manner that holds back its full power. I would gamble on it being best to take possession of the object ourselves."

"You're the boss here," White-Star replied. "Now a direct line to the mine entrance passes between too many buildings, where most likely they have guards keeping watch, ready to ambush anyone outside of their group. Chances are, there are guards right inside the entrance as well, just out of sight. I've seen two people

A Day at Georgie and Armand's Place

working around their ship. Other than that, they'd have a hard time with all the needed sentries, as this place is not designed to be secured. Our best shot would be to circle around a little bit more and make a direct line for the opening from the side away from the ship. There is no one on lookout and no place a guard could hide on that approach, so we should be in the clear."

"I shall follow your lead in this father. Let us proceed by your plan."

The two of them took off to the side to make their approach. There was little cover, making them cautious with every move. They got to the side of the entrance without confrontation.

"This is a real rookie operation," White-Star remarked. "I've not seen any sign of guards, even from the buildings. Wondering if they don't have too many men."

"I am not sure of their actual numbers. They also might not believe anyone would find them. There are many possible factors at work."

"Yeah, but still we should move quickly and assume there are guards everywhere."

"Agreed."

"We sweep into the entrance on three."

Gateway nodded.

White-Star held up three fingers and did a silent countdown. As his last finger lowered the two of them rushed around the corner and into the entrance to the mine.

They froze, ready for a fight, but there was no one there.

"This is just ridiculous," White-Star commented. "They can't be that confident. They know you're after this thing, right?"

"I never expressed any direct interest," Gateway replied. "They might believe that no one is pursuing them. This is a world that is avoided with penalties from the local space-faring races if they discover you on it."

"I don't trust that. You don't get far being this sloppy."

"We shall be cautious in our actions."

"Shh…"

The two of them fell silent in the still, near darkness. The sounds of movement came from far below them. It was muffled and distorted, but there was clearly activity in the lower levels of the mine.

"At least we know they're still here," White-Star remarked.

A Day at Georgie and Armand's Place

The two of them made their way over towards where the sounds were echoing from. The tunnel opened up into a chamber filled with soft artificial light, which was dominated by a carved shaft reaching deep into the planet. A series of stairs led down the shaft as well as what was clearly an elevator system that was powered up.

White-Star looked over the railing into the darkness, where a spot of light could be seen.

"Not too deep of a mine," he said.

"Any ideas of how we should best go about getting down there?"

White-Star looked around at what was available. He pulled up a cord of rope and tested its strength. It had aged well and was still strong.

"Do you remember how to rappel?"

The two of them got to work in properly securing the ropes to firm anchors before throwing them over the railings.

White-Star examined the elevator controls.

"Good, these are fairly basic," he remarked. "Once you hear the thing starting up, start dropping down. I'll be right behind you."

White-Star threw a switch and waited. A moment later the gears came to life, with the sounds of moving metal echoing through the cavern. He grabbed onto the prepared rope and took off down the shaft.

The two of them reached the level with the activity, their plan seemed to have worked. All attention was focused on the elevator. There were ten visible beings, all armed, each one watching the elevator.

White-Star gave a series of hand signals, to which Gateway gave a nod of understanding in reply. White-Star produced a plasma pistol, then gave a quiet countdown from three.

The two of them landed just past the railing. White-Star fired a series of plasma blasts and Gateway let loose with a wave of mythic energy. As the air cleared, all ten of the beings lay prone on the ground.

"This is going too smoothly," White-Star remarked.

"Something does feel off."

"I thought you said these were ruins down here?"

"That was my understanding."

"This is just a mineshaft kid. No way there are ruins down here. These walls are too solid."

A Day at Georgie and Armand's Place

Gateway stood, looking around as if he were having trouble seeing.

"Are you okay?" White-Star asked with a fatherly tone.

"I'm trying to sense the talisman," Gateway explained. "But there is no connection to magic at all down here. I do not believe I have ever been so cut off before. The one blast has left me nearly drained. I feel…disoriented"

"Well, let's grab this thing and get out of here. My guess is it's in that fancy box there."

Resting on a small work table was a wooden box with various symbols carved into its lid.

"Yes," Gaetway replied. "There is magic there."

Gateway rushed over and opened the box in a manner that made White-Star think picture a dehydrated person being given water.

There was a flash as Gateway touched the treasure inside the box. As his sight cleared up, White-Star saw his son lying unconscious on the ground.

"About time he got here," a voice said from behind him. "We tried to make it as simple as possible to find us."

A tall, thin being with ebony skin walked over to Gateway's body.

"Get him tied up quickly," the being commanded. "Even drained he's dangerous."

White-Star looked around to see that all ten of the beings they had taken out were now standing with their weapons pointed at him.

"Now just who are you," the ebony being asked as he stood in front of White-Star looking down at him.

"Just a merc for hire. And it looks like I'm back on the market. Don't suppose you have any openings right now?"

*****

White-Star found himself disarmed, but allowed to roam, as long as he didn't approach the cave they had taken the tied up Gateway to.

"So you're just going to hang down here?" White-Star remarked as he took a seat with six members of the group. They were passing around a bottle of something alcoholic while playing a card game White-Star was unfamiliar with.

"We're here until we get new orders," one of them replied.

A Day at Georgie and Armand's Place

"If that's what you're gettin' paid for, it works," White-Star looked at the body armor they were all wearing. "Now that is impressive armor. It took on my plasma blasts and the kid's mystic stuff. Where'd it come from?"

"Don't know. We were given it when we agreed to the gig."

White-Star shook his head and let out a low whistle. "Someone is spending big bucks just to take out the magic kid there and keep him down here for a time? Why don't I ever get gigs like this?"

"Everything about this has been a little crazy, but so far the guy's kept up with his payments, and that is really all that matters."

"Well said," White-Star replied. "What ya drinking?"

"Some homebrew Jah'do there makes. Strong stuff."

"Now that sounds like a challenge."

"Here. See what ya think." The hired gun held out the bottle to White-Star.

White-Star took the offered bottle, held it under his nose and sniffed. "Yeah, that is strong." He pulled the bottle to his lips and took a sip. As he lowered the bottle he faked a coughing fit.

Pulling his hands together he opened a hidden compartment in his watch and poured the contents into the bottle.

"Give me that before you drop it," one of them said, taking the bottle from him. It soon returned to being passed around.

The ebony being, who had revealed himself to be Captain Lito, emerged from the darkness and looked at his men.

"The mage is secure. Keep yourselves sober," Lito commanded. "The stories of Gateway make it clear that, even unconscious, without his powers, he's still dangerous."

"Yeah, I heard he took down a Darkening Beast before he learned to walk," Jah'Do remarked.

White-Star's mouth fell open in shock.

"Seriously?" He said.

"What, you don't believe the stories?"

"I just spent the day with the kid," White-Star replied. "You saw how easy it was to fool him and take him out. I mean, he didn't know enough to not grab that jewel you drained his magic with. Besides, I always heard it was his father who fought the Darkening Beast."

A Day at Georgie and Armand's Place

"Never heard any stories about his dad. His mother was a goddess though, right?"

There was a round of agreeing nods as White-Star took in a few calming breaths.

"He has a reputation that should not be overlooked," Lito stated. "So you will control your drinking. After the job is done, we will celebrate properly."

"Any call of my fate yet Captain?" White-Star asked.

"No. That will be decided once this job is finished. For now feel secure that I have not had you killed."

"Oh yeah, I'm very thankful for that," White-Star remarked with a friendly tone. "Any idea how much longer we got?"

"All is at the whim of our client," Liot explained. "Once he is done with his plans, he will send payment."

"What? Then you kill the kid?"

"Oddly enough, no," Lito answered. "We leave him here. Otherwise you both would be dead now."

"Fair enough," White-Star said, giving an agreeing nod.

One of the females of the group tried to get to her feet and fell over.

"I said no getting drunk!" Liot shouted.

"I'm sorry. Must have…" She trailed off into unconsciousness. One by one the other five slipped into similar states as Captain Lito continued to yell at them.

"They were right, that is strong stuff," White-Star commented. "Glad I only took a sip."

"Shut up," Lito said, clearly annoyed.

"Hey, it just looks like you might be in the market for some sober help right now. Sorry, but I know an opportunity when I see one."

"You've yet to earn my trust," Lito replied. "Stay here." The Captain moved back into the cave.

White-Star didn't waste any time. He jumped towards the nearest body and pulled off the armor and slipped it on himself. He had made note of all their gear early on. One of them had a set of small blaster pistols, that were only good for close combat, which was perfect for his needs here.

Two of Lito's crew came out of the cave while White-Star was rummaging for the pistols.

A Day at Georgie and Armand's Place

"Hey, get away from them," one of them said.

"Oh sorry, just seeing if he's still breathing." White-Star got to his feet quickly as the two of them were looking at their fallen comrade with some concern. "I think he's good though."

"Take that armor off."

"But I'm gonna need it."

"Why's that?"

"Because things are about to get real messy down here."

White-Star leapt between the two of them and jabbed the acquired pistols into the gap at their necks and fired a blast under the armor. They both fell to the ground.

"What's going on out here?" Lito asked as he emerged from the cave.

"I think I just ruined my chances for a job with you," White-Star replied.

Lito drew his pistol and fired several blasts. White-Star flinched as the blasts exploded just inches in front of him, with him barely feeling the impact.

"So that's how this armor works. Seems we're at a standoff now."

The other two crew members exited the cave and stood next to their captain.

"I believe we have the numbers still," Lito remarked.

"Won't the force field keep us from being able to hit each other?"

"We'll hold you down and remove it," Lito replied. "Slow enough movements won't activate the fields. Get him."

The two crew members moved toward White-Star.

"Okay now, just hold on a moment," White-Star said backing away. "You know, there was one thing you were right about."

"What are you talking about?"

"My son, Gateway there, he's dangerous and you should never underestimate him."

Lito and his crew turned to look at the cave. Gateway quickly rushed Lito, stabbing a knife slowly into the Captain's neck. White-Star took the opportunity to jab his pistols into the crew members necks and fired.

"Good to see you remembered how to get out of being tied up," White-Star said, a proud smile on his face.

A Day at Georgie and Armand's Place

"As I was being taught such skills since I was three years old," Gateway replied. "I must admit it is second nature for me."

"I wasn't sure. You seemed to be a little off with your judgment today."

"I am not in a healthy frame of mind. This world is detrimental for magic and those of us who are connected to it."

"Now let's get back to the Hotel. I get the feeling that something's about to go down there, and for some reason whoever's behind it needed you out of the way."

Ian Brazee-Cannon

The Balance

A gust of wind whipped over the hill as the great beast burst forth from its hiding place among the thick white bushes. Han'Gra stood her ground with her spear at the ready. Two wild golden eyes focused on her as the monstrous jaws opened. The creature let loose a chilling growl signifying its intent to devour its prey as it charged at full speed. It took to the air to cover the last of the distance between them. Han'Gra raised her spear, giving it a forceful shove, piercing the rough skin, driving deep into the flesh. Dark red blood spurted out, darkening the wispy white fur.

A Day at Georgie and Armand's Place

Han'Gra rolled away, dodging the massive claws that struck out at her. She could tell the spear had missed any major organs, prolonging the fight. Her aim had been off due to the quickness of the beast and the idea of making the creature suffer before its demise bothered her. Better to end it quickly, with a minimum of pain. Just because she possessed skills in dealing death and understood the need for it at times, didn't mean she enjoyed all the aspects that went along with taking on a job. She respected the balance of life and death, showing honor to the great god Rya'Je, overseer of existence.

Getting to her feet, Han'Gra rushed over to the bundle of spears resting in the back of her simple, two-wheeled, supply cart. She pulled forth a fresh one and turned as the creature closed in on her.

As the beast swung its deadly claw at her, she ducked to its right side and plunged the spear with all her strength into its side.

The gush of blood signified a far more deadly hit. Han'Gra was fairly sure she had gotten the creature's heart this time. She picked up another spear and rushed at the creature's other side.

The spear embedded itself firmly in the beast's flesh.

That was enough to drive the fight out it. The creature stumbled a bit, before collapsing onto its right side, snapping the spear imbedded there.

Han'Gra drew her sword and approached the creature. She held out her three-fingered hand and gently placed it on the creature's nose.

"I do apologize for taking your life noble being," Han'Gra said in a calming voice. "You are beautiful and I wish circumstances had been different. But you have been hunting the locals here, and, in the greater level of balance, it has come down to you encountering me. While you have every right to hunt and feed, your pray has every right to find ways to stop you. It is the essence of survival."

Han'Gra raised her sword and struck right between the creature's golden eyes. With a firm push the blade penetrated the skull, piercing the brain, bringing the creature peace.

Once there was no doubt that all life had left the body, Han'Gra took out her small daggers and began work to dig out both the creature's eyes. After she pulled them out she tied them to a tree branch to let their fluids drain dry.

A Day at Georgie and Armand's Place

As Han'Gra waited, she looked out at the clear brilliant green sky with its white sun. It was nothing like the skies of Shandry, her home world. Her quests had led her to dozens of worlds, each with its own sky, none of them matching the vibrantly colorful skies that were a living show of twisting lights and clouds she had grown up with. She awkwardly shuffled around on her skinny, boneless legs as she tried to not think about home.

Once the eyes had dried out, Han'Gra took them down and placed them in leather sheets which she wrapped up tightly and loaded onto the cart.

*****

It was an easy enough task to guide the cart down the hill, towards the town of Roedoblo. The gathering of people at the road into town was clearly going to be Han'Gra's next obstacle.

There were eight of them waiting there in the open. All of them Nagetins, with long furry noses and stubby tails. Each of them carried a sword, but they were not fighters. Their culture taught the use of trickery over direct confrontation. It was one of the main reasons they had to hire someone to deal with the beast. They had the numbers, but were unable to sneak up on it. Rushing it was out of the question for them, as not one of them was willing to risk their life in such an attack.

"Greetings," Han'Gra said, bringing the cart to a halt. "The beast has been slain. Its remains are still up there if you desire to verify the deed. You can return to your people and assure them it is once more safe to roam this area."

"We are grateful for your work," the Nagetin in the front replied. "Now we need you to hand over the eyes to us."

"No. I'm to deliver those to your council members who hired me. I'm sure they would be willing to allow all the villagers to get a good look at the eyes afterwards."

"I don't think you understand what's going on here."

"Oh, I fully understand," Han'Gra replied coldly. "I'm not sure you have grasped just who you are dealing with, though."

"We'd rather this go without you getting hurt."

A Day at Georgie and Armand's Place

"That will happen no matter what. It would go best for you if you back away now and let me continue on."

"I will give you one last chance," the Nagetin said, raising his sword.

"Do you really think I'm not aware of the four archers you are getting ready to signal? You're not warriors. I can smell the fear on you from here. There is not a one of you who could survive against me, even if you were to rush as one. Don't waste your lives just because your council is trying to be cheap."

The Nagetin looked around nervously and said, "We have the numbers. Just give us the eyes."

"I already told you, no." Han'Gra drew her sword and began to bend her legs.

The Nagetin's arm shook as he dropped his sword.

Han'Gra let out a frustrated breath as she hunched down, when the pressure in her muscles felt right, she released her legs, catapulting her into the air. Four arrows struck the cart where she had just been.

There was confusion and panic as Nan-Gra flew over the assembled Nagetins. She lashed out with non-lethal blows as they turned to face her. Four of them were now on the ground, rolling in pain.

There was no surprise when two of them took off at a furious pace as Han'Gra engaged the other two who were still standing there. They tried to put up a fight, but it was hopeless. Both of them fell quickly.

"If you value your lives, you will drop your bows and run for it," Han'Gra announced. Four bows dropped from the nearby trees, followed by four Nagetins, who took off at full speed, away from the area.

"Be glad I did not see the need for any deaths here today," Han'Gra said as she picked up the Nagetin that had done all the talking. "You live by the grace of Rya'Je and the respect for the balance of life. I shall update your council members of this when I meet with them in the Hotel."

Han'Gra dropped the Nagetin and returned to her cart.

There were no other disturbances on her way to the Hotel door. In fact the streets seemed to be even emptier than they should have been. The Nagetins clearly did not understand the idea of the

A Day at Georgie and Armand's Place

Balance, as revenge was a practice Han'Gra never took part in. No innocents would be harmed because of their council's attempt at betrayal.

*****

The musky aroma of abundant plant life relaxed Han'Gra as she entered the Jangul Lobby of Georgie and Armand's place. This wing of the Hotel catered to a more natural feel with large planters, filled with a truly unique variety of plants from dozens of worlds, filling large portions of the lobby and hallways. Most of the rooms in this area had dirt floors, some being filled wall-to-wall with dirt, making burrowing the only way to enter them..

The organic feel gave Han'Gra comfort; the Hotel was her home now and she foresaw no signs of that changing as there was little doubt her exile from Shandry would ever be reversed.

The leather bundles were tied together and draped over her shoulder. She had made sure there was no chance of dripping unwanted fluids. It was a mistake she had made in the past and had not left her in good standing with the Hotel staff.

Han'Gra had learned from her mistakes and now had a mutually respectful relationship with the staff.

She exchanged simple greetings with those she passed as she made her way to the Peachy Pegasus. She was driven to bring this endeavour to a quick ending and be done with her association with the Roedoblo Council. Such attempted betrayal went against the Balance; you honored your deals and paid for what you agreed to.

Ta'bith was manning the hostess booth as Han'Gra entered.

"Are the Nagetins here yet?" Han'Gra asked.

"Yes, they're seated overlooking the large room's stage," Ta'bith replied. "It seems they are Pendragon fans, as they were highly interested in catching his show."

"Of course they are." Han'Gra gave an acknowledging nod and made her way through the crowded restaurant. She could hear Conrad Pendragon's Derovian Chanting. She felt herself entering a state of arousal that she easily brushed away. Part of embracing the Balance was self-control . Her species rarely came to the Hotel and

A Day at Georgie and Armand's Place

she had no desire to engage in cross-species intimacy, as she viewed such encounters as disturbing. Control of her sexual desires was something she had come to terms with some time ago, fighting off the urges when they came.

Finding their table was not difficult- the seven Nagetins were in a celebratory mood that clearly made the Flayian Banker sitting with them a little uncomfortable. He had all four of his stubby hands on the table with all sixteen of his fingers tapping in an awkward rhythm.

Han'Gra walked up to the table, pulled the leather bundles from her shoulder and placed them in front of the Nagetins.

Pmur't, head of the Roedoblo Council paused in his inappropriate activities towards a female council member and looked up at Han'Gra.

"Our mighty slayer has returned," He said. "It is regretful that you..." He fell silent when he took notice of the leather bundles. "And what are those?"

"The creature's golden eyes," Han'Gra replied. "Delivered as evidence of completion of my task, as per our agreement."

"Uh... So there were no... difficulties then?"

"If you are asking about your band of would be robbers, no difficulties there. I dealt with them quickly."

"What about Non'ab!" One of the females let slip.

"Always good to have confirmation of deceit," Han'Gra stated. "But do not fear for your loved ones, I took no lives in our confrontation.

"Now please verify that I have delivered on my part of our agreement. Okada seems anxious to finish this up."

The Flayian Banker nodded his chubby head in agreement and said, "Yes, let's get this over with."

Pmur't rose and reluctantly untied one of the bundles. There was no denying the golden eyeball that rested before him. He untied the second one to expose that eyeball as well.

"Do you agree that all the terms of the contract have been met by Han'Gra?" Okada asked.

"Yes, I do," Pmur't replied solemnly.

"As you did attempt deceit, I will invoke the 'trustworthy' amendment of the contract. That would double the fee as well as free me from the

A Day at Georgie and Armand's Place

'Offspring' agreement," Han'Gra added. "Better hope the creature did not spawn any pups."

Okada handed Pmur't a clipboard and said, "Please initial here and here, then sign at the bottom."

Pmur't shook his head as he did as he was instructed.

Okada then handed the clipboard to Han'Gra, who signed and initialed where needed.

Okada looked over the paperwork, nodding as he doubled checked it all.

"All is in order," Okada stated. "The money is being transferred to Han'Gra's account." He tapped the back of the clipboard twice. Two copies of the paperwork fell onto the table. Okada handed one copy to Han'Gra and one to Pmur't.

"Good day," Okada said as he rose from the table and made his exit.

Han'Gra prepared to leave as well, but stopped and turned back towards the table.

"One of the reasons I conduct all my business inside of the Hotel is because of their well-crafted system," Han'Gra explained. "The Dragons realized early on that for a place like this to be able to fully accommodate the needs of so many worlds they would have to create and continuously update the business side of things. Their banking system is far more complex than anything found elsewhere in all the realities out there, with such a great amount of services offered. All my contracts are done through their systems, a system that only the most foolish try to cheat."

"Is there any point to this?" Pmur't asked, clearly annoyed.

"Their system is not structured to benefit cheats," Han'Gra explained. "It is set up in a manner that respects the Balance. You follow your agreement and the other side follows theirs, everyone benefits the most. I take no pleasure in receiving extra pay from you. You gambled, fought the Balance and you lost. I know your people are not wealthy, but here you are wasting what little they have. This Hotel and the Balance can serve you well if you let them.

"I wish a prosperous future for you and your people."

Han'Gra took her leave and headed over to the bar. A mildly intoxicating drink sounded enjoyable. Pendragon had finished his performance, now it was time for Georgie to begin his fashion show. While Han'Gra never

A Day at Georgie and Armand's Place

understood the concept of fashion, she did find it enjoyable to see the creative use of fabrics and colors in the various creations they showed off.

It would be a nice relaxing way to end the day.

An Interview with
Conrad Pendragon

The small crowd of employees that had been working in The Peachy Pegasus cheered as Conrad Pendragon and his band finished up their rehearsal.

"Bravo, bravo, you sound as lovely as ever," Georgie said, standing next to the stage applauding.

"Thank you Georgie," Conrad replied. "What did you think of 'Children of the Nexus'?"

"I loved it, but 'Suzanne's Story' will always be my favorite."

A Day at Georgie and Armand's Place

"I know, and I promise to include it in every show I do for you, handsome."

"Enough with the charm, I'm taken you know," Georgie replied, playfully flirting.

"I know, and it breaks my heart," Conrad playfully flirted back.

"Sure it does. Now there is a young lady that I know is more to your taste waiting over at the bar, hoping for an interview. Go and charm her my boy, I must finish up preparations. The show starts in just two hours."

Conrad looked over at the bar and saw a highly attractive brunette, with all the right curves, sitting there watching him.

"Her?"

"Yes, her."

"Oh Georgie, you're the greatest. Did she hear my Derovian Chanting?"

"No sweetie, she came in near the end of your set. Her name is Olivia Alba. Go and don't have too much fun, the show starts in two hours and you are my third act."

"If all goes well, I'll hold off the real fun until after the show."

Georgie hustled off backstage as Conrad headed for the bar.

He casually walked over to the reporter and said, "Hello, I'm Conrad Pendragon, I understand you're interested in interviewing me?"

"Yes, I'm Olivia Alba with Measures of Reality, the Cross Dimensional News Agency," Olivia said, holding out her hand.

Conrad took her hand, raised it to his lips and kissed it.

"It is a pleasure to meet you," Conrad said, displaying his most charming smile.

"Thank you. Now about that interview," Olivia replied in a fully professional voice.

"Yes, of course. I love doing interviews. Best to head back to my dressing room, as they will be opening the doors and this place will get flooded with our audience soon."

"Okay."

*****

Conrad offered Olivia a seat then made himself comfortable in the chair across from her.

"Would you like some water? Or maybe something from the bar?"

"No thanks, I'm good. I'm going to start recording now," Olivia said as she placed a device

A Day at Georgie and Armand's Place

on the small table between them. She pressed a button and a red light on top lit up.

"Right to business I see," Conrad remarked. "I like a woman who knows what she wants."

"This is Olivia Alba with Measures of Reality, backstage with Conrad Pendragon at The Peachy Pegasus. In just over an hour he will be performing as part of one of Georgie's big shows. This is where you got your start and seems to be a favorite venue for you."

"Yes, my first concert was here, before I had even recorded any songs. Georgie liked my voice and convinced me to give it a try. And there is nowhere else that you will find such a diverse crowd: with beings from thousands and thousands of worlds come here to see me proform, it's always a fresh crowd. And I don't believe I have distribution on all of them yet."

Oliva let out a meek laugh then asked, "You often use this stage as a platform to get a reaction for your new works."

"Yes, I find a live audience to be the best measure of how a new song is going to go over with the fans."

"Just now as you rehearsed, I believe I heard you playing a new song."

"Yes, that was 'Children of the Nexus', a very personal song for me."

"For the fans who are not aware, is that not a direct reference to where you grew up?"

"Correct, you've studied up on me it seems," Conrad remarked with a flash of a knowing smile.

"It's my job," Olivia replied manner-of-factly. "Could you tell us about what a Child of the Nexus is?"

"Now that is a bit of a long story. Not sure where to start."

"From the beginning would be best. We have time."

"Well, okay. As you know, I was born in the underground city of Hineser. Our civilization had moved underground several centuries before due to various events making the surface unlivable. There were strict laws about leaving the city, as the claim was there were dangers in the caverns outside the walls. I grew up in a very small, controlled world. I was actually involved with politics there, believe it or not.

A Day at Georgie and Armand's Place

"For our schooling we were grouped together with others of our age, from our district. These were the handful of people you knew since you were born as your friends, even if you didn't like them. You also knew all your neighbors and were familiar with just about everyone in the city. There were rarely surprises, and those were always dealt with quickly.

"As I said, it was highly controlled society.

"Then one day, not too long after we started working in our assigned departments, my career test placed me in politics, we were called together for what we thought was going to be a group assessment. When we got there, however, we found ourselves talking with total strangers.

"We knew there were levels to the government that were hidden, but never thought we'd get involved with them. We figured these were the people who cleaned up the unwanted messes while the average citizens looked away. There was a little bit of excitement in the idea of being part of a secret force.

"It was then we learned about alternate worlds and the fact that our city was built next to a nexus of realities. We were told that due to our various talents, that we as a group were to become a team to travel to different dimensions on missions for the government.

"There was some anxiety from others in the group, but I was all in from the get-go. Getting away from the cavern and seeing other worlds. It was more than I ever imagined possible."

As Conrad told his tale, his charming demeanor vanished being replaced with the look and posture of someone getting lost in thought.

"We went to our first world, saw a sun, a real sky, clouds, moons for the first time. It was amazing. We were so caught up in the idea of visiting a new world that we didn't think about how each of us seemed to have new abilities there. We wrote it off as being something that happened when you visited a different world. We finished the mission and returned home.

"It was hard to not tell everyone about what we had seen. The cavern suddenly seemed so small and confining.

"Every time they called us in, I never once hesitated. A mission meant I got to see and experience a whole new world.

"On one of those worlds my ability turned out to be an enhanced voice, that never fully went

A Day at Georgie and Armand's Place

away. Obviously, that is what would lead me to a career in music.

"After one long mission, due to a fluctuation in time, we had been gone from Hineser for a noticeable length. Questions were asked when we returned.

"This led to the revelation that our government had no idea about our missions and that we had actually been working for an interdimensional group that knew far more about what was really going on than our own leaders. All talk about the idea of other realities had been subjugated since the founding of the city, with the nexus itself being denied. It turned out our leaders were just as in the dark about this as everyone else.

"We also learned that during the time frame my schooling group was born, there was a spike in the nexus. For several weeks, one area of the city, the one we were all born in, was flooded with interdimensional energies. For the most part no one was affected by them, outside of us newborn babies. We were connected to the nexus, hence Children of the Nexus.

"What we thought was a regular occurrence of dimensional travel, turned out to be a unique ability of ours. Whenever we found ourselves in a new dimension, we synced up with that dimension. We gained abilities fitting with that world's powers. We became mages on certain worlds, or warriors of the gods on others. On tech worlds we would quickly take to understanding that world's mathematics and physics. On one water world we found we were able to breath underwater, still have no clue how, though."

"That must make Georgie and Armand's Place a little crazy for you," Olivia stated.

"Not as much as you'd think," Conrad replied. "I can feel the changes from area to area, but however they have this place balanced, it's not the same as actually being in a different dimension. Although I prefer recording my songs in the Hotel because there does seem to be an effect to my voice in certain areas."

"I'm guessing the Peachy Pegasus is one of those areas."

"Yes, it is. That's why I try to hold all my in -hotel performances here."

"Have you met other 'Children of the Nexus'?"

"I have. It's rare enough. Most areas with a nexus are viewed as being haunted or the like,

A Day at Georgie and Armand's Place

rarely does anyone intentionally build near one, let alone give birth by one."

"Is there a greater meaning to the song, since it is based on your actual past?"

"All my songs have a greater meaning to them. It's my art, my expression, my soul being put out there for all to experience."

"How poetic," Olivia said playfully.

"While I have enjoyed this time with you tremendously, Olivia, regretfully I do have a show to get ready for," Conrad said, with a slight frown. "However, if you wish to wait around until after my set, we could continue our interview."

"I think that might be a possibility."

*****

The place was packed, with a rush of beings making for the stage when Conrad took the mic. He knew his voice affected more than just the humanoids. He had been hit on by some species that even if he had been attracted to them, he would have had no clue how to seal the deal. It wasn't all about hooking up though. Conrad really did enjoy performing and he could feel the rush of the crowd. He felt empowered on stage.

During his performance, he kept an eye out for Olivia and was pleased to see that she had found a place near the bar and stayed for the whole show. He made sure to focus his gaze at her while performing the Derovian Chanting.

"Thank you, Peachy Pegasus," Conrad said after his final song. "I hope you all enjoyed our performance. Next up is the highlight of the afternoon, one of Georgie's infamous and often scandalous fashion shows. Stay put, order some drinks and enjoy. Love you all." Bringing his fingers to his lips, he blew a kiss to the audience.

Conrad took a few more bows before finally taking his leave.

He made his way through the backstage crowd, accepting praise, clasping hands, giving various salutes and being pleasant, as he edged ever farther to his goal. Many females from a large variety of species approached him with clear intention. Normally he would have started flirting with them and choosing a few to spend the evening with. Now, however, he had a goal and was not going to lose sight of the prize.

When he found Olivia standing outside his dressing room, he could not hide his smile.

A Day at Georgie and Armand's Place

"I hope you enjoyed the show," Conrad remarked, giving her a saucy grin as he opened his dressing room door.

"It was quite the show I have to admit,' Olivia replied. "You are impressive on stage. And from what I've heard, you're equally impressive in other areas."

Conrad's eyes opened wide at the implication. It was clear to him that the Derovian Chanting had had the desired effect.

"I guess I have something of a reputation."

"Why don't you come back to my room and we can see if that reputation is deserved."

"Sounds like a great way to end my day."

*****

Conrad found he could not keep his hands off of Olivia as they made their way through the Hotel. Olivia's hands were all over Conrad as well. They kept finding places out of sight to fall into and make out and sneak hands into each other's clothes.

Conrad was highly excited when they crossed a dimensional boundary that made him freeze up.

"What is it?" Olivia asked, kissing the back of Conrad's neck.

"I don't know... Where are we? I'm not familiar with this part of the Hotel."

"Just taking a rarely used hall to get to my room," Olivia explained, her hands moving into Conrad's pants. "I figured we have a little more privacy this way."

"Sounds good," Conrad replied, followed by a soft moan. "But something feels off here. It's almost like we're not in any reality."

"I'm sure it's just because it's a new area for you." Olivia pressed up close, making sure her breasts were rubbing against his back. "Let's just get to my room quickly and I'll find a way to make you think about other things."

"Uhh....yeah."

Conrad closed his eyes and let himself be directed down the hall, even as the odd feeling intensified.

When they came to a stop, Conrad opened his eyes and was puzzled when all he saw was a stone wall in front of him.

A Day at Georgie and Armand's Place

"Did we take a wrong turn somewhere?' Conrad asked.

"Oh no my dear," a voice other than Olivia's replied. "You are right where you need to be."

Conrad turned and watched as the form of Olivia faded away, with something else taking shape.

"What's going on?"

"Just need you to stay here for a while," the being that had taken Olivia's place said.

The being before Conrad was large and impressive. There was a clear sense of power to him. In the limited lighting the being's impressive physique appeared to be covered in dark stripes. There was something inhuman to his face that Conrad was unable to focus on.

"Wait a moment, was that you I've been..." Conrad reeled back in disgust.

"You weren't complaining a moment ago. Besides, you're really not my type either."

The being turned and walked through the stone wall without another word.

That was when Conrad got a good look around. He had no idea how it had happened, but he was now in a room of four stone walls with no doors or openings and whatever the light source was it was quickly fading. He rushed to where the creature had been to find the wall there just as solid as the other three.

"Oh shit," Conrad said as darkness engulfed him.

*****

Olivia had finally got herself backstage as the fashion show started.

"Olivia, what are you doing here?" Georgie asked when he noticed her.

"I'm looking for Conrad. I thought we were going to meet up after his set to finish the interview."

"So that wasn't you he left with?" Georgie remarked. "I'm so sorry my dear. Conrad can be such the inconsiderate scoundrel."

"Don't worry. It's not like I was going to sleep with him or anything. I have my standards."

"The Derovian Chanting did nothing for you?"

"I had gotten a warning he was going to chant, so I had picked up some special earplugs to

A Day at Georgie and Armand's Place

block its effects. I wouldn't be an effective reporter if I didn't prepare ahead of time."

"I could send a messenger to retrieve him if you need to finish the interview."

"Not necessary. I got enough to do my story."

"Well good. I'm glad it worked out," Georgie siad. "Now I need to get back to my show. I'll give him a piece of my mind next time I see him. It's not like him to standup a beautiful young woman like yourself."

"Thanks. As I have nothing else to do, I'm going to get back out there and enjoy the rest of the show." Olivia turned back into the crowd to find herself a fresh seat in the audience.

The Courtship of
Georgie and Armand
Part 2:
Young Dragons in Love

"They seem to be stable," Archmage Lionope remarked looking at the series of five doorways that lined one of the chamber's walls.

"Well, I hope so," Hax'georget' replied quietly. "I mean, we haven't actually tested them yet, but if everything is set up properly and the spells work as they're supposed to, we should have stable portals to four different worlds without having to give up our adjustable portal.."

"Which one shall we try first?"

A Day at Georgie and Armand's Place

Hax'georget' awkwardly shifted his weight back and forth from one leg to the other. "Oh, I don't know if we should. If they're not stable, we could get trapped on the other side, or if it were to detach while we walked through, there would be no way to tell where we might end up."

"Come now Hax'georget'," Lionope replied with a calm, reassuring tone. "You've been working on these for over a decade now. Have faith in your abilities. If things go wrong, then they go wrong. No way to know until you take that first step. Besides, I can summon my doorway from any realm. We are in no risk of being trapped."

"Right. You're right... of course."

"Why don't we try the marketplace at Xebulon? I understand there is a huge festival going on there today, with an emphasis on fashion."

Hax'georget' looked down at the nice white tunic that went well with his tan trousers. He had added a blue scarf to in place of a belt.

"I... I don't know. It would be somewhat disappointing to go and see clothes without being able to purchase anything."

"I believe you were the one who corrected the protection charm on Pickett castle, which would mean the payment for that should go to you," Lionope said, as he raised a small pouch of coins and shook it.

"You... I... I guess... Maybe."

"You are becoming a powerful mage. I am relying on you more and more because your skills are invaluable. It is your own insecurities that keep holding you back. These doorways are brilliant and my guess is they will work perfectly. It is time for you to reward yourself for all the hard work you do here."

"Thank you master," Hax'georget said as he politely accepted the coin pouch. He held it tight as he turned and opened the door to Xebulon. Looking through he saw crowds of beings roaming through the vast bazaar. "Looks like it's working."

"Move on my boy," Lionope said, giving the young dragon an encouraging nudge.

Hax'georget' stepped through the portal and breathed a sigh of relief as the sounds and smells of the festival overwhelmed him.

Lionope emerged right behind him and said," See, I knew it would work. Have a little

A Day at Georgie and Armand's Place

faith in yourself. Now I believe we both have shopping to do."

*****

Hax'georget' was glad he could hold his human form indefinitely now. He embraced being able to roam so freely, with no worries about accidentally transforming to his natural form in the middle of the crowd.

The scent of roasting meats and fresh baked pastries seemed to be everywhere. Dozens of stages had been set up, with entertainers of all manner filling them.

Hax'georget' found himself drawn to a puppet show depicting a young noble being on a quest to rescue his true love from an evil beast which had taken her captive. He was disappointed when the beast was revealed to be a dragon.

"I must say that's rather ignorant," Hax'georget' said loudly as he walked away. "I would suggest you get out and meet more dragons face to face before you pursue them is such an offensive fashion."

All his frustration vanished as he found himself watching a parade of young women in colorful clothes walking across a stage.

"Oh my, those are beautiful," Hax'georget' commented out loud.

"I rather like what you're wearing," came an unexpected reply.

"Oh, thank you," Hax'georget' said as he turned to learn the identity of his complementor.

Standing there, tall and proud with his grim visage, wearing a gorgeous black tunic, adorned in the fashionable manner of a high-class merchant was Armand.

"Oh... Hello Armand... You look... Well, handsome. Very handsome indeed."

"Thank you Hax'georget'. Enjoying the festival?"

"Yes, it has been very pleasant. How is your apprenticeship going?"

"Well. And yours?"

"Good, I guess... I just set up a series of instant doorways..." Goerige stuttered in a display of insecurity. " I'm sorry... I'm sure you have no interest in my mundane experiments."

A Day at Georgie and Armand's Place

"Instant doorways?" Armand asked with an intrigued bearing. "How are they different than portals?"

"Well," Georgie started, letting the enthusiasm of getting to explain his ideas to someone other than Master Lionope override his lack of confidence. "Portal spells are created at one point in time for a specific jump, then fade as soon as you end your spell, taking time to power up and use. Portals such as the traveling doorways, while simpler to power up, still take time and have to be reset for every trip. What I designed are basically doorways that you can set for a specific place and travel through whenever needed without having to power up or reactivate or reset the destination every time. Very useful if you have specific worlds you visit regularly or know you might need to get to quickly."

"Sounds like it would need a lot of power just to get one working," Armand commented quizzically.

"Somehow that was only an issue when trying to work a lone door. In my experiments, I discovered that if you make a series of doorways, they can actually pull forth needed energy from their destination points and distribute…"

The two of them soon found themselves lost in conversation as they roamed through the festivities. They both acquired some roasted meat on a stick to eat as they walked.

Their aimless wanderings led them to a dressmaker shop. Hax'georget' picked up a pale green gown for humanoids and raised it to his face.

"This fabric is so soft," Hax'georget' said. He took the garment and held it in front of him. "What do you think? Would this look good on me?"

"A dragon, publicly embracing clothing. You are a depraved one," Armand said with a slight trace of a smile.

"We're the only dragons around. Besides, you shouldn't be one to comment. Most others here will think I'm queer for looking at female clothes."

"True, although I will say that gown does appear to be something you would look pleasant in it."

"Thank you. Your outfit is well worn on you as well. Those colors work fabulously with your features, making you quite handsome."

Armand smiled.

A Day at Georgie and Armand's Place

"What was that?" Georgie exclaimed, a playful smirk on his face.

"What?"

"You smiled. I saw it. There was a break from your grimness."

"You are such a silly person at times," Armand said, his face returning to an emotionless scowl. "How you ever won that match between us still puzzles me."

"Why?"

"Because nothing about you fits with what one pictures as a powerful mage."

"Some of us are just too distinctive to fit into preconceived notions," Hax'georget' nonchalantly commented.

"A rational point."

Hax'georget' smiled playfully as he danced around holding the dress.

"I am tempted," he said, placing the dress back on the table. "I may come back for you."

"You are not a normal dragon," Armand remarked.

"No, I am not. Isn't it nice to be able to take a day off to enjoy such an event," Hax'georget' replied as he swallowed down the last bite of his roasted treat.

"I never take a day off," Armand replied coldly. "The Coulder is here on a mission. He told me to await his call. Until I saw you, I was becoming restless. There is so much ridiculousness going on here."

"Do you not know how to relax and have fun?"

"Not all of us have had the luxury of an easy life."

"What are you talking about?"

"Oh please, Hax'georget'krestdawn, of the royal bloodline of Sandoval. The family who claims to be the one true lineage of dragons, from the beginning of time."

Overflowing with shock, Hax'georget' replied, "How did you find out?"

"It was not a challenge, really," Armand explained. "There was an odor of them to you when we first met. And in the dragon circles they do not hide their progenies. There is a lot of talk about the young male who has taken up mage craft and has yet to produce a viable egg."

"Well, mating with females it just... odd... uncomfortable..." Hax'georget' moved from side to side, uncomfortable with where the conversation was going. "But that's not the point."

A Day at Georgie and Armand's Place

"Really, then what is?" Armand asked, crossing his arms, a stern expression on his face.

"I am not some spoiled royal," Hax'georget' muttered defensively.

"Have you ever been on the run for your life?

"Well, no."

"Have you ever not known where your next meal was coming from? Or even felt true hunger?"

"What are you talking about?" Hax'georget' asked, pulling back in anxiety.

"I am talking about life, real life," Armamd replied, becoming animated as he took on the feel of a professor educating a naive student. Holding out his hand he gestured towards the mulling crowds. "These frivolous events are held because most people need them, far more than someone who is clueless about the reality around him. The few who can take an actual day off to enjoy it are lucky. Many here are still working, still having to earn their way in life because they were not born to special families, even with all this triviality going on around them. If they can take a break and enjoy just a few minutes, they are lucky. These events give them a little joy in an otherwise harsh life that is created by those who claim royal privilege because of their heritage."

"I have never... Why would you?... No, I am not..." Hax'georget' said turning away from Armand.

Armand took a step back as Hax'georget's skin transformed to red scales. He quickly moved in behind and put his hands on Hax'georget's shoulders

"Ok, I'm sorry," Armand said in a controlled tone. "Just calm down. This is not the place to lose control."

"I..." Hax'georget' pushed Armand's hands off before shoving through the crowd and vanishing.

*****

Hax'georget' lay on his belly in a clearing he had found in the forest. He had returned to his natural form as soon as his clothes were off. He had paced around in a circle for a bit, growling and scaring away all the wild life in the area. Finally, he overcame the anxiety and was able to curl up and relax.

A Day at Georgie and Armand's Place

He had just stopped grumbling to himself when he heard the sounds of movement, followed by a now-all-too-familiar smell.

"Go away. I want to be alone."

Armand entered the clearing and said, "I've come to apologize." He gently placed the package he was carrying on the ground and held his hands out in a peaceful gesture.

Hax'georget' swung his head just a few feet from Armand's human form and blew out a blast of heated air.

"Was that really necessary?" Armand had not changed his stance, still looking Hax'georget' right in the eyes

"Why would you want to associate with a spoiled, lazy, stupid dragon like me?"

Armand shook his head and quickly transformed into his natural form. He stood slightly longer than Hax'georget' with his black scales glistening in the sunlight. While the two of them were different breeds from different realities, their key physical traits were similar, with the most obvious differences outside of scale color being the horn structure around their heads. Where Hax'georget's horns were straight, forming a single line down the back of his head , with two lines of notably shorter horns framing his jawline, Armand had a similar row on the back of his head, but it was the two larger horns that came out from each of his cheeks, curving out to the sides that really stuck out.

"I know I can be somewhat harsh at times, as I am not gifted in the skills of interaction. I believe I may have crossed a line with you today…" Armand trailed off when he realized Hax'georget' was looking at him in stunned silence. "Are you ok? Have you never witnessed another dragon transform before?"

"Oh no, it's just… Uh… Where did your clothes go?"

"What? My clothes?"

"Of course your clothes. I have to take mine off before I change or I'll rip them. Yours vanished as you transformed."

Armand shook his head in puzzlement. "Here I am trying to apologize and you are thinking about my clothes."

"Well, I guess that does seem a little rude of me," Georgie said, lowering his head slightly. "But we are talking about clothes here."

"I have never met another being like you," Armand said, smiling. "It is a simple spell that I might be able to teach you. Why don't we both return to human form so you can get dressed."

"Look, I made you smile again."

"Fine, fine." Armand returned to his normal grim face as he transformed.

Hax'georget' watched the change and then returned to his human form as well.

"Your clothes just appear and disappear as needed," Georgie stated, absentmindedly reaching out to touch Armand's shirt. "Why is this not taught as a necessary spell?"

Armand stood there, looking at the naked body of Hax'georget'.

"You're staring at me now?"

"I'm sorry, it is just that… Well you are an attractive individual in both your forms. I have never really found the naked body of a human appealing before now."

"What?" Hax'georget' moved his arms to cover his body, suddenly feeling bashful. He plucked up his clothes and quickly got dressed, hiding behind a batch of trees.

The two of them got right to work on Armand teaching Hax'georget' the spell.

"Now remember timing is important, so let's take it slow," Armand stated as Hax'georget' prepared to try it for the first time. "If you mess up and the clothes don't vanish quick enough, they could tear."

"I got this."

Armand closed his eyes and waited. When the distinctive sound of cloth ripping came, he opened his eyes to find Hax'georget' frozen in the early stage of transformation with a troubled frown on his face.

"I am so useless. Master Lionope humors me for some reason, but I'm a terrible mage."

"Come now Georgie, a terrible mage would never have bested me in that match."

"What did you call me?" Georgie asked with a curious smile on his face.

"Oh, I'm sorry," Armand replied with a true sense of contrition in his voice. "It's just Georgie seemed to fit you. If you would rather I…"

"No, I like Georgie."

"Ok then, Georgie, do not be so hard on yourself." Armand held a respectful, satisfied expression in hopes of being comforting. "I've experienced how skilled you are first hand"

A Day at Georgie and Armand's Place

"But my clothes are ruined." Georige poked several fingers through one of the larger rips on his sleeve.

"I guess you might just have to wear something else on your way back."

Armand picked up the package he had brought into the clearing with him. He pulled out the pale green gown Hax'georget' had been attracted to.

"Oh my. You got that for me?"

"I had planned it as way of an apology, but now I think I shall make it a reward instead. I even made the alterations on it before coming here. Let's keep you in the torn clothes until you learn the spell. Once you've earned it, then you can change into the gown."

Hax'georget' laughed, "I guess it only makes sense to not put such a lovely garment at risk."

As Hax'georget' moved to take hold of the gown, Armand pulled it back and said, "Not yet. It is your reward. First you learn the spell, then you get to feel the gown."

"You are such a cruel being." Georgie shook his head in a playfully, bratty fashion. "Fine, let's get back to it."

*****

With his focus now on gaining the gown, Hax'georget' was quick to master the spell. In little time, he was switching forms and vanishing the clothes with relative ease, finding it far more amusing than was normal for a grown being. Armand clearly felt that way as he shook his head.

"What was that for?" Hax'georget' said as he rested for a bit in his dragon form

"It's just… Georgie, you are so silly. Are you sure you're of the royal bloodline?"

"That is what I've been told. Now I have mastered the spell, the gown is mine."

"Of course. You picked that up far quicker than I did, but that should not be surprising after what I saw at Dela CoErwine. You will be a mage to be reckoned with once fully trained. At that point, I feel for any enemies you might gain."

"Now you're being the silly one." Hax'georget' returned to human form, covered in the ruins of his white and tan outfit. "I am nothing special."

Armand came up behind Hax'georget' to help him out of the tattered outfit.

A Day at Georgie and Armand's Place

"Holding onto such ideas is only going to limit you from..." Armand found he was resting a hand on Hax'georget's bare shoulder after removing the shirt and absentmindedly started gently rubbing.

"That feels nice," Hax'georget' commented.

"I'm sorry. I shouldn't have..." Aramnd backed away, holding his hands up in an awkward fashion.

"Don't be silly. I was enjoying that."

Hax'georget' turned and stepped out of his trousers. "Ok, now it's your turn," He said with a playful smile.

"What?"

"You have seen me naked in my human form. I saw you topless at our match, but now I think it is just fair I get to see what the rest of your body looks like."

"It is getting late and I am sure The Coulder will be calling for me any time now..."

Hax'georget' moved in close to Armand, their faces almost touching. "It's only fair. You claim to enjoy looking at me like this, I might like seeing your body as well."

"I have never met anyone like you," Armand said, as he backed up and began to remove his clothes. "Something about you..."

Once all of his clothes were off he said, "There, you happy now?"

"Oh, I do like the looks of this," Hax'georget' remarked as Armand stood there naked. He walked over and put his hand on Armand's chest. "And the hairs feels so... I like this."

"I think we've had enough for now," Armand said removing Hax'georget's hand. "We need to make sure..."

"You've never mated before have you?"

"I do not believe that is an issue. Besides, two males would not be mating. It would just be..."

"Pleasurable maybe?"

"I don't think..."

Hax'georget' had moved in so their bodies were touching. His hands were exploring Armand's body.

"I have heard beings attempt to mate for pleasure, but I have never found females to interest me. You on the other hand, I've never felt so excited about physical contact before."

A Day at Georgie and Armand's Place

"I generally find it best to avoid such contact…" Armand said, as he fought his discomfort.

"From the response of your body, I do believe you're enjoying this contact."

Armand closed his eyes and stood there as Hax'georget' hands continued their exploration. After a bit he opened his eyes, put his arms around Hax'georget', pulling their bodies together, and gave him a slight nip on the neck. He soon found himself moving his hands around Hax'georget's body.

"Oh, now we're being playful," Hax'georget' said as he returned the nip.

The two of them soon found themselves reverting to dragon forms, as they continued nibbling at each other's necks. Their hands never stopped roaming over each other's bodies as they shifted into their natural forms.

The clearing was soon filled with actions and sounds on a level never before experienced in the forest.

*****

Hax'georget' and Armand lay on the forest floor in the aftermath of their experimentation, their tails twisted together. Hax'georget' was nuzzling his head in Armand's chest.

"I must say, attempting to mate with you has proven to be far more enjoyable than actually mating with those females," Hax'georget' remarked. "If only my family would forget that nonsense and let me be. We should see what attempted mating as humans is like. I bet it would be just as fun."

Hax'georget' transformed to his human form and started rubbing Armand's black scales.

"This is so…" Armand started to say.

"So what?

"So unlike me," Armand admitted. "What is it about you? I have been around other dragons I have found attractive, but none of them have had this effect on me. I have never let myself…"

"You could just be humbled by me having defeated you. Or maybe you're scared I might best you again. I promise not to throw you around, unless that's something you want to try."

A Day at Georgie and Armand's Place

"I have no fear of you winning if we were to have another match. As I told you, I was going to study what happened and learn from it."

"You believe you can beat me next time?" Hax'georget' asked playfully.

"I know I can," Armand replied with a matter-of-fact tone. "And with our interactions today, I am confident that I know even more of your weaknesses."

"Why don't you prove it then? We can have a match now. But we will both stay naked, that should make it interesting."

"Another silly idea from you. No surprise there. Besides, there would be little point to me defeating you without any witnesses…"

"Oh, you like to be watched?" Hax'georget' said with a naughty laugh.

Armand changed to human form and, without a word, started getting dressed.

"I thought we were going to stay naked," Hax'georget' said hopefully. "Match or not, there is still a lot we should experiment with before we get dressed."

"The Coulder has summoned me. I need to get going"

"We need to find a chance for this again soon."

Armand paused and turned towards Hax'georget'. "This was an enjoyable diversion for an afternoon, but in truth it cannot happen again."

"What? Why?"

"I tried to explain to you before. I am not one to take a day off. This all has been…" Armand's face had returned to its full cold, impersonal state. "It is just not something I can justify doing again. There are far greater concerns that need to be dealt with. The Coulder and I have been working hard on making things right and we cannot afford to let distractions of the flesh get in the way of our work."

"I was just a distraction?"

"No, you are something truly special." Armand put his hands on Georige's shoulders. "Never forget that. Our encounter here will always mean something to me, but I must be above such things for the greater good."

"You're not making any sense," Georgie said, his face filled with worry.

"I wish I could explain it all to you."

A Day at Georgie and Armand's Place

"Then explain," Hax'georget' said in a pained voice.

"I can't. Just understand that soon there will be a time when any of those connected to the Nine will have to choose sides for the fate of all. It will happen. At that time, I hope you choose the right side. Even with your skills, when events take their inevitable turn for the worse, it won't be enough if you choose wrong. And I won't be able to protect you."

"You're speaking gibberish now?" Tears started to fill Hax'georget's eyes.

"I wish I was, my sweet Georgie." Armand put his hand gently on Hax'georget's cheek.

Nothing else was said as Armand took off into the woods.

*****

Back in Xebulon, Hax'georget' found himself roaming aimlessly, his thoughts a clouded mess. He was wearing the gown with his blue scarf as a belt, his tattered outfit left in the forest.

"There you are Hax'georget'," Lionope said as he rushed over to his student. "Where have you been? You've been ignoring my summons and there is much we need to talk about. Klacki'Nicoo, Chatwell and The Coulder were all here today. They have informed me of some new information that has me greatly worried."

Hax'georget' said nothing as he nodded solemnly.

"Looks as if you've had a troublesome day as well. There is clearly something upsetting you."

"I am sorry master," Hax'georget' replied. "It's a personal matter that I should not trouble you with. I shall make sure it does not affect my studies."

"That would be impossible," Lionope commented. "One's emotions are always in play to the rest of one's life. Cutting yourself off from your feelings will only cause you more grief in the end. If you wish, I shall pry no farther, but understand I am here to help you as needed."

"Thank you, but it is truly personal. Although you might want to know about a warning I received from The Coulder's apprentice."

"Oh yes, very much."

A Day at Georgie and Armand's Place

Hax'georget' recounted his day to his master, leaving out large parts that he felt were of a more personal nature. He made sure to give the warning word for word though.

"Interesting," Lionope said. "That would seem to reflect the feelings coming from The Coulder and the others."

"This all seems too dramatic," Hax'georget' commented.

"I guess it's time to fill you in on how The Nine Masters of the Realms came to be and the lesson that it is best to avoid the affairs of gods from all realms, no matter their claims." Lionope paused and put up a privacy spell.

"We do not know when the fighting began, but a truly long time ago a body of gods began a conflict that raged across the realms. Due to the nature of their war, most who were drawn into were fully unaware of whom they were fighting for, or at times even that they were in such a war. These gods manipulated mortal beings far beyond the normal manner of most other gods. While billions of mortals were dying daily in their names, without knowing why, the gods themselves avoided direct action against each other. While their anger towards their brethren was real, they fought it out as if all of existence was nothing more than a game board for them to settle their disputes with.

"After a point, many of the more powerful mages of the time were getting worried about the effects these battles were having. As races were being wiped out, worlds would vanish without warning, the whole system was being twisted and through our connections, we knew the essence of our magics were being contaminated.

"Several hundred of us gathered together on a neutral pocket realm to discuss what was to be done. That was when the rogue goddess, who would become known as Crystalline, came to us. She had been keeping an eye out for mortals who might be able to help her end the conflicts. She had already worked out a plan on how to bring it all to an end, but the others would notice the direct actions of another god, while mostly ignoring us mortals.

"There was little debate, as her plan sounded well thought out and made sense. And we were not the only ones she had recruited. There were thousands of mages, masters from all the disciplines involved. Crystalline had built up a force unlike anything seen before or since.

A Day at Georgie and Armand's Place

"That's when the gods discovered her plan. All hell broke loose as the fighting moved into a new, personal level. There were battles between the mages and the gods that destroyed whole realities."

Lionope fell silent for a moment.

"What we experienced in that war... There is no way to describe it. In truth, none of us will ever recover from what we saw... What we did..." Loinope took in and released a big breath. "When the dust settled, when the fighting finally came to an end, there were only nine of us left. Nine out of so many thousands. We survived because we came together and worked out a spell that used all of our abilities on a level that bordered on suicidal. It took all nine of us working together, with a mindset that came from true desperation.

"The ritual we performed was a true one-shot, that could never be repeated or duplicated, which is best for all of existence."

Lionope paused again before saying, "Obviously it worked.

"Crystalline was the only one of the gods left. To keep the final eleven other gods from reforming she had to remove their powers. This she did through the use of jewels formed in the moment of creation of the first reality. Each crystal held the full power of a god, the primal energies of creation and destruction.

"She took those crystals and framed them in silver, with the name and story of the god they were created from engraved in the metal."

"The Hearts of the Gods..." Hax'georget' said in realization.

Lionope nodded his head. "Yes, the name is literal. They are, in essence, the actual hearts of those gods.

"Crystalline decided it was best for each of us to take one and guard it while she dealt with the other two. Her biggest goal was to keep them separate from each other, as one was dangerous enough on its own. For anyone to possess two or more... There was only darkness down that path.

"Since each of us resided in a different realm, this was a rational, feasible plan. We each were to secure our Heart in our home realm, in a manner of our choosing, to keep them safe, never to have them on our person.

"As far as each of us knows, the others all followed through with the agreement. I must assume that, like me, they have kept up with

A Day at Georgie and Armand's Place

checking in to their hiding place and that each of them are still secure. It is our pledge to guard the Hearts that links us."

"You had talked about the possibility of me needing to take on a burden if you took me on as an apprentice," Hax'georget' commented.

"Yes, this is the burden that may fall upon you if I fall into the final release from the physical world. It does seem as if there is little choice now but to show you that path fully and allow you to make the decision yourself about where we go from here. Understand, no matter what, once you start this journey, it will change everything."

"I think... I... No, I know I am ready to help you with this burden," Hax'georget' said solemnly. "What does this have to do with Armand's warning? Do you believe others of the Nine might be plotting to use their Hearts?"

"Since Crystalline gave us these burdens, we have had recurring discussions about what we should do, as the goddess left us no real instruction outside of keeping them apart and from being used by anyone."

Lionope took in a deep breath. It was clear that he had felt weighed down by keeping all this from his apprentice. An aura of discomfort still lingered as he continued, "The simplest train of thought is to keep them hidden, which has been what we've done so far. The argument against this is that sooner or later someone is likely going to find one or more of them and use them. It means we each have to be persistent in guarding our Heart.

"Some of the Nine feel that restricts us too much.

"There is an argument that says we should use them ourselves and keep them on us at all times. This of course opens the door to personal corruption as well as the greater possibility of someone else getting ahold of them.

"There is nothing rational about that idea. I have no doubt that it would lead to a new war of the realms.

"The third and most rational possible solution is to destroy them."

"How would you destroy such a powerful talisman?" Georgie asked in serious inquisition.

Lionope gave a prideful smile, seeing that his student understood the full depth of the dilemma.

"That is the problem. We do not know. Several of us have been looking into the possible

A Day at Georgie and Armand's Place

methods but have come up with nothing. By my calculations, if we tried to destroy one of them, it would take out several realities in the process. Any experiment to test that has too high a cost."

"Does anyone know what happened to the other two?"

Worry filled Lionope's face.

"That is what is causing all our troubles now. The rumors have it that they have been found and are now in play. We have yet to confirm this though.

"Just the idea that they are being used means we need to be on our guard and ready for action.

"It doesn't help that Crystalline seems to have vanished. For a time, she would check in with each of us, even if just a vague appearance to leave us aware she was watching. While she rarely interacted with us, she was still seen. Last sighting of her was several centuries ago."

For several long moments nothing was said.

Hax'georget' broke the silence and said, "So what do we do next?"

"If you are truly ready, I will show you my greatest secret and let you take on part of the burden. After that I am not sure what we can do, but we prepare for all possibilities."

Hax'georget' looked down at his dress and rubbed his hands over the comforting material.

"All of this puts my trivial desires into perspective."

"I will have none of that thinking from you," Lionope replied. "Just because there are new burdens in your life does not mean you have to stop enjoying living. If anything, now is the time for you to make sure you get the most out of those 'trivial desires' every chance you get. That will be one task I will require you continue with."

Hax'georget' laughed as he said, "I guess if you pronounce it a task of my training, I have no choice but to commit to it."

"Good, now we best return home. There is a lot I need to show you."

A Day at Georgie and Armand's Place

A Question of Jurisdiction

The continuous grumbling of the waterfall's mass impacting the crystal-clear pool echoed through the cavern walls that made up the far side of the Bonita Lobby. Novick had always found the noise reassuring and relaxing. It was a big part of why he took on the position of Lobby Manager. It was his job to maintain this area that he loved and felt so at home with.

He was seated at the edge of the pool, taking in a big breath of the humid air. His white fur-covered hand gently stroked the surface of the water as he watched the hustle of the lobby.

"You look relaxed," came a soft voice from the pool. Four dark bulbous eyes and a greenish-gray half sphere of a head were poking out of the water. Beneath the surface its slick-skinned six limbed body wadded calmly with its short tail slowly wagging back and forth.

"Hello Jess'iah. It's been a smooth flowing day so far," Novick replied. "How are things going in the Aquarian Casa Lobby?"

"Smooth down here as well."

"I saw some beautifully illuminated creatures swim by recently that I had never seen before."

"Ah yes, the Glan-na-vals. They do stand out when in motion. Once at rest their light show ends and they become almost invisible. They rarely leave their world, so we don't see them too often here."

"Gotta love the endless variety of species we get to experience. It is one of the more enjoyable aspects of working for the Dragons."

Jess'iah climbed out of the pool onto a large flat rock and glanced around the lobby. She opened her wide mouth and let out a quick series of loud croaks. The sounds echoed through the vast caverns. Her whole smooth body vibrated as she chuckled while watching various beings look around for the source of the sound.

A Day at Georgie and Armand's Place

"I never grow tired of the acoustics up here," Jess'iah said with a laugh.

"You're never around when it's a madhouse. Those acoustics can get real annoying when it becomes hard to hear what the person in front of you is saying, being drowned out by an argument the couple on the other side of the chamber is having."

A blue scaly head broke through the surface of the water and gurgled out, "Ma'am, we have an issue with a double booking of a lava room."

"Let me guess, the Muscrians?"

"Yes sir."

"Gotta go."

"Have fun," Novick said as his friend leapt back into the pool, her stubby tail catching at just the right angle to produce a strong enough splash to get him in the face as it broke the surface.

Novick smiled as he got to his feet and smoothed out his tan vest.

"Guess I should get back to work myself."

The morning had been fairly average, with nothing too crazy going on, as a workable crowd of customers had flowed through.

A group of nocturnal flyers had been impatient, gathering on the hallway ceiling to sleep. As that was not an unusual occurrence, just a regular nuisance, the staff was more than prepared to deal with them and get the group in a cavern room with minimal confrontation.

"Loy and Drog, so nice to see you again," Novick greeted a couple of flat bodied creatures with eight legs, two manipulating appendages and a set of large feelers on their heads, that he recognized as regular customers. "I believe Dyers has the itinerary we put together for you. We found a few new worlds I know you've not been to yet, for your excursions."

The two of them rose up to stand on their back four legs, both replying in their soft voices at the same time.

"Whooo there, slow down, one at a time," Novick said, maintaining a pleasant smile.

A few minutes later he had finished his conversation and began surveying the lobby, when a brash voice, with a demanding tone, drew his attention.

"I believe I spoke clearly and slowly, but if you still are unable to understand my request, then I can restate it yet again for you," the voice

A Day at Georgie and Armand's Place

was saying. Overwhelming arrogance echoed in every word, which was resonating throughout the chamber. Most of the beings in the lobby had paused to listen to the confrontation that was drowning out all other noise.

"Well no, I understood what you were asking," came the muddled reply. "It's just that, I'm not sure that it's allowed."

"Of course it's allowed! Otherwise I wouldn't be here having to explain myself to a low-level peon, who clearly has been poorly trained."

Novick rushed over to the desk where the confrontation was taking place.

"Jaya, is everything alright here?" Novick asked the large, pink-skinned employee with one large eye protruding out of what on most beings would be a snoot.

The lightening of Jaya skin showed his relief at being able to hand off the troublesome individual. "Oh sir, I'm glad you're here. This gentleman is asking to be allowed access to our backrooms."

Novick turned to face the man in question. He was a short creature with two long, skinny arms that would have to be held up when he walked to keep them from dragging. His head was as big around as his stubby body, and half the size. Two tufts of gray hair shot from either side of his head in points. He wore a black suit tight around his body that had the feeling of business dress for his species. On his chest was a pouch attached to his shirt, that had papers sticking out of.

"Hello sir, how can I help you?" Novick asked.

The man looked Novick up and down before replying, "Are you in charge here?"

"I am Novick, the Lobby Manager for the Bonita Lobby."

"Manager, good. I hate dealing with peons. Now, we can get down to business. We have left you four notices already, none of which we received a response to, which is why I now have to come here. And as you have yet to address any of the violations, it is clear that I will need to do a full audit of your maintenance records."

"I have no idea what you're talking about sir. Who are you again?"

The man stared up at Novick with a frustrated frown.

"Is this how you treat all government representatives?"

A Day at Georgie and Armand's Place

"No sir," Novick replied. "But I don't know what government you're from even."

"Is the whole staff here so poorly trained or just really stupid?" The man moved his right hand to his left shoulder, where he smoothed down the shirt in order to better show off the patch he wore there. It was a blue circle with one red line and one yellow line making an 'X' across it, with something in an unfamiliar language written below.

"Is that supposed to mean something?" Novick asked

"How could they let you be a manager when you clearly have not had even the most basic of business training. I am starting to think we may have to close this whole place down until the entire staff has attended the proper classes."

"I'm not sure you understand just where you are," Novick remarked.

"Yes, and that has been one of the larger problems with this establishment. I was unable to find a business name anywhere around the entrance and there is not a 'Georgie and Armand's Place' registered with the Department of Business. A silly name to begin with, but then to have no easy way to find the place, there is a clear lack of business skills being used to manage this facility."

Novick raised his paw to his forehead and scratched. He took note of a crowd gathering nearby to eavesdrop on the exchange.

"Why don't you come back to my office and we can figure this all out there," Novick said.

"Finally, a step in the right direction."

*****

Novick's office had been designed to continue the cavernous feel of the Hotel wing. His desk, cabinets and shelves were all shaped from the actual stone that formed the chamber. The chairs had been decorated to resemble the stone. A series of lights made to resemble bioluminescent fungi lined the room for illumination.

Novick moved behind his desk and turned to offer the man a seat, but the man was ignoring him. He stopped at the first bookcase he came to and started to look through the binders that rested on it.

"Umm, excuse me, but I can't let you do that," Novick explained.

A Day at Georgie and Armand's Place

"Let me?" The man continued his exploration of the paperwork. "I showed you my credentials, there is no 'letting me' at this point. You are to allow me full access to anything I decide I should have access to."

"I saw no credentials," Novick replied. "I don't even know who you are."

The man turned towards Novick and once more flashed the emblem on his shoulder.

"I still have to ask, is that supposed to mean something?"

"What kind of amateur business is this when a manager is unaware of the badge of a Senior Facility Inspector and Regulator."

"A what now?"

"Is there anyone working here that has the slightest clue?"

"Can we stop with the insults?" Novick stated. "I don't even know who you are, let alone what world you're from or why you think you have any jurisdiction here."

"There's the problem, everything you just said was pure nonsense," The Man said, an indignant look on his face. "I am an officer of the Government, assigned to investigate complaints against businesses. My name is none of your business, as this is not a personal call. Seeing you are a business that has had several complaints filed against it, and have nothing on the records as even existing, as well as clearly having no proper training for any level of your staff, I recommend you show me full respect. I can have you closed down indefinitely with just a call based on everything I have already seen today."

"Wow, on your world they have an interesting system. Not sure how it applies here though."

"'My world'? What nonsense are you talking about?" The Man stared at Novick as if he was mad.

"You really don't know where you are, do you?"

"I am in an unregistered hotel, that is clearly being illegally run, that has numerous complaints filed that have been ignored, with a fully untrained staff that is overly unaware of the proper procedures when dealing with a government official."

"I've heard tales of this kind of thing happening, but never thought I'd have to deal with it," Novick mumbled. His calm demeanor was

A Day at Georgie and Armand's Place

nearing its breaking point. "Now where is that doohickey?"

The man continued going through the binders as Novick searched through the desk drawers.

"I'm curious if you can even read anything in them," Novick remarked.

"Why wouldn't I?"

"Not sure how the spells work."

"Spells? What nonsense are you on to now?"

"You're not supposed to be here, so the magic is making you see what you expect to see. Chances are what you think you're reading, is whatever you believe would be in our books."

"Well, so far I am not surprised to see that this place has horrid bookkeeping and is losing money regularly."

"And those aren't even accounting books," Novick replied with a stressed chuckle.

"Your attempts to confuse me will not work," The Man stated coldly. "Chances are this place will have to be closed down due to the high level of violations I keep seeing everywhere."

"Right," Novick replied absently. "Oh good, here it is." Novick pulled out a small blue crystal fixed at the end of an ebony wand.

"Now, just to confirm before I use this, you are declaring openly and honestly that you are a government official from your world?"

"Enough with the games, I have shown you that I am a Senior Facility Inspector and Regulator."

"Just needed a final declaration of that," Novick explained. "Now I can do this."

The Man turned towards Novick with a large frown on his face. "Do what?"

Novik held the wand out towards the man and gave it a mild flick. A blue spark shot out, hit the man square on his forehead.

"Attacking an officer of the government is a major offense and is punishable by…"

The Man froze, staring wide eyed at Novick.

"I'm guessing you're seeing my real form now," Novick remarked. "Good, now we might be able to get this settled."

"What in the name of the Great Moderator are you?"

A Day at Georgie and Armand's Place

"Me? I'm a slodrew, from the planet Anwood," Novick calmly replied. "Understand, you are in an interdimensional hotel that is owned and run by dragons."

"This is madness." The Man turned and opened the door. He froze in his tracks.

A group of large pinkish tubular creatures were writhing past.

"Oh good, the Swarh'jan contingency made it. They were not sure if their annual competitive crawling event was going to happen. We had the regular lower caverns reserved and set up for them just in case."

"Those are giant worms…"

"Might want to watch what you say. That term could be viewed as offensive to some of our guests."

The Man closed the door, stumbled to the nearest chair and collapsed into it.

"You look like you could use a drink. Does your species drink water?" Nocik pulled out a pitcher of cold water from the cooler cabinet behind his desk and set it before The Man. "We have a lot to talk about."

*****

"... Outside of the door to your world, none of the Hotel actually is physically in your world. While some of it may technically be in your dimension, and it gets tricky in how all that works, in the end you have no jurisdiction here."

The Man had sat and nodded his head every so often as Novick sat across from him, giving him a full rundown concerning the Hotel, trying to keep to the official disclosure as much as possible.

"If you were an average individual having wandered in here by accident, we would have cleared your memory of this place, then sent you on your way, but, as you made it overly clear you were a government agent who sought us out, it gets a little complicated."

"I... I still need to file a report..." The Man mumbled as he jerked his head in frustration. "you're still in violation of..."

"I'm not sure you're getting this. Your government's policies don't apply here. I can promise you, Georgie and Armand make sure things are safe for all, as well as accommodating as much as possible to the needs of every hotel

guest. Whatever violations we may be in
according to your government, are irrelevant."

"Yes, well... I ... Not sure if there's a
form for that."

"I can see if Armand is available to meet
with you to work this out."

"One of the dragons..." The Man's face
changed color as the blood rushed from it. "I think
I'll pass on that."

"Well there's only so much I can do
for..." Novick started to explain. "It might help if
I knew your name."

"Odd request, as I am an administrator
and this is a business management dealing. Best
not to make any of it personal, as is standard
protocol."

"Bureaucracy at its finest."

The lack of a reply led to an awkward
lingering silence.

"I have a lobby to run," Novick said,
getting to his feet. "Not sure what else I can do for
you."

"How do I explain all this? They will
request paperwork..." The Man stood up as well,
with a nervous shake in his stance. "The whole

department will have to reinvent how we do things."

"Why don't you try this. File an unfinished report with a 'need a form 27b-6, in triplicate, from Internal Reviews before being able to proceed,' note on it."

"I'm not sure what a 27b-6 form is."

"Through an odd alignment of universal causality, all bureaucracies have such a form," Novick explained. "Most people are unaware of its existence. Those who know what it is, dread them and will do everything they can to avoid the task, including making paperwork vanish into the endless loop of 'passing the buck'."

"That sounds suspect."

"I guess you could just explain the Hotel to your bosses."

"Uh… I think I will try the 27b…" The Man said, pulling forth some paper from his pouch.

" Stroke 6."

"Right, 27b-6." The Man scribbled down the information shoved the paper back in the pouch.

"Now I really do need to get back to work," Novick said as he opened the office door.

A Day at Georgie and Armand's Place

The Man looked out into the cavernous passages of the Hotel with a great deal of caution. Several dozen different species passed by as he stared out into the lobby.

"This is just so…" The Man mumbled.

"Understandable reaction. Now let's get you back to your world."

They cut through the colorful traffic of the lobby. The Man froze as he took notice of the wall of doorways. Hundreds of doors, lined up along dozens of levels, each different and unique.

"This isn't right," The Man said looking around frantically.

"Of yeah, the spell would have altered your perception upon entering. I assure you, this is where you came in at."

"How do I get home?"

"Just go through the door that you feel connected to."

"What?"

"You're still connected to your world," Novick explained. "Trying to visit other worlds gets tricky, but finding one's way home from the Hotel, all you have to do is let yourself go with the flow."

"You're serious."

Novick gave The Man a reassuring smile followed by a gentle nudge.

The Man began to walk up several sets of stairs that he did not remember having come down. He soon found a familiar feeling door. He looked down at Novick with a questioning look, then turned back to the door. With a cautious move, the man opened the door and was relieved to see the familiar, well maintained uniformity of his home city.

The Man turned and looked over the Bonita Lobby, with its amassed variety of creatures going about their business.

When the Man turned back to walk through the doorway, he found himself looking at the cavern wall. He was still holding the door open with a doorframe there, but the welcoming cityscape had vanished. From the noises that were coming from all around him, it was clear others were having the same problem.

"Okay everyone. I'm not sure what's going on, but no need to panic here," Novick said from his place in the center of the lobby. "We'll send out messengers right now and get this taken care of as…"

A Day at Georgie and Armand's Place

The whole of the lobby shook with a clasp of thunder echoing through the caverns.

"Oh this can't be good," Novick mumbled as everything went dark.

Ian Brazee-Cannon

Gears and Noise

"What the hell did you do to this rig?" Pods yelled from deep with-in the large arrangement of gears. "One of these days this amateur rigging crap is going to bring it all down."

"I can do basic maintenance on the motor without you just fine," Lonna replied. He stood with his green arms crossed, picking at a piece of dry skin, that was in the midst of shedding off. "I replaced the spring unit yesterday and it was all in tune then."

"Yeah, and now it's all off by point oh oh seven of its prime rhythm."

A Day at Georgie and Armand's Place

"No one would ever notice, let alone care about such a miniscule difference."

"And once more we see how pride in one's work is slipping away."

A tall dark figure arrived at the scene. It floated towards the open access panel that Lonna was standing next to while talking to Pods.

"Greeting Lonna," The figure said.

"Not sure why you're here Myts, Pods is just over reacting as usual."

"Is metal head here?" Came Pods' voice. "I need your electro torch thingy going buddy."

"And why is that?"

"I need to fix a spring."

Pods' top half popped out of the collection of gears, upside down, obviously hanging on to something with her feet, holding a giant spring in her lengthy, flexible hand.

"See this line?" Pods asked, holding the spring out towards Myts.

The cold metallic face of Myts' headpiece bent down to look at the end of the spring.

"Ah yes, I do."

"Well, cut through it with your torch."

"That is a barely noticeable amount to cut off. Will it actually make any difference?" Inquired Myts.

"Do I question you about your computers stuff?" Pods replied. "Trust me, this thing is out of rhythm."

"Fine."

A metal appendage stretched out from Myts' dark cloak. At its end an arch of electricity was being produced. With a quick but precise movement, an almost unperceivable piece of metal was sheared off of the spring.

"Is that what you wanted?" Myts asked.

Pods gave a good look at the end of the spring through the magnifying lens of her work helmet.

"Oh yeah, that looks perfect. Wait here though, just in case."

She vanished back into the gears.

"Now what happened here?" Myts asked.

"Yesterday one of the timing springs snapped," Lonna explained.

"Which would not have happened if someone had kept the winding to its recommended levels," Pods added.

A Day at Georgie and Armand's Place

"As is my job, I got in there and replaced the spring," Lonna continued. He scratched at the dark, wiry hairs on his chin. "And everything was working fine this morning when Pods came for her inspection."

"A point oh oh seven deviation in the prime rhythm is not fine. We'd have to adjust the timing every twenty-seven days to make up for the slippage."

"We already adjust the timing every thirty days as it is."

"Yet we don't have to do much in those adjustments, because it is tuned to function that precisely."

"See what I have to deal with?" Lonna remarked.

"You did request to be her apprentice," Myts stated. "I could have told you she is this anal when it comes to her machines."

"Everyone told me that. I just didn't think anyone could be this difficult." Lonna closed his large yellow eyes and shook his head.

Pods fully emerged from the gears, dropped onto her feet, her coveralls had a fresh layer of grease to them. She reached back in and pulled out her tool belt, which she flung around her waist. She slid her long, flexible feet into her waiting slippers.

"Those who seek perfection in their work are justified in being difficult. Now wind it up to capacity, no farther and hit the lever."

Lonna moved over to the large key and twisted it three and a quarter times, feeling the proper amount of resistance on it. He then turned and released a large lever.

The sound of gears moving quickly flooded the area. Pods stood quietly listening. A series of reassuring nods followed.

"That fixed it," Pods said. "The steam batteries should be good and stay charged indefinitely, if the daily windings are done right."

"So we're done here?" Lonna asked.

"Yes. Now you need to get to The Steamy Room and check on their autotrons. Grover had reported a batch of them were stuttering as they moved. I'll finish the morning's rounds, then join you there."

"Fine."

The young man left the two tech-based Sacred Gatekeepers alone.

"You are rather rough with him," Myts commented.

A Day at Georgie and Armand's Place

"If he's going to work with gears, my gears, he's going to learn how to take care of them."

"And how long did it take you to get to your level of skills?"

"A few centuries."

"And he has been at it how long?"

Pods let out a stubborn laugh. "Hey, I'm gonna teach him the way I teach. He sought me out after all."

Myts shook his headpiece in response, a gesture Pods knew was not natural for him. Myts copied a fair amount of bipedal movements as part of his attempts to fit in with them.

"Could you not have cut that spring yourself?" Myts inquired.

"Well yeah," Pods admitted. "But your torch leaves a far smoother end."

"Does that make a difference in the performance?"

"Not really. I just like knowing everything I fix is as precise as possible. Do you have a pressing engagement to attend to?"

"Your timing was amazingly impeccable," Myts remarked. "I had just finished my full diagnosis of the master systems, with a gap in my schedule."

"Well, timing is one thing I know and excel at. That, and getting into those tight places, where I use my magic touch to make good things happen." Pods stretched out her lengthy arms and cracked the knuckles of her extremely flexible fingers.

"Was that one of your sexual innuendos?"

"You're finally catching on."

"Your humor is odd, but over this last century I feel I have learned to read you."

"Getting there, metal head," Pods replied playfully. "Now if you'd learn to enjoy being with a woman, you might understand my references."

As always there were no outward signs of a response from Myts. "I told you, my people grew away from the need for physical relationships long ago. Besides, there is no point to you, a female, engaging in sexual acts with another female. Sexual contact is supposed to focus on the reproductive needs of a species."

"See, this is why you need to get some. If I can get you laid, then you'd see why I do it. Although I have no idea what your biology is like, since you stay inside that freaky suit of yours."

A Day at Georgie and Armand's Place

"Actual contact with another's flesh is so…" There was a shiver in Myts' artificial voice. "Disgusting to begin with. The idea of having intimate contact? For nothing but an attempt at physical pleasure? I can only imagine the revoltingness of it all."

"Yeah, well, to each their own, I guess," Pods replied with a mock shrug of surrender. "Why don't you join me for rounds. Might do you good to learn the gears?"

"As it would do you well to learn the fine art of computers."

"Your circuit boards are so boring," Pods remarked, stretching the last few syllables out for over a second. "All those processors and diodes and chips, just sitting there quietly, working or not working without any outward signs."

"If only I could get you to appreciate the eloquence that is a properly constructed mainframe system," came Myts' direct reply.

The two of them had been making good time through the hallways to Pods next stop, when she came to a sudden halt.

"Do you hear that?' Pods asked.

"There are a great many sounds here," Myts replied. "Please be more specific."

"The rhythm in this wall…It's off. Real off."

"Let me tune in and see," Myts said. He floated without a sound for a few moments before adding, "There does seem to be a frequency in there that does not belong. I do not believe it is part of any of your workings though. I would hazard a guess to say it is something that has been added."

"Probably some guests deciding they got the right to mess with hotel machines again," Pods said with a frustrated shake of her head. "They can be incredibly witless at times."

*****

An hour later, the two of them were at yet another access way which Pods had disappeared into.

"Nothing out of place in here," Pods yelled.

"The undesired reverberations seem to be increasing," Myts replied. "Yet with all our wanderings, I have yet to determine a possible origin point for them."

A Day at Georgie and Armand's Place

"I've noticed that myself," Pods said as she emerged. "They're not fading or becoming stronger in any direction. It's coming from everywhere. None of my gears seem to be affected, though."

"I've been running various simulations. Nothing about them should interfere with any of the Hotel's systems."

"You think the mystic folk might be doing something crazy now?"

Myts took a moment to ponder the idea. "While I believe that is a possibility, if it were one of the other Gatekeepers, we would have been informed. I believe it might be best at this point to alert Armand and request a magic trained Gatekeeper to assist us."

"Agreed."

"I have sent the request to one of my stations to direct a messenger to the Dragons and the other Gatekeepers, top priority."

"Have them meet us at The Steamy Room," Pods stated. "I need to check in with Lonna."

*****

In the back of The Steamy Room, Lonna stood over the fourth autotron he had opened up. Just like the other three, he could see nothing wrong with them. They were fine-tuned, most likely by Pods and should be working smoothly. As with the other three, he closed the fourth one up, wound it to its most effective strength and watched as it tried to walk. It would start up just fine, then after a few steps there was a shakiness to its moves.

"And you don't feel any oddness in your joints?" Lonna asked.

"None sir," the autotron replied.

"And there are no signs of anything magnetic happening. Somehow you're out of rhythm while everything about you is working fine."

"Not an enjoyable state to be in."

"I believe you," Lonna replied.

"You've not yet found the problem I see," Pods remarked as she charged in.

"There doesn't seem to be a cause to the problem," Lonna replied coldly. "I already examined four of them, and they each looked to be in tip top condition."

A Day at Georgie and Armand's Place

"Of course they are, I maintain them. If you would come here, D-42-A, if I'm not mistaken."

"Yes, that is my designation."

The autotron walked over to Pods, trying to move as smoothly as possible.

"Do you hear it?" Pods asked as she put her ear to D-42-A's chest.

"Yes," Myts replied. "The same frequency is emitting from this construct."

"Yet, not all the autotrons are having this problem. My money's on they're all from the same batch, with the same start-up modulations."

"What are you two talking about?' Lonna asked.

"Something questionable is occurring concerning odd vibrations that seems to be having an adverse effect on these autotrons." Myts replied.

"How long has this been going on?" Pods asked

"Two days ago I started having mild shakes," D-42-A answered. "My batch brothers were experiencing the same problem. And you are correct, so far it has only been those from my batch who have been affected."

"I'd suggest we change your functional tone," Pods remarked. "But that would also change your matrix itself, which would give you a whole new personality. I'm guessing you like who you are."

"Yes, very much."

"My recommendation is you guys should take some time off until we figure out what's going on here. Now where are those other gatekeepers?"

"I shall check," Myts replied. He fell silent as he switch from external to internal communication.

"Okay Lon-Lon," Pods started, looking her apprentice in the eyes. "What's your thoughts on a strange noise going through all the systems, yet only seeming to have a bad reaction with one group of autotrons? Well, as far as we know."

"You're actually asking for my opinion?" Lonna replied, startled at being asked.

"Yeah, I gotta find ways to sharpen that mind of yours after all. Right or wrong, get you thinking and it might become a regular thing."

Lonna put his hand to his chin, rubbing it gently in concentration. "If this is happening all over, then the autotrons are not the target or the cause."

"Right, because then it would be more limited."

"Is it only around areas with clockwork, or is this beyond that?"

Pods took a moment to think before answering, "While I've focused on checking my obligations, I have noticed the same noise coming from walls empty of gears."

"So it might just be clockwork picks it up better?" Lonna suggested with a hint of apprehension.

"Yeah, that would be fair to say."

"That would suggest the target is larger than this area… Maybe the Hotel as a whole."

"That can't happen," Pods replied, her going blank over fear of the concept. "The Dragons have crazy defenses up against such things."

"We have no clue how those work," Lonna remarked. "But from what D-42-A told us, this started off small and has been building for a few days. I mean, you haven't even noticed them until today. And you notice everything. Sounds to me like someone has been testing the limits."

"Damn," Pods said, a sense of realization covering her face. "Where the hell are those other Gatekeepers? This just moved to a new level of 'we may be screwed'."

"I am unsure if my message got through to them," Myts answered. "I have been trying to grasp just what my stations are reporting to me. It appears the Messenger Routes have vanished."

"What? You sure your computers aren't flaking out on you?"

"They are running as effectively as any of your contraptions, if not more so. If they are reporting the Messenger Routes have vanished, then the Messenger Route have vanished."

"The crap is hitting the gears full force now," Pods replied. "And the mess may just be beginning."

"If I properly have grasped the meaning of that phrase, then I agree," Myts stated. "I have activated all my security protocols that are possible from here. Several of the systems seem to be off line though. I do not believe this to be a coincidence."

"Lonna my boy, I think we need to go into lockdown. First priority is to secure my wing, then see what's going on with the rest of this place."

A Day at Georgie and Armand's Place

"Sounds rational. I shall follow your example and put my wing in lockdown until we know more. Here, take this." A robotic hand emerged from Myts' cloak with an earpiece in it. "As our wings are not separated by a magic realm, we should be able to communicate with my technology. You will be able to exchange dialogue with me instantaneously as needed. Just put it in your ear."

Pods took the ear pieces and gave it a disgusted look.

"You're lucky things are getting crazy." Pods put the earpiece in her ear, clearly uncomfortable.

Myts took off at a high speed, as Pods and Lonna hurried off to their work.

Pods opened up a hidden chamber behind the wall of the hallway

"We put in all these safety systems, never thinking we'd have to use them," Pods remarked as she pulled the first of a series of levers. "Let's hope we're over reacting and won't see it all in action."

"Do you really believe we're in danger?" Lonna asked.

Pods took in a deep breath and replied, "Well. It's not supposed to be possible to attack the Hotel, I mean this is Georgie and Armand's Place. On that same note though, I have seen a lot of impossible stuff happen in this hotel over the centuries."

"Is it too late to quit as your apprentice?"

"It was too late the moment I said 'yes' to you. Now let's get moving, I've a feeling we have one long afternoon ahead of us."

*****

"What's next?" Lonna asked as they rushed through the halls.

"That's easy. We just need to access…" Pods paused.

"Okay, now what?"

"Do you hear that?"

"When have you ever asked me that question and I've been able to say 'yes'? Your hearing is way too…"

"Shh," Pods said, waving at Lonna to be quiet. "I'm trying to listen."

Lonna rolled his eyes, but stayed as silent as possible.

A Day at Georgie and Armand's Place

"There are new sounds getting mixed in with the vibrations," Pods explained. "These new ones aren't regular though. No pattern to them."

Lonna tried to concentrate to hear for himself, but the vibrations were still beyond his ability to pick up. "What's that mean?"

"No idea," Pods flashed a devious smile to her apprentice. "Looks like we need to climb into some gears and see what's going on in our walls."

The two of them hustled to the closest access panel. Pods wasted no time in opening the panel, slipping off her sandals and climbing in. Lonna followed as well as he could.

"Are you hearing it now?"

"Yeah," Lonna siad, excited to finally have some idea of what Pods had been going on about. "It's a... cracking sound?"

"That's what I'm hearing. It's coming from over here." Pods gracefully swung through the maze of gears, switching between holding on with her feet to her hands as needed, passing between the large moving components with a sense of timing that was hard to believe was not rehearsed. Lonna as usual, had no way to keep up.

"Hey watch out," Lonna yelled as he saw the ceiling above Pods start to move in a manner it was not supposed to.

Pods looked up in time to dodge the articles that fell out of the opening that had formed. She was able to reach out and catch the group of clearly confused long, wiggling creatures.

"Calm down, you're safe," Pods said. "Lonna, see that these guests get back into the Hotel proper."

Pods handed off the bundle of squiggly creatures to Lonna. There was a chorus of quiet, almost inaudible murmurs.

"Please do file a complaint, as we here at Georgie and Armand's Place are always striving to improve our customer service," Pods replied, not looking away from where she was focused. "I assure you that we are actively working on repairs as we seek to ensure the issue is resolved."

"So what is…" Lonna started to say.

"Ah ah," Pods said, holding her finger out. "Help the guests, then return and we can talk business."

Lonna took the guests out and placed them on a decorative table.

A Day at Georgie and Armand's Place

"You should be fine here," Lonna said. "Feel free to relax there for as long as you need to."

He rushed back into the machine room.

"Ok Pods, what is going on?"

"Still no clue. We just don't admit everything is falling apart in front of hotel guests."

"Those guys were from a World With-In section right?"

"Yes."

"We are not connected to any of the World With-Ins though."

"Right."

"What am I missing here?"

"A lot, but then again for once so am I," Pods replied. "Take in a big sniff now."

Lonna did as he was instructed.

"What did you smell?"

"Ammonia? Maybe vinegar? Dead fish?" Lonna replied, the puzzlement clear on his face. "There's a lot of smells that shouldn't be here."

"Good, you're learning," Pods remarked. "You know I keep my gears clean, never gonna have a bunch of odors in the machine areas."

"Are we getting leaks of atmosphere in here?" Lonna asked as he glanced around nervously.

"It seems my teachings are having an effect on you," Pods replied with a sense of pride. "Yes, atmospheres from other areas of the Hotel are coming through these cracks."

"What areas do we neighbor?"

"None that would cause this?"

"What does that mean?"

Pods dropped down next to Lonna and looked around. There were cracks forming in the ceiling, the walls and the floor.

"Those vibrations seem to be weakening the foundations of the Hotel itself," Pod explained. "Here at the edges of our wing, the barriers that keep all of it stable, are coming undone."

"That's... How is this possible?"

"No idea."

"So what do we do now?"

"I'll update Myts through his little piece of junk," Pods said tapping the earpiece. "Then, as before, we're in lockdown. We secure our wing. If all hell breaks loose, we deal with it."

A Day at Georgie and Armand's Place

On with the Show

"Get ready everyone. This is Conrad's last song,"
Georgie instructed as he moved around backstage
looking over the models. He held his hands close
to his breast. "You all just look so incredible. The
beauty I'm seeing here… I'm almost in tears."

The line-up of various beings, most of
them humanoid, gave their quiet expressions of
enthusiasm.

Georgie made his way down the line,
adjusting bits and pieces of the outfits as needed.
He had kept all the models in their soundproof
dressing rooms until after Conrad finished with his
Derovian Chanting, to ensure their focus would be
on the show itself, not their sexual urges.

Now they were all lined up in their first outfits for the show.

"Thank you Peachy Pegasus," Conrad said from on stage. "I hope you all enjoyed our performance. Next up is the highlight of the afternoon, one of Georgie's infamous and often scandalous fashion shows. Stay put, order some drinks and enjoy. Love you all."

Applause echoed through the stage area as Conrad and his band gave their final bows, thanking the audience as they exited.

Conrad was met with handshakes and celebratory comments as he made his way through the crowd backstage.

"That was incredible," Georgie remarked.

"Thank you," Conrad replied absently, his mind clearly elsewhere.

"Go get her boy," Georgie said as he patted Conrad on the back.

The models watched and waited as the stage was cleared and reset for them.

Once all was ready the house lights went dark. A sole spotlight flickered to life, focusing on Georgie standing at his podium. He was wearing a short dark Green chiffon dress with a v-neck, accessorized with a silver and jade belt modeled to

A Day at Georgie and Armand's Place

look like a flowing river. He wore a simple, pale, pearl necklace and a yellowish-amber leaf brooch on his left breast to finish up the ensemble.

"Welcome one and all, you beautiful creatures, to today's show" Goerige announced in an enthusiastic voice. "As always, I take pride in my search across the worlds for new and exciting fashions from designers of such skill and vision that there are no words to describe the grandeur of their creations. For this show I personally picked three beings who I felt showed truly unique revelation in their designs and styles. I can only hope the outfits you get to see and experience this afternoon leave you with the sense of awe they left me with.

"First up we have Madam Er-Ard and her fabulous designs inspired by the sulfuric oceans of Corkell, and the diverse life found there."

Applause filled the place as Georgie gave the podium over to the impressive form of Madam Er-Ard. She was humanoid, standing at nearly 7 feet tall with crimson skin and a hefty, muscular build. Her grey dress was highly revealing, with her four breasts on full display, barely covered by thin straps of material.

Backstage, Georgie headed for his dressing room to switch into his next outfit.

Before he could open the door, the stage manager Ande Garrett rushed over.

"We got a problem," Ande said in her soft voice.

"Is it Crix again?" Goeige let out a frustrated breath. "He volunteered for a fashion show, which means he's going to have to wear fashion. No parading out naked on stage this time. Besides, blue really is a great color on him."

"No sir, it has to do with J'Haricot's clothes."

"We did the fitting for them yesterday," Georgie replied. "Tell him there is no time for alterations now."

"That's not it."

"Oh, not grubbers... We put up a protection ward against those pests."

"If only it were that simple."

Georgie fell silent with worry for a moment before replying, "Okay, what happened?"

"Well, they seem to have vanished."

"What? When?"

A Day at Georgie and Armand's Place

"On their way from storage to here," Ande explained. "As he was to finish the show, his were the last crates to be moved out. The first crate made it, but the other three and the teams moving them are… well, gone."

"We still have time," Georgie stated as he strengthened himself up, a focused look on his face. "Summon all the available messengers. Have them run a search pattern on all halls between here and there, with permission to investigate any guest rooms the search might led them to."

"I'll get right on it."

*****

Thirty minutes later Georgie emerged from his dressing room wearing a tight-fitting black outfit that was little more than straps of smooth material in a crisscross pattern, doing next to nothing to actually cover his body. Silver balls of fluff were placed around the outfit in the configuration of various constellations from the homeworld of the outfit's designer. They would glow in darkness, to give Georgie an ethereal presence when he took the podium again.

He found his place at the side of the stage where he could watch the rest of Madam Er-Ard's presentation. He was pleased that he had not missed much and was feeling relaxed as the models efficiently showed their stuff, putting on a well-received show.

Georgie was worried when he saw no sign that Ande has returned yet.

"She's taking care of it all," Georgie said to himself.

Madam Er-Ard concluded her segment of the show and took a bow as the crowd applauded. The stage went black as she exited

Georgie and Madam Er-Ard met and hugged at the side of the stage.

"Thank you, thank you, thank you," Georgie said as they released. "Your creations are just so amazing. I love them all."

The glowing balls on Georgie's outfit had the desired effect as he made his way on stage. Once at the podium, a spot light illuminated Georgie.

"The beauty of those extraordinary clothes just leaves me breathless, which for a dragon is saying a lot." Georgie paused for a laugh. "I have no doubt we will continue to see great things from

A Day at Georgie and Armand's Place

Madam Er-Ard. And while it will be difficult to accept that there is still more remarkable fashion of that quality out there, our next designer will prove that lightening has struck you twice this afternoon. I present to you from the volcanic regions of Kerkekazor-3, Oanna-Jay."

A round of applause followed as the form of Oanna-Jay came on stage. Ze was about half the height of Georgie but held a stance that made zir appear much larger. Ze wore a leather vest of muted colors with a curtain of leather strips hanging down from zir belt. Ze extended zir wings and flew up to the special platform attached to the podium for zir. Ze folded zirs wings in a manner that made them appear to be shoulder pads connected to a cape.

"Thank you Georgie, for that charming introduction," Oanna-Jay said in a lackluster voice. "It is always something of a pleasure to encounter someone who understands the importance of fashion for all beings at a level far higher than most can ever hope to comprehend."

Georgie took his leave and was excited to see Ande striding around off stage.

"Do we know where the crates are?" Georgie asked.

"Um… No," Ande answered.

"I cannot believe our messengers forces were unable to find them. They are a highly skilled group."

Ande bit her lips nervously before replying, "It seems most of your messenger force has gone missing as well, along with the messenger routes."

"The messenger routes have gone missing?" Georgie replied in puzzlement. "That doesn't make any sense."

"I just spent way too much time at the Sundseth Lobby, having a very similar conversation. As far as I can figure, there is a lot going on right now in the Hotel that is not making sense."

"Oh my, this is troubling." Goerige held his hand up to his forehead and started rubbing. "Should I end the show now? Armand must be alerted."

"He's aware of it all. He was able to get this message delivered here for you." Ande handed Georgie a black envelope, sealed with Armand's finger print imprinted in the wax.

"Oh, a black envelope," Georgie remarked. "He knows how serious this is."

A Day at Georgie and Armand's Place

With a quick flick, Georgie broke the wax seal and opened the letter.

My sweet Georgie,

I am informing you that right now the Hotel is experiencing a unique amount of unusual issues. At this time I have all available Gatekeepers investigating and am taking my normal active role in dealing with the problems.

I know your show is important to you, so go ahead and finish up. Give your audience a memorable experience as you always do. Once you are free to join me, I am sure we will already be working on a solution and be in the midst of clean up.

Best to keep this as a need to know issue for the time being as to not incite a panic.

Love Always

Armand

"He is so thoughtful," Georgie said with tears in his eyes. "I want all available hands back there with J'Haricot now, we will do whatever is needed to give him the show he deserves. We will finish the show."

Georgie had to spend some time calming J'Haricot down, while keeping the details secret. He was not happy that he had only a fourth of his outfits to work with as well as so little time to figure out how to flesh out his stage time. The stage staff was doing all they could to get J'Haricot anything he needed. When Georgie suggested the use of some of his J'Haricot's-designed outfits, there came a spark of inspiration.

"I believe I see where this shall go," J'Haricot said as he looked through the outfits Georgie had pulled from his dressing room. "Now leave me with my models. I have a miracle to perform."

Georgie got back to his dressing room and changed into a red half-dress with black stripes that covered only the right side of his body. He took a red scarf and draped it over his left side and put a loose-fitting black belt on. He topped the outfit off with a headpiece of red and black feathers that curved around the head with a black feather partially covering his right eye.

Oanna-Jay was finishing up as Georgie made it to the stage. Ze took a cold bow, unfolded

A Day at Georgie and Armand's Place

zir wings and flew off the stage as the lights went black.

"Your fashions are as inspiring as always," Georgie said to Oanna-Jay at the side of the stage.

"Thank you," Oanna-Jay replied in a dreary tone. "It is always a treat to display my visions at your shows."

The two of them exchanged familiar bows before Georgie prepared to take the stage.

Ande was backstage already, pacing nervously.

"Is he ready, or do I need to amuse the crowd for a bit?" Georgie asked.

"J'Haricot says all is ready to go," Ande replied.

Georgie took in a deep calming breath before emerging on stage.

"Oh the sights we have seen today," Georgie said once at the podium. "What beauty. What craftsmanship. Oanna-Jay is truly a unique creative mind. But we still have one batch of remarkable fashions to bear witness to today. Due to unplanned circumstances, I can honestly say I do not know what we are in for with our next presentation today. Knowing his genius, I am sure we will have quite the show ahead of us though. I now present J'Haricot."

J'Haricot confidentially emerged onto the stage. He wore a form fitting green dress with white accents, that showed a clearly feminine figure. His mustache and patch of a beard were covered in silver glitter, giving his face a sparkling effect when the light hit it.

"My show today is truly a surprise for all of us involved," J'Haricot said as he took the podium. "Instead of focusing on just my new creations, we will be looking back through my works and seeing the evolution of my style to see how I came to where I am today."

Georgie was relieved as he left the stage. It sounded as if J'Haricot had salvaged a show from what could have been a disaster.

He rushed to his dressing room and quickly switched into a simple blouse with white flowers on a dark blue background with matching slacks. He knew it was time to be practical and get to business.

"Ande," Georgie said as he returned to back stage. "We have a lot to do. As soon as J'Haricot is finished, you will need to get it all

A Day at Georgie and Armand's Place

shut down quickly and get everyone on their way. There will be no time to linger today."

"Yes sir," Ande acknowledged. "I'm guessing this has something to do with what Armand wrote you."

"That is not for you to worry about my dear. Let the show finish. There is something I need to check on and then, most likely, I will be seeing to other matters."

Ande clearly knew better than to question Georgie. She nodded her head in understanding and rushed off to get to work.

*****

In a small room behind the stage, purposely out of sight and made to go unnoticed, Georgie stood with his left hand on the diagram that covered the stone wall there. A light hum filled the cramped chamber and the lines of the diagram lit up with flashing patterns.

"Oh my, this is not good," Georgie said to himself. "I can't see the rest of the Hotel... That should not be possible."

Ian Brazee-Cannon

Encounter in the Library

Stephan leaned over the large tome he had found and lumbered over to the desk. It was a massive book, the likes of which he had never seen. After another enjoyable encounter with Alejandra, he decided he wanted to learn all he could about the Hotel. Kwando had recommended he check out the library, which he at first took to be a joke. A library in a hotel? It was clear that Kwando was trying to make him look foolish. Once Alejandra ensured him it was a real thing, he headed out to see what was there.

The Grimm Hall Library was as otherworldly feeling as just about everything else Stephan had seen in Georgie and Armand's Place.

A Day at Georgie and Armand's Place

The bookcases were impressively hand carved with each one being unique, showing the subject matter of the books on them through the carved designs. Various reading areas were scattered around, each one filled with differing styles of chairs, leaning posts and other devices for resting on, depending on one's biology. The musky odor of aging paper and ink that dominated the facility, finalized the sense of historic splendor.

The Librarian, Liemen, was a pleasant, knowledgeable fellow. He sat on a large cushion with his six crab like legs tucked around the sides. He was using his four upper appendages to organize the various trays of books he was working with. His four eyes, each on its own flexible eyestalk, shifting back and forth between the work at a nauseating-looking pace. Stephan realized he had already acclimated to the bizarreness of the Hotel when he didn't flinch from Liemen as he was greeted upon entering the library.

"When you don't think twice about a giant crab creature greeting you, then you know you've accepted the weirdness," Stephan thought to himself.

Liemen had directed Stephan to The Incomplete History of Georgie and Armand's Place, which was an impressive looking manuscript. It was large, both in actual size and in thickness of pages, although a great deal of the later pages had yet to be written in. The cover was hand worked leather, with images of two dragons beautifully shaped into the front. Each page was hand written, with various diagrams and illustrations masterfully drawn to properly highlight the writings.

Even the areas that talked about spells and magic that went completely over Stephan's head, he still found fascinating.

It was an oddly recorded history, in that there were no dates and it jumped around, clearly being written long after the actual events and in the order of when the stories were told rather than the order they happened. A fair amount of the tales trailed off at places, going into a related story without concluding. There were clear gaps in information, some of the names changed around as the stories got told and at times it drifted into odd ramblings. Whoever had taken the dictation, copied down what was being told to them without editing.

A Day at Georgie and Armand's Place

Stephan found a few interesting stories about the earlier days of the Hotel, even though there was nothing to suggest how long ago they had happened. With all his reading, he was no closer to understanding the workings of the place. If anything, he ended up with more questions. The mysteries of Georgie and Armand's Place were keeping themselves well protected.

As Stephan was learning about the first attempt that was made to build a full underwater wing for the Hotel, a black spot appeared on the page. It was a big black dot that moved slowly down the pages, giving the impression it was reading what was there.

"Hello" Stephan said to the spot. "Can you talk? I just wanted to say, it is a little rude to rush onto a book like that while someone is reading it."

The spot finished its trip over the current page and flowed on to other books. Stephan watched as it moved quickly over any closed books, taking some time to 'read' through any open books it ran across. It circled back to The Incomplete History of Georgie and Armand's Place. It started 'reading', but soon lost interest and moved on. Stephan turned to the next page, a move that seemed to attract the spot. It came back and 'read' the open pages.

He got his first good look at the thing. It was a large black dot, but so black that it hurt Stephan to look at it. There was absolutely no light at all being reflected off it. From his perspective, it came off as a blank area, not a physical object. Blinking his eyes a few times and not looking directly at it seemed to fix the problem.

"I guess you want to read, but can't turn the pages," Stephan remarked. "I'm surprised they don't have something setup to help you. Why don't you go ask Liemen if there is something he can do?"

The spot made no reply. It reached the end of the open pages and waited at the edge of the book.

"You might want to learn how to ask," Stephan said as he turned the page. Once more the spot went through the process of reading the open pages and then waited for Stephan to turn to the next one for it.

"This is getting old." Stephan turned the page, then headed for Liemen, who he realized was now talking with Armand.

A Day at Georgie and Armand's Place

"…and now the messengers have vanished. Your spot issue will have to wait for another day," Armand was explaining.

"Are you talking about that spot?" Stephan said, pointing to The Incomplete History of Georgie and Armand's Place where the spot was finishing reading what was open. "I was going to ask if you had a way to help it."

"Help it with what?" Liemen asked.

"It seems to want to read the books. I've been turning pages for it, but I'm hoping there's an easier way to help the thing."

Armand took several quick, cautious steps towards the book. As he neared, the spot began to move on.

"We need to catch that thing," Armand said.

"So it's not a hotel guest?" Stephan asked.

"No, it's magic of some manner," Armand replied. "A spell I'm not familiar with."

"How do we catch a spell?"

"I have ways. Now where did it go?"

Stephan looked to the direction the spot had moved. There was no sign of it.

"No idea."

"We need an aerial perspective for this," Armand stated. He stood up straight. Where there had been a well dressed man, now there hovered a small winged mammal who swiftly began making strategic flyovers around the library.

Stephan moved over to stand next to Liemen and asked, "Where do their clothes go?"

"That is what you're worried about at a time like this?" Liemen replied.

"Is the spot dangerous?"

"If Armand doesn't like it and has broken from his plans in order to hunt the thing down, I am going to say 'yes'."

"Still wondering where his clothes went."

Liemen blinked all four of his eyes in unison as he pondered the question. "I don't really know. It's magic and knowing the Dragons, they most likely have spells in place to keep their outfits safe and taken care of when they change form."

"Makes sense."

Armand hastily went into a dive. Stephan looked to where he was heading and glanced at the spot. The painful sensation returned. He shook the pain off and tried to follow the spot without looking directly at it.

A Day at Georgie and Armand's Place

Liemen sprinted towards the spot with a staff of some kind held between two of his upper appendages. As Armand flew down at the spot, Liemen placed the staff in the spot's path and made a brief incantation. The spot came to a sudden halt as it tried to pass the staff. It moved around looking for an opening. Though there was no visible barrier, it could not move any farther in that direction.

Armand landed on the spot and attempted to dig his claws into it. With a pain filled yelp, Armand jumped away and began circling over the spot.

"Touching it is not an option," Armand remarked. Even in the new form, his voice still held all its authority and power. "We will have to contain it. Man person, I need you to retrieve the emergency box from behind Liemen's desk."

"Me?" Stephan replied. He made his way to the large desk. "What am I looking for?"

"Wooden box, just to your left," Liemen answered.

"This?" Stephan held up a small wooden box.

"Yes, take it over to Armand."

As Stephan neared, Armand returned to his human form. Stephan noted that his suit reappeared, as if part of the transformation, still perfectly pressed.

"Keep an eye on the spot," Armand said, taking the box. It seemed to have grown in size once Armand opened it.

Stephan took off after the spot, which was moving faster than it had before. He was keeping pace with it until it quickly took a corner. Stephan followed, but the spot had vanished by the time he made it around.

"For a spell, that thing's pretty clever," Stephan remarked.

"Don't compliment the thing," Armand said joining him. "Now hold this." Armand handed Stephan a clear glass cube. "If you see the spot again, press that against it."

Armand once more took the flying mammal form and returned to his searching.

Stephan looked at the glass box, then gave a once over to the library.

"You know, the thing was interested in the book," Stephan said. He walked over to where The Incomplete History of Georgie and Armand's Place still rested. "Well, it's worth a try."

A Day at Georgie and Armand's Place

Stephan turned the page, making sure to shuffle the paper, making as much noise as possible.

"Oh look, I turned the page," Stephan announced.

Both Armand and Liemen looked over at him.

"There it is," Armand stated.

The spot was moving towards where Stephan waited. It moved up the side of the table and onto the opened book. As it started to 'read' Stephan moved the glass cube onto it. The cube changed its shape as the spot appeared to be fighting being pulled in.

"It's much stronger than I thought," Armand said, now standing next to Stephan. He pushed Stephan out of the way and held his hands above the cube, making various elaborate motions.

Stephan watched in pure fascination as the spot seem to be battling with Armand. The dragon would obviously cast a spell through the cube, which would agitate the spot, which would then lose a little of itself into the cube, before catching itself and halting the progress.

"Stand back," Armand said. As Stephan followed the instruction, Armand raised his right hand and slammed it into the cube. The backlash of energy knocked Stephan to the floor.

Blinking his eyes, as he tried to remember where he was, Stephan was able to climb back to his feet. Liemen stood looking over the mess of books that had been flung around that area of the library. Armand stood, holding a glass container in his hand that was filled with a mass of black goo. His full attention was on the blackness.

"We got it?" Stephan asked.

"Yes, thank you," Armand replied. "This was clearly more than the minor task I had originally envisioned."

"What are you going to do with the thing?"

"The spell itself is broken," Armand explained. "It was made to destroy itself if caught. All that is left is its original ingredients."

Stephan got a closer look into the glass. What had been the black spot was now black goo with various bits and pieces of things mixed in it. Instead of getting a headache from looking at, now Stephan felt disgusted by it.

"I will need you to come with me," Armand stated. "You ended up with a better look at the spell than anyone else. You will need to be debriefed on what went on in here."

"Yeah, I guess," Stephan replied. "You'll stay human for that. Right?"

"Not by me. I'm going to have one of the Gatekeepers take that task. I have other priorities."

"Gatekeepers? Like the purple ball guy?"

"Purple ball... Sna? No, there are others who are better at interrogation and will be able to get the information out of you."

"I don't know if I need to be interrogated. I'll openly tell everything I know."

"I believe you. However, there is a chance you have knowledge that will need a little digging to get out. No need to fear our Gatekeepers in this. They will do no harm to you. I would be far more fearful of what the owner of this spell is up to. If the Hotel has been breached by more magic on this level, there is a powerful being here that needs to be dealt with."

Stephan fell silent as he followed Armand down the hallway.

"Oh shit, what have I gotten myself into?" Stephan thought. *"What kind of being can make a dragon fearful?"*

Ian Brazee-Cannon

The Courtship of

Georgie and Armand

Part 3:

Lies, Betrayal and Death

"Are you ready for today?" Lionope asked. He was holding an elaborately inscribed silver frame with a deep red crystal centered in it.

"I think so." Hax'georget' replied.

"If all goes as planned, this will change everything."

"I know."

"No matter what, after today you will no longer be an apprentice,' Lionope said, a proud smile on his face. "You will be able to go out there as a journeyman and earn a title of your own."

"Do you really think I'm ready?" Hax'georget' asked nervously looking at the ground.

"You've been ready for some time," Lionope reassured. "I've just been keeping you around for my own selfish reasons. Besides, I doubt you would have left before we finished. Understand, I would never have been able to figure this method out on my own. You have been the key to all of it."

"Thank you Master."

"This is the last you will be calling me that. I have never cared for that title, and I look forward to never hearing it from you again. You are undeniably my equal, if not my superior. Knowing you, it may take some time to get out of the habit."

"I will try Ma- Archmage."

"Now let's get to Dela CoErwine and see about changing the fate of reality." Lionope slid the frame into a leather case that was clearly made specifically for it.

"Right, but what should I wear?"

"Of course…" Lionope let out a polite laugh. "I would recommend wearing formal, male clothing for this. Best to look good and not be wearing something that will take attention away from the matter at hand."

"Oh, I think I know the perfect outfit," Hax'georget' excitedly replied.

"Then go get dressed and be quick about it. We have a lot to do."

*****

There was a crowd gathered in the lecture hall when Lionope and Hax'georget', dressed in a well fitted green tunic with burgundy trim and a brown leather jerkin, arrived. The hall was not yet packed, but word had gotten out that one of the Nine Masters of the Realms had a reality altering demonstration to make. Seats up at the front had been reserved for the other members of the Nine, but so far L'Jerdak, Master Joh, The Enchantress Allidy and Royal Chatwell were the only ones there. Mmm'ddeliommm, Sna, Je'Garramone and Jesillip were sitting with them.

"It is good to see you made it," Hax'georget' said to the group. "I was not sure

A Day at Georgie and Armand's Place

who of the former apprentices would be able to make it today."

"If this is as big a deal as we have been led to believe, missing it would have been a true error of judgment," Je'Garramone said.

"I think we're all interested in what you and Lionope have been working on," Sna remarked.

"Besides, some of us are still apprentices and had no choice," Jesillip added.

"And you will remain one until you start showing signs that you are ready," L'Jerdak said. "There are times I think you have no desire to become a journeyman mage."

"Maybe he's just too caught up in your beauty and incredible fashion sense to want to leave you," Hax'georget' suggested.

"We do not have that kind of relationship," L'Jerdak replied.

"Are you sure?" Hax'georget' asked, gesturing to Jesillip. His scales had tightened up, pulling his body in, making him noticeably smaller. This was clearly a nervous reaction. "I'm thinking you two might need to have a talk."

"Yes, I do believe you might be correct about that," L'Jerdak said with an amused smile.

Hax'georget' made his way onto the stage and helped Lionope prepare the apparatus they had been working on over the last few months.

"Are you sure we should be drawing this much attention to our work?" Hax'georget' asked.

"If the other two Hearts of the Gods have been found, this will be the best way to flush out whoever has them," Lionope replied. "If we really are headed into an end game concerning them, I am not going to wait and just react. This is what we have been working for all these years, we will now be the ones to draw the line and see who crosses it."

"I just have a feeling this is not going to end well," Hax'georget' commented.

"That is a wise judgement, but in truth when it came time for it all to play out, it was never going to end well."

Hax'georget' looked back at the audience and saw that Klacki'Nicoo, Dwar Kwando, Magus Ebright and Schilt had found their seats.

"Chances are he won't be here," Lionope said.

"I... what?"

"Armand. Chances are he won't be here. And if he is, I don't see him being open about it."

A Day at Georgie and Armand's Place

"Why should I care about that self-absorbed bore?" Hax'georget' replied.

"After your day at Xebulon, you have been truly obsessed with him," Lionope remarked with a knowing glance.

"I don't know what you're talking about." Hax'georget' turned, picking up a piece of the apparatus, looking around for a moment and then putting it back where it had been.

"Of course. Let's get back to work."

*****

Lionope gave a wave of his hand and extinguished the flames from all the candles in the room except for the ones around the stage. The sudden darkness put a quick end to the personal conversations and mindless chatter, bringing silence to the lecture hall.

"Good day and thank you for coming out for this unique demonstration," Lionope said. "I am Archmage Lionope and with me on stage is my assistant, the Journeyman Mage Hax'georget'. I can back up the claim of uniqueness as there is only a chance of seeing this ten more times at the most. I am sure you have all heard of the Hearts of the Gods, yet not a dozen beings in this chamber have ever seen one. Hax'georget', if you would please."

Hax'georget' removed the silver frame from its leather case and held it up for all to see.

"This artifact is in truth the heart of a god. There are a good deal of stories and myths about the creation of the Hearts, I leave you to feel free to believe as you will. How they came to be is not as important as how we go about dealing with constructs such as these. That is an issue that has long been debated. Lock them up and forgot about them. Use them to 'better' the realms. Or find a way to be rid of them. I have never hidden my views. We will be far better off without them and the clear path of corruption that will come with ever using them. But how does one destroy something this powerful, without releasing the power and destroying the world they are on? I will let Hax'georget' explain the process." Master Lionope moved to the side of the stage after motioning to his former apprentice with a slight bow to the audience.

A Day at Georgie and Armand's Place

Hax'georget' placed the Heart on the stand they had been setting up and turned to face the audience.

"Umm... So as Mast- Archmage Lionope explained, dealing with such artifacts can be devastating," Hax'georget' explained. "In the destruction of them, you release a lot of energy and it has to go somewhere. The legend of Da'Voob has it that a religious war caused one of the high priests to destroy the Sphere of Neshatian. The war was ended that day because there was no one left to fight it, most of the continent having been leveled, with Da'Voob becoming an uninhabitable wasteland.

"Dealing with a Heart of the Gods, we have an even more powerful artifact. All signs pointed to there being no way to destroy them without causing incalculable devastation. We had to ask the question, where can we go with all the energy? And the answer was 'everywhere'."

Hax'georget' took a pause. The desired look of confusion on the faces of the audience amused him. His presentation was working. They were clearly listening to what he was saying.

"We looked at the idea that with near infinite realms, why does all the energy need to be released into just the one you're in? Most mages have the ability to wander through the realms, so why couldn't we let the energy do the same."

Hax'georget' turned and motioned toward Lionope, who had been adjusting mirrors.

"Now instead of letting the full force of the energy blast through where we are at, we can divide that force between worlds," Lionope said as he took over. "Opening and sustaining a single portal takes a lot of energy. You generally open your portal, walk through and let it close behind you. We are going to open hundreds of thousands of portals at once, maintain them as long as needed and let them fade on their own. And while all these portals will be small, any good mage knows that portal size is not the real issue. In order to do this, we will be tapping into the power of the Heart itself to maintain the portals that will be used to destroy it."

There was the anticipated flow of murmuring through the crowd.

"Now that you know what we are about to do, this is your last chance to leave," Lionope stated. "While if we do make a mistake now, there is nowhere you could run to on this world. Anyone without faith in us, feel free to be ready to open

A Day at Georgie and Armand's Place

your own portals in a test of speed and skill if you are correct."

There was a round of awkward laughter.

"Best to be quiet so we can focus on the task at hand."

Lionope nodded to Hax'georget' and the two of them began.

With one hand on the Heart of a God, Lionope waved his other three hands around, pulling forth small holes in midair. Hax'georget' moved and adjusted the mirrors around, forming an expanding barrier of unseen forces that were holding the increasing number of miniature portals in a spherical formation around the Heart. Both of them were working up a heavy sweat.

After some time, Lionope pulled his hand free of the Heart and held all four of his hands over the concentration of portals. The openings moved with his gestures, spreading out, covering the heart from every side.

"Hax'georget' now," Lionope said.

With a wave of his hand, Hax'georget' caused a small opening to form at one point of the sphere of portals. He placed two fingers into the sphere and made a motion with his other hand. Once his hand was glowing, he touched it to his other wrist. The glow flew through is hand, into his fingers and disappeared into the sphere of portals. Hax'georget' pulled his fingers free, the miniature portals rearranged to cover the gap. Hax'georget' and Lionope both moved away to opposite sides of the stage as a maddening hum from with-in the portal sphere grew louder.

Much of the audience rose to get a better look at what was going on. They were knocked off their feet when a blast flew out from the stage with a loud pop that shook much of the library beyond the lecture hall.

There was silence as the crowd took time to ensure there was no real damage done.

On the stage Lionope and Hax'georget' were cautiously approaching the smoking mess that had been their apparatus. The mirrors and stands were all knocked over, some broken and bent up, but most had survived with minor damage.

The two of them dug around in the center of the mess, until Lionope found what he was looking for.

Lionope walked to the front of the stage and held up the blackened silver frame. The jewel

A Day at Georgie and Armand's Place

that had been in the center of it was gone, all that was left was an empty frame.

"A dangerous artifact has been destroyed and hundreds of thousands of worlds just suffered a minor inconvenient wind," Lionope said. "The energy has been dissipated, across the realms, and we are all safer for it."

After a long moment of silence, the audience broke out in applause.

Hax'georget' stood just behind Lionope with a satisfied smile. He did take note however that not everyone in the lecture hall seemed pleased.

"It seems not everyone here agrees with our actions," Hax'georget' whispered to Lionope.

With a subtle, knowing nod Lionope replied, "We have just upset various power games and made enemies. Now we wait and see who comes for us."

"We just destroyed our most powerful weapon," Hax'georget' remarked. "Does that not leave us vulnerable?"

"Very much so," Lionope answered. "That is why they will come for us. And then all this game playing will end, everything finally revealed."

Hax'georget' swallowed nervously, not
looking forward to the coming action.

*****

It took some time before the crowd
emptied out of the hall. Most came up to the stage
with compliments and questions for Lionope and
Hax'georget'. They had already decided on some
throw away answers for certain questions, to keep
anyone from putting it all together.

There was an uncertain silence lingering
once all that remained were the seven members of
the Nine and their former and active apprentices.

Klacki'Nicoo broke the silence by saying,
"What were you thinking? You had no right to do
that without consulting us first."

"He was the guardian of his Heart,"
Magus Ebright replied. "It is, in the end, his
decision as to its fate."

"I find I agree with Klacki," Dwar
Kwando said. "This changes everything. We all
should have been involved in making this call."

"And then we would be going around in
circles yet again with the same old arguments,"

A Day at Georgie and Armand's Place

Master Joh stated. "Action has now been taken. More action will undoubtedly follow."

"I thought we had agreed to make it all or nothing, in order to keep some level of balance," L'Jerdak remarked. "If half of us destroy our Hearts, those who keep theirs will become more likely to use them."

"The balance has been broken for some time," Lionope said. "I do not believe I am the only one that has used my Heart to sense the lost two are in play and have been used. They are connected after all."

"All the more reason not to be destroying the ones we have," Royal Chatwell replied. "If someone new has that kind of power, we'll need everything we have to stop them."

"I think you miss the point of my actions," Lionope said with amusement. "The game needed to change. The arguments needed to change. Our undeserved sense of superiority needed to change. Now the choice is out there. Everyone knows there is a way to destroy the Hearts of the Gods. It is now up to each of you to decide what to do with this knowledge.

"Hax'georget' and I will remain here for some time. We will reset the apparatus and have it prepared, in case anyone might wish to follow our example. Now please take your leave, as we have work to do."

The group left quietly at the clear dismissal. Everyone knew there was nothing that could be said to change things.

"What's next?" Hax'georget' asked

"We clear this mess up and wait. They will all return, as will our missing member. At which point a new mess will present itself."

"I don't like any of this."

"Neither do I,' Lionope admitted. "We made our choice here. We cannot undo it. Now we move forwards and deal with the consequences of our actions."

*****

Magus Ebright was the first to return. She walked up to the stage, pulled her Heart of a God out of its leather case and handed it to Lionope.

"I want to have it set up to go as the next one to be destroyed once the others start showing up," she said. "Now let's go over the spells. As this is my responsibility, I will be the one to take the action that finishes it."

A Day at Georgie and Armand's Place

"Of course," Lionope replied. "Let us get started."

Several of the former apprentices returned next. While each of them were journeyman mages now, their link to the Nine meant they were connected to the Hearts of the Gods and the fates of those artifacts. Je'Garramone, Sna, and Mmm'ddeliommm had formed their own little group, often working with their former masters. It was not at all surprising they would be the ones most interested in being present as the fate of the Hearts of the Gods play out.

"You two really switched things up today," Sna remarked as Hax'georget' approached them.

"That was our desired goal," Hax'georget' replied.

"And now we sssee a sssecond heart ready to be dessstroyed," Mmm'ddeliommm added. "We are witnesssssssesss to fate unfolding."

"Not all of the Nine will follow this," Je'Garramone said.

"I just ask that you, my friends, be cautious if you choose to remain here," Hax'georget' stated. "I do not want to see any of you hurt due to the backlash from our actions."

"In the end we are all connected," Sna replied. "In the end we are choosing to be here and are ready for the consequences that may come with it. If there is negative reaction, you will need all the allies available to you."

"Thank you." Hax'georget' gave a nod, then turned and returned to the stage.

At some point Master Joh had appeared and was now talking with Lionope and Ebright as they went over the preparations.

L'Jerdak and Jesillip returned, walking side by side with a noticeably different relationship than when they had left. L'Jerdak had a leather case at her side.

"So far the turnout is what I expected," Ebright remarked. "I am thinking we should get to dealing with mine, as the next to show up will most likely attempt to stop us."

"As you wish," Lionope replied.

Hax'georget' found he was not up for conversation and seated himself off to one side to watch as Ebright dealt with her Heart of a God.

Lionope got to work creating the mini portals as Ebright took to making the adjustments. Master Joh's silver form hovered over the stage, zir eyes clearly focused on the action there.

A Day at Georgie and Armand's Place

As the covering of portals blocked out the Heart of a God, a full-sized portal opened at the front of the stage. The intimidating form of The Coulder emerged, standing fully erect to give his impressive build a fully demanding presence, hanging by leather straps over his bare torso were two Hearts of the Gods.

"You will end this madness now," The Coulder announced. "I shall take possession of the Heart. And that goes for anyone here who is thinking of ignoring their responsibility."

Neither Lionope nor Ebright responded to the demands. Hax'georget' had sprung from his seat and was preparing his defensive spells. The others in the audience were doing their own forms of preparations for a conflict.

"Lionope, don't make me do this," The Coulder stated.

"You are in control of your own will, not I," Lioniope replied, continuing with his work. "Whatever you do is fully of your own volition."

Four more portals opened up throughout the lecture hall, at strategic points to the stage. The Enchantress Allidy, Klacki'Nicoo, Schilt and Armand emerged from those portals. Allidy wore her Heart of a God on a silver chain around her neck. Klacki'Nicoo was seated on his Heart of a God, riding it around like it was a vehicle. Schilt had a Heart of a God that had been fashioned into a belt around zir waist. Armand had two Hearts of the Gods attached to the long leather vest he wore.

"Listen to him for once Lionope," Allidy pleaded. "This has crossed the line of madness. Pull back and let us resolve this in a civil manner."

"As The Coulder seems to have Chatwell's Heart, I believe we have gone past being civil," Loinope pointed out. "Or do you believe Chatwell gave it to him willingly?"

Allidy looked down in discomfort.

"And Schilt seems to have zirs Master's Heart," Lionope remarked, still not looking away from his work. "Yet Kwando is not here. Do you suppose he uncharacteristically transferred his responsibility to his apprentice at a time like this?"

"He was not willing to wield the power," Schilt replied. "I was. Sacrifices have to be made for the greater good."

"Are you trying to convince us or yourself with that?" Asked Lionope.

"Enough of this." A bright blast of orange flew from The Coulder's hands, hitting Lionope in

A Day at Georgie and Armand's Place

the chest, sending him flying off the stage, crashing in the seating.

"Too late," Ebright said. She touched her finger to her wrist and sent the blast of energy into her Heart of a God. She quickly slipped off the stage and took cover right as the loud pop sounded, knocking The Coulder off the stage, landing heavily on his ass.

Hax'georget' reached out to the seat in front of him, preparing to leap over it and join the conflict. He found his hand encountering an invisible barrier.

"I need you to stay out of this Georgie," Armand said, his normal grim visage showing signs of great stress. "Once The Coulder ends this chaos, I'll convince him that you were just following your Master's orders."

"No," Hax'georget' replied. "Now release me. If need be we can have our rematch now."

"I don't want to fight you."

"Then don't. Take down your spell and stand aside."

"I can't"

"Then I will."

Hax'georget' raised his hands quickly, shattering the invisible barrier and sending Armand smashing into a wall.

As Hax'georget' took off towards the stage, Armand leaped onto his back and wrestled him to the ground.

*****

Lionope had gotten to his feet and released a binding spell towards The Coulder. It found its mark and was restraining its target when Lionope noticed that The Coulder did not have any Hearts of the Gods on him. There now stood five identical The Coulders in the lecture hall, each of them ready for a fight. Lionope found himself being lifted off the ground as The Coulder, who had the Hearts of the Gods, raised his fists.

"Thanks to learning how to use the Hearts, all my spells are more powerful and quicker to summon," The Coulder explained. "You have no hope of beating me."

Ebright flew into the air and released several blasts that knocked two of the duplicate The Coulders onto their backs. She landed between them and fired two more blasts into the

A Day at Georgie and Armand's Place

prone forms of the duplicates. They quivered as they turned to ash. The real The Coulder convulsed in pain.

Lionope was released and landed on his feet. With a wave of his left hand, the bonds around the duplicate The Coulders tightened, until the being burst in an explosion of ash.

As the real The Coulder spasmed once more, L'Jerdak and Jesillip each threw a binding spell around him and pulled him into a seat where they continued to add to their spells.

Schilt took a leap and went flying towards the two of them, when a purple blast hit him square in the chest. Je'Garramone was flying straight at him with Sna and Mmm'ddeliommm right behind her.

Klacki'Nicoo flew in on his Heart and intercepted his former apprentice and Mmm'ddeliommm.

"This should keep you two out of trouble for now," he said as he cast a blue globe around them. "Now be good and sit tight."

A moment later the globe exploded with a pop and the two mages flew out, releasing agressive blasts at Klacki'Nicoo.

*****

The Enchantress Allidy had leaped in front of Magus Ebright. The two of them were standing, looking at each other, spells at the ready.

"Destroy her," yelled The Coulder.

"I... I can't," replied Allidy. She lowered her arms and fell into a seat sobbing.

Ebright was clearly relieved as she turned her focus towards The Coulder.

Lionope had turned the last duplicate to ash and joined Ebright in front of The Coulder.

"Now to end this," Lionope said.

"Yes, I agree," The Coulder said, with his eyes closed and a confident smile on his face.

As The Coulder opened his eyes, two blasts shot out through the bindings, shattering them while flinging L'Jerdak and Jesillip into the air. The black strips that covered The Coulter's body glowed as he rose to his feet. He reached out one hand towards Ebright and gave a quick wave; a black tendril flew out, piercing the defensive spells the Magus had summoned as well as her chest. The tendril vanished, allowing the lifeless body of Ebright to fall to the floor.

A Day at Georgie and Armand's Place

Lionope sent a continuous series of blasts at The Coulder, all of which would have been deadly for a majority of beings.

"I have tapped into the true power of the Hearts," The Coulder stated. "None of your feeble spells can hurt me."

"We'll see."

Lionope leaped into the air, daggers of blue energy forming around his upper fists. The first one looked like it would connect with The Coulder until Lionope realized he was now frozen in midair, almost touching his opponent.

"Enough of this," The Coulder said as he raised and lowered his right hand quickly. Lionope's body ripped itself apart and vanished in a blast of blue sizzling energy and a puff of smoke.

*****

Hax'georget' fought his way to his feet after stunning Armand with a spell right to his face. He froze once he looked around the lecture hall.

Schilt held the two halves of Je'Garramone's body in zir hands.

Sna, and Mmm'ddeliommm were caught up in what looked to be a losing battle with Klacki'Nicoo.

L'Jerdak and Jesillip lay in unsettling positions across a row of seats.

The Enchantress Allidy sat with her head in her hands.

The Coulder stood smugly looking at a cloud of smoke that had just been Lionope.

"You were useless," The Coulder said as he turned to face Allidy.

"I told you we shouldn't force a fight here," Allidy replied.

"It matters not at this point." The Coulder reached over and took the chain with her Heart of a God from around her neck. "I'll take this. You are no longer needed."

"What?" Allidy said. The Coulder raised and lowered his hand once more. The Enchantress gasped as a sizzling blue energy shot out from The Coulder's hand and overwhelmed her before she vanished in a burst of smoke.

"Hax'georget', here," came a quiet voice.

Hax'georget' turned to see Rodfire in his natural form at the doorway. He rushed over to join his friend just outside of the lecture hall.

A Day at Georgie and Armand's Place

"Where have you been?"

"I'm sorry, The Coulder showed up, killed Master Chatwell and thought he had trapped me."

"Did you see the madness?" Hax'georget' asked, glancing back through the doorway.

"I saw," Rodfire replied with a solemn nod of his head.

"We need to stop him."

"We're not powerful enough," Rodfire remarked. "Best to retreat for now. The Coulder clearly is showing no mercy today."

"We have friends still alive in there," Hax'georget' pleaded, holding back tears. "We have to do something."

"Let's just run away, the two of us," Rodfire suggested, brushing Hax'georget's cheek with one of his tusks. "And forget this madness ever happened."

"I... I can't," Hax'georget' said as he turned and walked back into the lecture hall.

*****

Once back in the lecture hall Hax'georget' transformed into his natural body, collapsing part of the balcony as he grew. The Coulder was picking up L'Jerdak's leather case from where it had fallen.

"At least they got to die together," Schilt commented with a screeching laugh.

"Lionope's dragon is still alive," The Coulder remarked. "Armand, deal with your playmate."

Armand jumped in front of Hax'georget' in human form and stood there.

"Move or I will smash you," Hax'georget' said.

"Turn back to human and work with us" Armand suggested. "Once we have all the remaining hearts, we can use them to govern over all the realms. We can put an end to the corruption and greed that causes so much pain and suffering."

"Like what we just saw here?"

"That was different. It was regretful that they had to die, but they didn't understand."

"By your logic, neither do I," Hax'georget' stated. "Master Lionope was following my plan. I'm the one who figured out how to destroy the Hearts. Now I'm going to destroy The Coulder."

A Day at Georgie and Armand's Place

"You heard the beast," The Coulder said. "Kill him, we don't have time to play around. Now what am I forgetting about?"

Armand changed into his dragon form with the two Hearts of the Gods still on his chest and stood face to face with Hax'georget'. He curled his claws into fists and begun to draw power into them.

Hax'georget' drew his own power in preparation against Armand's actions.

"Please Georgie, don't make me do this."

Hax'georget' made no reply.

"I can't," Armand said. He lowered his hands and turned towards The Coulder.

"Worthless beast," The Coulder said. "Despite your lineage, I always got the impression you were not worthy of that heritage."

Now with four Hearts of the Gods, The Coulder started to grow. He quickly became as tall as Armand.

"I like this size," The Coulder remarked. "It feels right for a new god to be of an impressive size."

The Coulder pulled back his arm, held his fist back for a moment, pulling energy into it. Once he had a powerful charge, he released it as if he were throwing a ball. The yellow orb of energy flew towards Hax'georget' who was producing his defensive spells when Armand leapt in between them. The orb burst through Armand's defensive spells and exploded against his chest. He fell to the floor, a large circle of his scales cracked and smoking.

"A pity you sacrificed yourself for nothing," The Coulder said. "I will finish you off once I have killed your friend here."

Armand opened his eyes and looked up at Hax'georget', "I'm sorry Georgie."

Hax'georget' reached over and pulled the two Hearts of the Gods off of Armand's chest and placed them on his own. He turned to find The Coulder laughing.

"Two to four, I still have the advantage."

Hax'georget' closed his eyes, took in a big breath and prepared his spells, drawing power from the Hearts. A yellow orb smashed into his defensive shield. He opened his eyes and saw The Coulder preparing another blast.

*****

A Day at Georgie and Armand's Place

The Coulder continued laughing as he threw blast after blast at Hax'georget' in an unrelenting attack. The resulting backblasts tore through the walls, floor and ceiling of the lecture hall leaving The Coulder and Hax'georget' standing in a smoking crater.

Finally, The Coulder paused to see his work. His laughter soon faded as he saw through the smoke the form of Hax'georget' coldly standing there, unfazed.

A weak voice was laughing in a deep roaring grunt.

"Now you get to face Georgie," Armand said, his uncharacteristic laugh chugging from his injured body. "If this is the last thing I witness, I will greet death highly amused."

As The Coulder turned his attention back to Hax'georget', a red blast struck him. His shields held as he was thrown back. Several more blasts soon followed.

As he was being bombarded, The Coulder decided to shrink back to his regular size in order to be a smaller target. His eyes adjusted from the temporary blindness caused by so many bright flashes to find Hax'georget' had returned to his human form and was floating right above him.

"Oh crap," The Coulder said as a series of blasts flew into him, shattering his defensive spells. Another blast struck his body directly and sent the Hearts of the Gods flying from him. The last blast left little of his body intact.

As Hax'georget' prepared for another assault, Armand reached out with one of his claws to block his view.

"Georgie, I think he's finished," Armand said in a weak growl.

*****

Hax'georget' shook his head. As his senses cleared, he realized he was now floating above the ruins of what had been the lecture hall. The head and other pieces of The Coulder rested burnt and beaten at the edge of the stage. Klacki'Nicoo flew around in a panic above him.

Without warning Hax'georget' found himself falling. One of Armand's claws quickly moved to catch him.

"Now this is too good of an opportunity," came the clicking voice of Schilt. "Most of the Nine are dead. No one left here strong enough to

A Day at Georgie and Armand's Place

stop me. The Hearts are mine. All I have to do is
finish off the two of you"

Rodfire, in his human form, leapt from the
back of the hall towards Schilt, causing zir to
misfire a magic blast that had been aimed at
Hax'georget as ze turned to see who was coming
at zir.

The two of them were now caught up in a
wrestling match.

Sna and Mmm'ddeliommm joined
Hax'georget' and Armand.

"We need to get out of here," Sna said.
"And quickly."

"We're in no shape to move right now,"
Armand remarked. "And I doubt the two of you
are going to be able to carry us."

"Turn to human form and we'll take care
of it," Sna instructed.

"We mussst hurry," Mmm'ddeliommm
said. "Massster Joh isss about to finisssh thisss."

"Wait, how did we all forget about Master
Joh?" Armand asked.

"It isss zir nature to be forgotten and ze
knowsss how to ussse that magic."

"But what is ze going to do?"

"Finish all this," Sna replied.

Armand reverted to his human form. His dark skin was covered in black burns, cracking and seeping blood. He pulled the barely conscious form of Hax'georget' close to him.

Sna raised all four of his tentacles and the two dragons in human form lifted into the air.

The four of them made their way through the debris and into the more structurally sound area of the library.

They turned and saw the silver shivering form of Master Joh hovering above the stage where a reconfigured set up now stood. A hand emerged from zirs flowing cloak and placed zirs Heart of the Gods into its place on the contraption. Thousands and thousands of mini portals flew from zirs cloak and spread out into the remains of the lecture hall. Joh's hand touched the Heart of a God and a beam shot out from the silver frame, hitting each of the other six full frames and two empty ones that were now scattered around the stage.

Klacki'Nicoo found himself thrown to the ground as his Heart froze in midair.

The green imp looked surprisingly relieved as he stood up and watched the spectacle before him.

A Day at Georgie and Armand's Place

Schilt screamed out, "No." as ze tried to hold on to zirs Heart of a God which was becoming red hot.

Rodfire held his arm around Schilt to limit zirs arm movements.

"You idiot, let me go or we will both die."

"I do not fear death," Rodfire replied. "I thought a warrior like you would not either."

The scene was soon blocked as thousands of mini portals moved into place, sealing off the lecture hall.

Time seemed to stand still until the release of energy shook the walls around them. The blast burst free and flew through the halls, leaving a distinctive path of destruction throughout the whole wing of the library.

The mini portals vanished to reveal a rain of dust falling into an empty crater where the lecture hall had been.

Hax'georget' sat up and looked at the destruction around him.

"We should go," he said. With a glass-eyed look, Hax'georget' raised his arms, made a quick motion and opened a portal right beneath them.

"What do we do now?" Sna asked as he flew around the cavern anxiously.

"I don't know," replied Hax'georget. "Are we sure the other hearts are destroyed?"

"Massster Joh told usss ze could dessstroy all of them with zirs ssspell," Mmm'ddeliommm answered. "It appearsss ze dessstroyed everything in there with zir."

"Those are the only two Hearts of the Gods left." Hax'georget looked at the two silver artifacts that he had dropped on the floor in front of him when he had sat down. "And only the four of us know this."

"That seems correct," Sna replied.

"And the Nine are all dead now…" It was clear that Hax'georget was doing all he could to keep his emotions from overwhelming him. He knew now was not the time to grieve, that would come soon enough.

"We destroy those things and move on with our lives," Armand said entering the room, holding his chest and grimacing in pain.

"You get back to bed," Hax'georget commanded.

A Day at Georgie and Armand's Place

"This is too serious an issue, far more important than my wellbeing right now," Armand replied. "You and Lionope were right; we all just saw firsthand the corrupting effects of that kind of power. The Coulder had noble ideas at one time. Schilt may have always been aggressive, but not blood thirsty. Allidy and Klacki'Nicoo were clearly not themselves. And my mind... We don't need to talk about that."

"But you did the right thing in the end," Hax'georget said, leading Armand into a chair. "What if the need for that kind of power arises in the future?"

"This is the same argument our masters fought, we're just on opposite sides now," Armand commented.

"It was different when there were eleven of them out there. Now with just two... Do we have the right to destroy the last two of them so callously?"

There was silence as the four of them looked towards the two silver artifacts on the floor in the middle of the room.

Ian Brazee-Cannon

End of the Day Part 1

"Armand destroyed my information gathering spell, it seems. His timing could not have been better; I gained the knowledge I needed. Let us remerge and prepare for the end game."

The figure stood up and faced the other identical versions of himself that were in the room.

"We will need to act swiftly. Everything is in place, but that will all be undone if the Dragons are given any time to investigate."

The identical forms lined up, walking into each other until only one remained.

"I am complete again. Oh, it feels good to have all my power back in one body." The figure

A Day at Georgie and Armand's Place

rotated his neck and stretched out his arms, before releasing a satisfying breath.

In the room was one large wooden chest. The figure opened the chest and pulled forth a belt made up of five silver frames with inscriptions carved into them, each with its own red crystal. He held it up, a satisfied smile on his face. He put the belt on, tightening it securely around his waist. He gave a good shove to the belt to ensure it was not going to slide off.

He closed his eyes and took in a big breath.

"Yes, I can feel that everything is in alignment."

The figure plucked up a leather bag that was filled with scrolls and three blackened silver frames and exited the room.

*****

"I don't think you understand how imperative this is," Shea Blossk explained to the black box that served as sentry for Armand's office. "It is of utmost importance that I see Armand now."

"That may be your beliefs, but in the end Armand is the one who gets to make those determinations," the box replied in a direct, emotionless voice. "If you state your full claim, it will be delivered to Armand with haste and he will make the determination as to its importance."

"Fine, let him hear this," Blossk said, not hiding zirs frustration. "A mysterious individual who I had never met before, was asking questions about maps of the Hotel and of the Gatekeepers. He paid me for my time by giving me a Sacred Heart of the Gods right before he took off. As things seem to be getting a little chaotic around here, I felt it might be of his benefit to know all this."

"In my office now," Armand said, as he entered the reception area from the Hotel. The door to his office opened as he rushed past his sentry. Blossk wasted no time in following.

The office was minimally decorated, with a large practical desk dominating the room, accompanied by several comfortable looking chairs, a few perches and leaning posts lining the front of the desk. The few bookshelves were filled with neatly organized binders, but there were no signs of personal mementos. The air was filled

A Day at Georgie and Armand's Place

with a neutral, sanitized smell that gave off no triggers one way or the other. There was nothing frivolous to be found here. This room was about one thing and one thing only- business.

Armand placed a glass container that seemed to be filled with some black slime on the desk.

"You weren't even in here?"

"I am rarely in my office," Armand explained. "The Hotel would fall apart if I attempted to run it from a desk. Now you better not be wasting my time. Show me the Sacred Heart and tell me the full story. I will know if you are lying or leaving anything important out. This is not the time to get on my bad side."

"Of course," Blossk replied. Ze pulled forth the silver frame from inside zirs jacket and handed it to Armand before ze recounted the story of the meeting.

Armand was focused on examining the Sacred Heart as he listened to Blossk's story. It was clear he heard every word as he remained silent.

"As the information regarding various incidents around the Hotel started to come my way, I felt there might be a connection and knew it was best to inform you of what I had inadvertently taken part in."

"I will not tolerate games from you, especially right now," Armand warned. "I know you are here only because you are doing what you can to play both sides. It is fully your nature. Do not presume to be fooling me on any of this."

"One has to protect one's position," Blossk replied, zir hands held out in a non-threatening manner.

"I do not care about you little criminal empire." Armand's sharp eyes made contact with Blossk's. "Do not betray us and you will live."

"Of course. I would never…"

"Now what do you know of these scrolls you told him about?"

"Nothing really. I was awaiting their delivery here to have them properly examined."

"Then I suggest you get them here now, as I will be taking part in their examination."

"That's not going to be possible I'm afraid; I recently received notice that our friend Fringe seems to have been involved in attacking the warehouse they were being held at. It looks like he stole them and then vanished."

A Day at Georgie and Armand's Place

"Must be one of his religious crusades." Armand's glance fell to desktop as he deliberated. "Chances are he will burn them for being evil or full of corruption. As they are most likely not of his faith, he would not use them. He would also not be working with this mysterious person. That's not his style. We need to focus on the more significant happenings."

"I guess that makes sense."

"Why do you think anyone would pay for information with a Sacred Heart?"

"Maybe he was unaware of its true value," Blossk replied, then paused to think it through. "He might be showing off, making it clear that for him it was trivial. He also might be trying to send a message through me to others, possibly you even."

"There is a message here," Armand replied. "I know much about this exact Sacred Heart. He knew you would be giving it to me, as he knew you would play your little games. You are merely a pawn in his game now, nothing more."

Blossk was filled with anger that ze couldn't express openly here. Ze had worked hard to be the king, not the pawn. Never the pawn again.

"What is our next move?" Blossk asked

"Our next move?" Armand flashed Blossk his cold stare. "You will return to your suite and wait there. You will allow any of my people access to your communication network, as I have the feeling right now your lines of communication are flowing better than ours."

"And what of my Heart of a God there?"

"I will be keeping it for the time being."

"But you do acknowledge it's mine?"

Armand let out a frustrated breath. "Once this is over we shall talk about its fate. For the time being it will remain with me."

"Of course. Would you like me to hunt down Fringe for you?"

"Not a priority. Besides, if he does not wish to be found, none of your people will be able to find him. Now go, but be ready for us. I have a lot to do and will most likely be needing your services here soon."

"Right. I'll have my people ready."

As Blossk turned for the door, Armand commented, "Are you aware there is no power left in this Heart?"

A Day at Georgie and Armand's Place

"What?" Blossk gave Armand a shocked look. "How can you tell?"

"I'm a Master Mage and I know the Hearts well. Somewhere along the way, this one lost its power. And there is a change in its nature; it's not what it once was."

"You don't think I had anything to do with that?"

"Of course not," Armand said in his matter-of-fact voice. "Such a change would take power far greater than any you have access to. But it does say a lot that you willingly gave it over to me without knowing it was a nothing but a shell of its former self."

"But it is an actual Heart of a God?" Blossk asked, a hint of worry filling zir voice.

"Yes, of that there is no doubt."

"And you admit it's mine?"

"That is not yet decided. Now go."

As Blossk left, Armand picked up the glass container with his free hand. He stood there for some time looking at the two items he was holding.

"Well my old master, it looks like you somehow survived. Even for you, this is a long game to be playing. What am I not seeing here?"

*****

"This is 100% unacceptable," Georgie exclaimed in frustration. He was backstage at the Peachy Pegasus. Ande knew better than to try to give an actual reply. Something had happened in the short time that Georgie had vanished as J'Haricot finished up the show.

"Find me a way to get a hold of Armand. I want to know what is going on in my hotel."

"So do I," Armand said, as he walked up to Georgie. He moved in close and took Georgie into a tight hug in an unusual public display for him. "We are under attack and need to organize," he whispered into Georgie's ear.

"Everyone out, now" Georgie commanded in a stern voice. There was a chaotic hustle as no one questioned him when he used that tone.

Once the room was clear the two dragons enacted a privacy spell.

"I know the connections between areas of the Hotel are failing. What's going on?' Georgie asked.

Armand held out the Sacred Heart.

A Day at Georgie and Armand's Place

Georgie let out a surprised gasp. "How did you get that out of the vaults without me there?"

"I didn't," Armand explained. "This was given to Blossk today."

"How is that possible? It takes all four of us to get access."

"This is not one of ours."

"What? Whose is it?" Georgie moved in to get a better look at artifact.

"The Coulder's. There is no doubt of that. I've held this thing too many times and know these marking by heart."

"Master Joh destroyed them. There was nothing left."

"We don't know what really happened in those last moments," Armand stated. "At least one clearly survived, which suggest the others might have as well. The thing is there is no power in this one. It's very nature, the way it is supposed to connect with reality, the very elements that were the driving force behind how it functioned, have been altered. It's a different artifact than when we last dealt with it. My guess is the same goes for the others that may have survived. My guess is it has taken The Coulder all this time to power the Hearts anew in order to use them against us."

"You don't think he's still alive? I don't remember what happened, but we both saw his remains. There was little left of him before Master Joh cast his spell."

Armand cringed at the memory before replying, "Someone is right now acting on what looks to have been a long, thought out plot against us. What has come my way so far fits with my old master's style. I spent over a century helping him with his last great push for ultimate power, I know how he works. You know as well as I do there are magical ways to cheat death and The Coulder was the kind of wizard to have studied many of them."

"We can't let him have our hotel," Georgie said with determination.

"I agree. We need to call in the Gatekeepers and hold our first war council."

"That sounds so extreme."

"My love, when we started all this, we knew we'd have enemies. For all these thousands of years we've been lucky. Now, however, we are at war. In some ways this is history repeating itself, we need to make sure the outcome is not the same this time around."

Armand pulled Georgie in tight as tears of worry rolled down his face.

A Day at Georgie and Armand's Place

"Pull it together," Armand said. "We are going to get through this and our hotel will still be standing when it's all over."

*****

Stephan sat at the table looking at the cloud of blue smoke that hovered above it, who had been introduced as Lou'y. At present there was one tentacle hanging out of Lou'y, lightly tapping the table. Throughout the interrogation it had produced a number of appendages for various uses as needed. The tentacle seemed to be its go to for when it was thinking.

"I'm still confused. Why were you speaking with the spell?" Lou'y asked.

"I thought it was a fellow guest that needed help," Stephan answered.

"Do you normally assume spots are living beings?"

"Not before today," Stephan replied. "I'd like to point out, I am right now talking to a blue cloud and on my world, clouds don't talk. This doesn't seem to be the kind of place one should make any assumptions regarding sentience."

There was a silence as Lou'y seemed to have been caught off guard, pausing his tentacle in mid tap.

"I see your point," Lou'y resumed. "Now what were you reading that it seemed to find so interesting?"

"The book was 'The Incomplete History of Georgie and Armand's Place' and I was at a story talking about the first try to make a fully underwater area in the Hotel. Didn't seem too interesting to me, although there were some impressive looking illustrations showing the designs of it and the wreckage after it all fell apart. Most of the diagrams made little sense. Maybe if I knew the Hotel better I'd understand it."

"That was an old project that was highly mismanaged as well as poorly placed," Lou'y remarked. "After that Armand made sure to be highly involved in every new wing as they were added. Now why would this spell be interested in information about a wing that has been off limits for millennia?"

"No idea," Stephan said, leaning back in his chair.

"Yet you caught it because it was interested in the information enough to risk capture. What did the book say about that area of the Hotel?"

"I guess it was going to replace some old…"

Lou'y suddenly pulled in its tentacle and seemed to freeze as it floated there.

"You ok?" Stephan asked.

"Yes I'm fine, just got a summons from Armand. You are free to go about your business. Just make yourself available on request if we have more questions."

"Of course."

*****

There was no hiding the worry on Armand's face. The Eli Craig Ballroom was the Hotel's largest events room. It was also the most suitable for holding the first meeting ever with all the Sacred Gatekeepers. It would be full, but not packed and possessed customizable seating that would be accommodating for the wide variety of needs. And while there would be some chaos as the crowd gathered, the acoustics would allow for Georgie and Armand to be heard by all, over the noise.

They knew this would be a unique gathering, as Georgie and Armand were the only two to know the identities of every Sacred Gatekeeper. Before now all the meetings had been held in small batches, normally grouped together by neighboring wings or by areas of responsibility. Due to security reasons and the impracticality of calling them all together, there had never been a good rationale to hold such a meeting before.

Now that this level of a gathering was taking place, the Dragons were not filled with assurance by the low number that had showed up.

"There are not even a hundred of them here yet," Georgie commented. He was bobbing with nervous energy.

"I am aware of that," Armand replied.

"How bad are things out there?"

"I know we have several hundred Gatekeepers who put their areas on lockdown as is the set protocol," Armand remarked with a reassuring tone. "That should be, at some level, comforting. We have trained them and they are doing what they can to protect their areas of the Hotel. I am more concerned about the amount of Gatekeepers who are straight out missing. Reports have stated that various sections have vanished,

A Day at Georgie and Armand's Place

with most of the World's With-In, areas used heavily by our messengers, just not being there anymore."

"Has The Coulder really become that powerful?" Georgie asked, pacing mindless back and forth. "Our security is second to none across the realities. With every expansion we instigated measures that would keep them secure beyond perceived time. And our power source will never run out. This should not be possible."

"My dearest Georgie," Armand put his hands on Georgie's shoulders, halting his stride. "One thing you should have learned by now in all our years and all our journeys that brought us here, is that nothing is impossible. Everything has a weakness, even our little Hotel. The Coulder has found that weakness and has been slowly exploiting it. We've become too relaxed over the millennia. It's what happens when everything runs smoothly for such a long time. Once this is over there will be changes in our procedures."

"Oh, my love," Goergie moved in to hug Armand. "Always thinking about the administrative needs, even as the enemy is at the gate. If not for your clearness of mind, I don't think there'd be any hope."

"Nonsense you silly thing. If need be, I know you would be able to take charge and claim victory. Now let us get out there and mobilize our defenses." Armand held Georgie, doing all he could to keep his own doubts from showing on his face.

*****

All the discussions among the Gatekeepers gathered in Eli Craig Ballroom quickly ended as Georgie and Armand took the stage. They had assumed their dragon forms knowing their natural bodies demanded a level of attention and respect from just about all other species.

"Thank you all for coming," Armand said. "I am going to cut to the chase. As I am sure you are all aware, right now the Hotel is under attack."

The Gatekeepers made agreeing gestures in a solemn moment of rapport.

"Information has come our way to paint a picture of this being a well-planned operation that has been in the works for some time, by a powerful individual who has a history of going after ultimate power. This hotel houses a great

A Day at Georgie and Armand's Place

deal of secrets, that only Georgie and I know of, secrets which would be truly dangerous for this individual to get a hold of. Now we must pool all of our resources, look into all options and make a plan of defense to keep this being from his goal."

A round of respectful agreeing replies followed.

"You will break into groups based on your areas. I want each of you to compare what you know is happening in your lobbies, we're looking for high concentration of activity and any patterns that may give us an idea of where this attack might be coming from. We do not have much time, so be precise and to the point. If you think you have found a point of attack, act on it immediately as you send someone to inform us. None of you would be here if we did not trust your judgement and skills.

"We need Mmm'ddeliommm and Sna to meet with us backstage now."

*****

There was no time wasted in getting backstage. Both Sna and Mmm'ddeliommm approached the dragons, who had resumed their human forms, waiting for them to speak first.

"It seems our past has come back to try and destroy us," Armand explained. He produced the Heart of a God. Both of the Gatekeepers got a good look at it and flinched.

"That was The Coulder's if I'm not mistaken?" Sna commented.

"But it wassss dessstroyed when the Nine fell."

"So we thought," Armadn replied. "It looks like The Coulder survived and is coming after the Hotel. You are the only two besides us who would recognize him and know what he is capable of. You were there that day. We cannot allow the Hotel to suffer the same fate of The Library of Dela CoErwine."

"Seems oddly symbolic holding our meeting in the ballroom we named in remembrance of that day," Georgie remarked.

"If The Coulder isss alive, could othersss have sssurvived asss well?"

There was silence as they pondered that idea.

"We can't worry about that now," Georgie said, breaking the silence.

A Day at Georgie and Armand's Place

"Right, we need to be focused on the present," Armand replied. "We can look into the ghosts of our pasts once this is all over. I need the two of you to head out there. You know what to look for. Use Blossk's network to pass information, ze has agreed to give us full access to zirs resources."

"No time to waste," Sna said as he floated away with Mmm'ddeliommm following.

"Let us get back out here and see what ideas they have come up with," Armand said.

The two of them returned to the stage and approached the edge. Before they had a chance to address the gathered Gatekeepers a thunderous roar echoed from all sides of the theater. The room shook violently as the lights flickered, before all went dark.

Frightened breathing was all that was heard in the pitch dark as those gathered there took a few moments to come to their senses. Several spheres of light shot out and illuminated the theater with assorted other forms of light now being produced by the Gatekeepers.

"Oh this can't be good," Georgie remarked.

End of the Day Part 2

"I need all of you to calm down and gather together around my desk," Nirron said. His faint red glow was the only light in the lobby.

The sounds of crashes and panicked ramblings kept most of those in the Nona'He Mountain lobby from hearing him. There were still the stirrings of chaos coming from all areas of the surrounding darkness. Even those who had come to the desk were still clearly uneasy.

Nirron reached under his counter and produced two glass containers with rubber plugs on their side and one of them had a narrow extension that was capped off. They were obviously designed to connect together. He

A Day at Georgie and Armand's Place

carefully pulled out the plugs on both containers before bringing them together and shaking them vigorously. After a few moments of the liquids inside mingling, there was a strong glow coming from the mixture.

In a quick motion, Nirron popped off the cap and chugged down the liquid. Soon his natural luminescence glowed stronger, illuminating a large amount of the lobby in an eerie glow. It was enough to attract the attention of most of the guests.

"Everyone needs to settle down," Nirron said with all the authority he could muster. "There is nothing to be gained by panicking."

"How can you say that when we're trapped here?" Replied a creature covered in layers and layers of fur to the point where none of its body could be seen. It was standing at a doorway with the door wide open. There was a blank wall on the other side. Many of the other lobby doors were fully open as well. Instead of a variety of worlds that should have been seen through them, there were only more blank walls to be found.

"Well, yes that is clearly a problem," Nirron replied. "However, nothing of significance will be gained by being careless. It is best that we all gather in the safety of the open lobby, where my bioluminescence can best benefit everyone."

"What's going on?" Came a yell that was soon followed by a chaotic chorus of repetition of the question.

"Quiet down," Nirron said over the voices. "I do not know what has transpired. For now, we need to have faith that Georgie and Armand are on top of things and will be resolving this as soon as possible. As we wait, it might be best to start processing the proper forms for any of you who desire to seek compensation for your inconvenience."

A sense of purpose seemed to overcome the crowd as individuals who had fought the idea of approaching Nirron were now interested in being part of the group.

"Now if everyone would form orderly lines in front of each manned station we have, we will get the process started," Nirron explained. "Anyone who is uncivil while in line will be made to go to the back. Now let's get to it."

Nirron took his place at his desk and watched as the lines formed. It was going to be one of those days.

A Day at Georgie and Armand's Place

*****

There had not been much to do during their time floating in the abyss of swirling dark clouds. Every so often voices could be heard from somewhere off in the distance, although it had quickly become clear that all distances were distorted by the fogginess.

Kra had spent some time trying to get his bearings and was able to determine that, in essence, they were still in the hotel lobby. After a considerable amount of effort, he had found one of the walls. Without gravity and the effects of something in the fog making it difficult to move, as well as not being able to see more than a few inches in front of you, there seemed no point in doing anything outside of floating aimlessly.

Then the vibrations came. There came the sounds of various structures cracking from all directions

Somehow the swirling become even more disorienting. Some of the noises that echoed through the clouds made Kra glad there was no one nearby. He now knew to be cautious as at least one of the noises suggested there was someone's sick floating around out there.

"Still being productive I see," Colliven remarked, briefly moving into sight.

"Like you're doing anything that'll make a difference," Kra replied.

"I'm manning my assigned lobby. You're the messenger, who should be getting word to someone of our peculiar predicament."

Kra flapped his wings a few times until he had moved far enough that the rodent was no longer visible.

"I'm putting in for hazard pay for today," Kra mumbled as he returned to letting himself float aimlessly in the void.

*****

The last of the books had been returned to its shelf when the shaking had begun. Now Liemen stood in the dark, with a fresh pile of books at his feet.

"Now what?" He mumbled before casting an illumination spell. What he saw caused him to drop down on all ten appendages for a moment.

A Day at Georgie and Armand's Place

Just about every shelf in the library had emptied their contents onto the floor.

"Why am I not surprised?" Liemen remarked. "I'm calling break time."

Liemen deactivated his spell, returning the library to darkness. With his legs he shifted all the books around him away in a big circle. As soon as the space was cleared, he curled himself up into a ball and shut the world away as he took a much-deserved nap.

*****

"Is this what you call 'safe for all'?" The Man asked.

One of the advantages of being in a subterranean wing of the Hotel, it had only taken a few moments for those with natural bioluminescence to begin producing enough light to illuminate the lobby back to a functioning level.

In the midst of the confusion, Novick found himself at a loss.

"I need everyone to remain calm as we sort all this out," he said over the growing level of aggressive grumbling. "Let me check with Jess'ish to confirm the status of the Aquarian Casa Lobby. Then we'll confer about our next step."

Novick neared the crystal pool passage to the underwater lobby and found himself walking through a thin layer of water. The waterfall had shifted slightly, but the water was still falling into the pool. However, where once the water flowed into the Aquarian Casa Lobby, it was now overflowing into the Bonita Lobby.

Novick raised his claw to his face and anxiously rubbed his furry chin.

Looking down into the receiving pool he saw a bottom to it, about a foot under the water. The portal to his friend's lobby was gone.

"I believe some manner of explanation is due," came the voice of The Man as he neared Novick.

"Yeah, that would be nice,' Novick replied. "Wish I had one."

*****

Ande pulled out another large box of candles from backstage and placed it on the edge of the stage. Every table now had several candles burning. Luckily most of the patrons left after the

A Day at Georgie and Armand's Place

show had ended, but it was a rare afternoon for the Peachy Pegasus to be empty. While the place was no longer packed, there was still a good crowd lingering when things went black.

"Any word of what's going on yet?" Ande asked Groat when she came to get more candles to distribute.

"Nothing," Groat replied. "We've tried everything, but there is no communication with the rest of the Hotel at all."

"I see more people have shown up."

"It looks like we're still connected to quite a few hallways,' Groat explained. "Everyone that got trapped in them are slowly finding their way here."

"Makes sense, I guess," Ande replied. "Hopefully we'll get a mage of some level in here soon before we use up all the candles."

"What was Georgie planning with all of these?"

"A few years ago he had the idea of doing a show by nothing but candle light," Ande explained. "We did a few run-throughs and it was looking amazing, until several brillios came on stage for an aerial display and one accidently released its bladders. We figured it had not been paying attention to where it had sucked in its air for flying from and gotten something flammable into its body. The blast was brilliant, but putting out the fires and all the repairs kind of got Georgie rethinking things. When he works with flames now, they are magical and controlled."

"Every time I turn around someone has a new crazy story about this place."

"There's a lot of history to this hotel."

"What happens if they can't fix whatever's going on?"

Ande took a moment to think before answering, "Not gonna happen."

"There is still the possibility."

"Well, everything is possible."

"Would we be lost in some void?" Groat asked, trying to hide her worry.

"If we really are separated from the Hotel…" Ande paused in thought. "No idea how that works. Best not to dwell on such things. Let's get these candles out there, looks like more people coming in."

*****

A Day at Georgie and Armand's Place

When the shaking came, Orr'koor'lon wasted no time in activating the reinforced barriers around his tank. He was never one to wait for catastrophe to happen before preparing for it. Grasping firmly onto the resting platform attached to the ceiling to keep from being stirred around violently in his water, he was pleased as the secondary walls began to rise into place.

Then all went dark. In the darkness Orr'koor'lon heard the cracking sounds from the walls.

"This is troublesome," he remarked.

There was a loud pop followed by a rushing flow of water. Orr'koor'lon let go of the platform and dove as deep as he could, fighting against the currents wanting to drag him out of his enclosure.

Feeling around he was able to figure out that the secondary walls had not quite made it half way up, but that should be enough to reinforce the lower half of his room.

Once the flow of the water stopped, he quickly went to his emergency kit and tried to activate it. There was no power to it, forcing him to open it manually. First thing he did was release the bioluminescent algae into the water. He could see that just over half of his room still had its water. None of his terminals were on-line and all of the filtration systems had shut down. The forcefields were down, but the emergency barrier was now covering that part of the walls.

It did not take long for Orr'koor'lon to become impatient, trapped in what was left of his room, with no way to keep the water clean or get out in his walker.

He soon found himself swimming in circles, reciting theoretical physics problems as he stirred up the algae to create different patterns.

*****

Han'Gra looked out over the railing at the large stage. They had pulled out a great number of candles and were using them for illumination. It seemed to be working well for them, although the larger beings were all gathering up near the stage instead of spreading out.

Up in the smaller bar the employees had pulled out a batch of globes that they shook to activate, that were now casting light for everyone up there.

A Day at Georgie and Armand's Place

The Nagetins were in the midst of a display of panic, squealing and yelling out nonsense.

"Quiet down," Han'Gra said. "Your cowardliness serves no purpose and will only aid in creating more anxiety."

"How can you be calm when we all could die?" Pmur't asked.

"There is the chance of death with every breath you take," Han'Gra replied. "Just because the odds of death have increased, is meaningless by your own reasoning. We do not know what is really taking place right now. Our efforts will be better spent working together in a calm atmosphere to ascertain the situation and look for possible solutions."

The Nagetins were clearly ignoring Han'Gra, as they bundled together, tightly, in a fury ball of shivering flesh.

"There is something attacking the Balance here in the Hotel," Han'Gra said quietly to herself. "By the wisdom of Rya'Je may there be those who can save that Balance from being destroyed."

*****

I returned to the den of evil in hopes of discovering what the sinful creature is up to. There is no sign of him, although it is clear whatever vile plans he has been working on, they are in motion now.

There is madness taking place in the cesspool, different, more intense, than what is usual. The stranger has clearly been working hard to create chaos.

For what ends?

He must be truly powerful to have caused the violent shifting that took place. There is now a misalignment of the segments of the Hotel. It is possible to move from one to another, but it is not easy. Any casual being will find themselves trapped where once there was a passage. Only mages or those who are at a higher level of understanding will be able to find safe pathways now.

The darkness was clearly added to aid in keeping the sinful masses confused and vulnerable.

Even in the complete lack of light, I am unaffected. My glorious mission empowers me to the point that such nuisances will not force me to halt.

A Day at Georgie and Armand's Place

It is clear that a power struggle is going to take place soon for control of this unique dwelling created and fouled by the dragons. Maybe the corrupt forces will cleanse each other in the process.

Unlikely.

There will be a victor, of that I am sure. Or if not, there are those who are ready to fill such a void that would be left.

My mission has always been clear - I am to cleanse. I am to fight the rising tide of sin and wickedness at every turn.

Yet now there are too many variables that could empower the sin, feed the wickedness and spread the corruption.

I have no choice but to get involved, but I clearly am not ready to confront the dragons or this new player in their wicked game. There is much repentance for me to do before I am worthy of the power to actively take part in such a confrontation.

That means I must watch and be ready to take whatever actions will keep the potential corruption at its lowest.

I do not like this level of uncertainty. When actions are not clearly right or wrong, that leaves an imbalance. Working in the grey areas puts one in danger of losing one's soul. I must be careful in the path I will be walking. There will be no room for error.

Time to make a prayer, this time for clarity of mind.

The coming conflict will be a test in and of itself.

I pray my soul is worthy.

*****

The room felt as if it had been ready to crumble around them before all went dark.

Bloosk stood motionless in the full darkness, Prags could be heard chirping loudly in panic from his perch. Bloosk had been working with Colby on the best way to ensure they had operatives properly dispersed throughout the Hotel in case events played out for the worse. Ze had not been prepared for it to happen so soon.

"Oh… This is not good, not good at all," Colby mumbled.

"I am guessing your screen is not coming back on," Bloosk stated. Ze had gotten up, found Prags and placed him on zirs shoulder, calming

him down. "Nor will any of our electronics be
working. Chances are good that magic will be
limited as well. Most likely simple personal spells
should work, but anything that will need power to
be drawn… Well, my mages, get us some light at
least."

In moments, three lumination orbs floated
in the office. The dozen gathered individuals stood
in silence as Bloosk looked out the window behind
zirs desk at the nothing that was there.

"It seems we have no way to connect to
our people in other areas of the Hotel now,"
Blossk remarked. "We are fully shut off."

"It does appear so," Colby replied. "I am
not sure how this is even possible. The Dragons
are powerful and they have always made it clear
their security protocols are of the highest level."

Blossk rubbed zirs chin as ze deliberated.
"And you know as well as I do that all of that is
true. That means their enemy is a force on their
level. I had hoped to be a player in this end game,
but it might be best to stay on the sideline, even if
it has been forced on us."

"Are you saying we are going to just sit
tight and wait for everything to play out?" Colby
asked.

"Not much else we can do," Bloosk stated, with zirs face reflecting zirs relaxed state, as ze accepted the ever less predictable series of events. "However, we will take this time to look at all the possible outcomes and strategize on what will put us in the best position in each one. I want it so whoever comes out on top we will be ready to roll with it and keep our power structure."

"Right," Colby said as he pulled out a bundle of blank notepads from the desk and started writing. "Should we begin with the Dragons being destroyed and this newcomer taking control of the Hotel?"

"Might as well."

*****

"Well that didn't help things any," Pods remarked. She was hanging upside down, in the darkness, her feet gripping tight to a gear that had been held in place as the rest of the world shook violently. "Lonna, I need a shootout from you to know you're not dead."

"Not dead, just wishing I was," he replied. "What just happened?"

A Day at Georgie and Armand's Place

"I would say the beginning of the end," Pods remarked. "Or maybe the Hotel had a bad case of indigestion, a really bad case. Most likely magic related would be my guess. That stuff is always causing problems. At least now we get to recalibrate all the systems."

"You have one odd idea of what we should be happy about," Lonna stated.

"Why would anyone be upset over getting to work with gears? Now get on your feet and let's get started."

"How do we work without being able to see?" Lonna asked as he blindly tried to feel his way around.

"Oh, yeah, it is a little dark now.". The sounds of something being revved filled the chamber. A moment later the soft light of a handheld lantern broke through the darkness.

"Just look at this mess," Pods remarked, setting the lantern down. There were gears, pistons and springs scattered everywhere, with several bent or busted. "Looks like we'll be able to keep ourselves busy for some time."

Now that he could see, Lonna was able to find something to grab onto and pull himself to his feet.

The whole chamber was littered with the remains of the machines. There was no clear way to start fixing anything without first clearing everything out and basically start building from scratch.

"Do you think the other motors are like this as well?" Lonna asked.

"Most likely," Pods answered.. Her gaze was shifting to take in every corner of the chamber. "We are at the edge, where things were already weakening. My guess is, whatever hit the Hotel, the closer to the edges, the more damage done."

"Yeah, those cracks are really bad now," Lonna remarked.

The two of them took a moment to look at the ceiling and walls to see large cracks everywhere.

"Yes, they are worse, but nothing should come through now," Pods explained as she took a closer look into one of them. "there's only the void in them. We are fully disconnected. All the more reason we need to get to work. The sooner we get the motors up and working the sooner we can get this wing of the Hotel functional."

A Day at Georgie and Armand's Place

"Are you looking at the same mess I'm seeing in here?" Lonna asked with a hopeless look on his face.

"Yes, of course I am."

"And you're that optimistic about getting things working again?"

"Beyond a doubt," Pods said with a mischievous smile. "These are my machines, my motors, my gears. I know them and I know we can get everything back in shape with less effort than you imagine. We just need to get our butts in motion and get this done."

"Alright, you're the boss. Where do we start?"

*****

"Hello! Anyone out there?" Conrad yelled. He had given in and had been peacefully napping when the vibrations hit. As he couldn't see anything before, his little prison world had not changed with whatever was going on beyond it. He figured he might as well take the chance that somehow the violent shaking might be a sign that something had changed.

"Damn, there are some impressive acoustics in here," Conrad remarked. He then went through a series of yells at differing tones.

"If I get out here, I'll have to find a way back to do some recording. This echo is just amazing."

He took his place in the center of the room and started singing the first song he ever wrote.

"Oh yeah, that is amazing. Seems like I got time, might as well go through them all."

*****

Stephan had made it back to Alejandra's room and told her all that had happened. He had been surprised at how quiet Kwando had remained while he told his tale.

"There is something big going on in the Hotel," Kwando stated once Stephan had finished. "If the Dragons have called all the Gatekeepers together, that means things are going to get worse. We need to be ready."

"Right," Alejandra replied. "We need to go find the Gatekeepers and see what help we can be."

"We do?"

A Day at Georgie and Armand's Place

"What are you thinking?" Kwando said. "We need to stay here, where it is safe and we can weather the coming chaos."

"Not going to happen," Alejandra said as she left the suite and headed into the Hotel.

Stephan and Kwando quickly followed. They were moving quickly as Alejandra was not wasting time

"I'm thinking ghostface here might be right," Stephan remarked. "I'm sure the Dragons and the Gatekeepers can handle whatever is going on. We'd most likely just get in the way."

"We'll see. But I am going to offer my services, just in case," Alejandra said.

"Oh foolish child, this cannot end well," Kwando said. "The boring one has the correct idea. Let's head back to…"

Without warning, the hallways violently twisted and shifted beneath their feet and then all went black.

"What the hell was that?" Stephan said.

"That is the Hotel making it clear how dangerous it is to be out of the room" Kwando replied, his faint glow was the only light to be found.

"That doesn't matter now," Alejandra said, looking back at the emptiness that the hallway now led to. "We can't go back."

"Then we should find a safe place to hold down until this is all over," Kwando suggested.

"No," Alejandra stated defiantly. "I'm not just going to sit back on this one. There is clearly too much at stake right now."

"But we are trapped in this hallway," Kwando replied. "So you might as well settle down."

"Really, Kwando, that's how you're going to play this one out?" Alejandra stood with her hands on her hips, staring down the ghost.

"What do you mean?"

"You're a spirit and I know you roam the Hotel when I'm away on my jobs. The hallways are meaningless to you, because the Hotel doesn't work by hallways alone. I have no doubt you know how to travel around the Hotel as the Gatekeepers do."

"Well... It is just..." Kwando started to bob up and down as he floated in a sign of frustration.

A Day at Georgie and Armand's Place

"You are going to lead us to the Dragons," Alejandra explained. "And we are going to see what help we can be."

"Well Kwany, I get the impression our lady is not going to take 'no' for an answer," Stephan remarked. "While I agree with you on the idea of staying safe, I'm thinking we'll be better off sticking together and following Alejandra, as I'm sure she would just go off on her own otherwise."

"He's right. I'm going to do this, with or without your help."

"Fine." Kwando paused and looked around. "There is a quick passage just over this way. Let's see if it's still connected. Even if there is still a connection, using them will be risky with how unstable everything is right now."

Alejandra conjured up a lumination orb, "Lead the way."

*****

Floating above the balcony the figure looked down at the darkness that now filled the view. A few specks of light had turned on in various corners of the Hotel, but most were lost in the blackness.

The figure rolled up the scroll he had been reading from and placed it back into his satchel. He wore a confident smile as he placed three empty, blackened silver frames on the railing.

"Now to get down there and end this once and for all."

He floated over to the controls, unaware that his satchel nudged the wheel slightly. He pressed down on the globe next to the wheel and floated through the portal that opened.

End of the Day Part 3

There was quiet mumbling among the Gatekeepers as everyone stood around awkwardly, some wondering if that was the end of the shaking, others suggesting the worst of it should be over now.

"How is any of this possible?" Georgie asked quietly.

"He's had millennia to put this together," Armand replied. "And we have clearly been too confident and arrogant in our own security. After all this time with no major issues, we thought we were untouchable and became complacent."

"What do we do?"

Armand folded his hands together and pressed them to his chin as he paused for a moment of thought. "Well, if we survive this night, we learn from it and create an even better security structure, working even more with our Sacred Gatekeepers for new ideas."

"And what about right now?"

"I'm not sure," Armand answered, clearly frustrated. "I wish we had more information."

"We know what he'll go after," Goergie stated, anger dominating his tone. "His goal has to be our vault. How would he gain access though?"

"Not sure, but he seems to be playing his end game now. He must believe he has a way in."

"How could he even know where it is?"

"No idea," Armand confessed shaking his head. "We can get there first using our balcony and confront him before he gets to the Vault."

"Agreed."

"But just in case, let us disperse our people as well as possible. If all the Gatekeepers are out and about repairing the damage, it will give a show of strength on our part."

"Right."

Georgie walked to the edge of the stage and let out a strong voice that no one was able to

A Day at Georgie and Armand's Place

ignore, "The time for discussion is over. We need for you to break up into teams of five, preferably with a variety of skills to each group, and begin recovery efforts. We need you to act quickly and efficiently in combing the Hotel and finding ways to repair the damage. We will leave it up to all of you to work together and decide how best to achieve this, as we have full faith in you and your abilities. Now Armand and I will be taking off to deal with the greater issue at hand."

Georgie jumped off the stage and headed out of the theater with Armand right behind him.

"Seeing you take command like that, impressive as always, my love," Armand commented. "I'm a little turned on right now."

"If only we had time," Georgie replied.

*****

"This is crazy," Stephan remarked. "We're flying blind, literally, through the Hotel, hoping that we'll somehow end up where we're needed. Does this sound at all rational?"

"It's not," Kwando replied coldly. "I can lead you around in circles all you want, my dear, but without a real destination, there is little point to doing anything."

"Not sure if I like the two of you agreeing with each other so much," Alejandra said. "I'm not going to claim anything about this as being rational or thought out. And I'm all for hearing something productive from either of you instead of meaningless bitching, more fitting to an old cranky sage who has long lost her gifts and is just bitter towards reality, than the two individuals that have pledged to help me."

Awkwardness filled the air as both accountant and spirit were at a loss for a reply.

"Let's take a moment and go over what we know before blindly taking another passage," Stephan said, breaking the eerie silence. "We are assuming whoever is behind this is trying to do what, take over the Hotel?"

"That would be my guess," Kwando replied.

"It's the most likely scenario," Alejandra added.

"So… How would someone do that?" Stephan asked.

"That gets a little tricky," Alejandra admitted. "The Dragons have to have a powerful source of magic to do what they do with this place, but they've never been foolish enough to make that known. All signs point to them having one or more of the Hearts of the Gods hidden in their vault. And no one knows where the vault is."

"Hearts of the Gods?"

"Ancient artifacts of great power that one of my ancestors, as well as the Dragons, were connected to," Kwando explained. "There are all manner of rumors and stories associated with them and their fates, but Georgie and Armand play a large role in the end of all related tales. It is believed that they ended up with several of them and that is what is powering the Hotel."

"Why not," Stephan commented. "Fits with everything else around here."

"But that does not help us figure out how to locate our foe," Alejandra replied.

"Well, can't you use your spirit sensing stuff to find people?" Stephan asked.

"If I knew who I was looking for I could seek out their soul," Alejandra answered. "But we don't know who to search for or how many are involved in this. And with so many beings in the Hotel, trying to pinpoint one soul would be next to impossible, even if the connections were still there."

Stephan bit his lip and bobbed his head slightly as he thought it through. "You'd think he'd be about the only one moving freely around the Hotel right now. Can you look for souls that are in movement like that?"

"I don't know," Alejandra said as she looked over at Kwando who shrugged. "I guess it's worth a try."

Alejandra closed her eyes and took in a deep breath.

"There are still a few strong links through the Hotel," Alejandra remarked. "So many souls hiding away in fear. There's Nirron, he's a little stressed. Lots of interesting souls around here, lots of... Now there's an old, powerful one I'm unfamiliar with... It's moving with purpose, no fear in it. Upset over something, but determined nonetheless."

"Sounds like our guy," Stephan said. "Can we head him off?"

"Not sure," Alejandra said as she sent the location to Kwando telepathically. "What's our quickest route to him?"

A Day at Georgie and Armand's Place

"Hmmm, easy enough to get there," Kwando replied. "I think I know where he might be headed. Come, this way."

*****

A few twists and turns later the three of them found themselves in an area of the Hotel none of them were familiar with.

"I've been to some obscure parts of this place, but this area... It's lifeless," Alejandra remarked. "Makes sense the vault would be around here."

"Even for the Hotel, this place is eerie," Stephan replied.

Alejandra waved and her lumination orb vanished.

"Why'd you..."

"Shh, someone is coming," Kwando whispered, as he vanished into a wall.

Alejandra and Stephan backed up and found a column to hide behind.

In the darkness they could make out a large figure making its way down the corridor. There came a few mumbles of cursing as the figure passed, clearly focused on his task at hand.

Alejandra had to take a moment to regain her posture herself as he passed.

"What is it?" Stephan asked in a whisper.

"The power radiating from him... I've never felt anything like it."

"Are you going to be okay?" Stephan moved his hands to her back for support.

"Yeah, just a little overloaded. Now that I know to be ready for it, there shouldn't be such a reaction next time."

"Next time?" Stephan replied in shock. "With what you're saying, we need to relay what we know to the Dragons and get out of here."

"He's right," Kwando said as he emerged from the wall.

Alejandra said nothing as she pushed past Stephan and headed after the figure. Stephan and Kwando silently followed.

They found themselves going through corridors that had an unfinished aspect to them. They were bare and empty, the walls unadorned. There was an overall oddness to the design with unfinished openings in the walls at hard to reach heights.

They followed the figure into a large chamber with elaborately carved stone pillars that depicted numerous forms of underwater life. There was a series of service counters that were attached to the walls. On the other side of the chamber was a large hole in the wall and floor that had clearly not been planned.

"Now this is starting to make sense," Stephan remarked.

"What, do you suddenly know where we are?" Kwando asked sarcastically.

"Actually, yes I do," Stephan replied. "This is the Dragons' first attempt at an underwater wing of the Hotel. I was reading about it when the whole spot thing happened. This is the information it seemed so interested in. It had a real impressive sketch of this lobby here and a close up of the hole there, that showed some of the older area that they accidentally collapsed into when they did their first pressure tests."

"So we are in some of the oldest areas of the Hotel?' Alejandra asked.

"Yeah, I guess."

"Kwando, go now. Tell the dragons where we are. We'll do what we can to slow him, but we won't be able to stop him."

"Right away," Kwando replied as he floated up into the ceiling.

"Wait a minute, we're going to do what now?" Stephan asked.

"I know you're not a fighter or mage, but here and now we have little choice. We're going to get in there and slow him down in his goal any way we can."

"I don't know about this."

Alejandra leaned in and gave Stephan a strong kiss.

"I'm going in there, alone if needed," Alejandra said as she produced a new lumination orb that was much brighter than her last one. "I'd rather have someone by my side though."

With that encouragement, Stephan shook his head then sprinted to catch up with her so that they entered the hole together.

*****

"Should we go straight to the Vault?" Georgie asked as he and Armand entered the balcony.

"I'd rather stop him before he got there," Armand replied. "If only we knew what path he planned to take."

A Day at Georgie and Armand's Place

"Well, with the regular hallways all in chaos the easiest path would be to…"

Armand turned to learn what had silenced Georgie.

His life-partner was looking at the three blackened silver frames that were resting on the balcony's railing.

"He was here," Georgie said in a quiet voice. He reached out his hands and recited a spell. Ribbons of silver energy flowed from his hands and filled all the corners of their personal suite before flowing back into him. "He's gone now. The place is clean."

"I guess he wanted us to know he isn't afraid of us," Armand remarked. "If he does have five Hearts of the Gods, then he has the upper hand. However, we won't be intimidated."

"But if he gained access to the portal here…"

"If he was in the Vault already, we'd know. Maybe he got confused with operating the wheel. Let's open up the viewer and see if we can find him."

"He was last seen headed into your first try at an underwater section," came a wispy voice.

Both of the dragons turned. Energy sizzled at their fingertips as they both activated aggressive spells, ready for a fight. They found Kwando's transparent form floating there giving off its soft blue glow.

"I apologize if I startled you," Kwando stated. "I was a little surprised that I was able to enter this area."

"You are Alejandra's spirit guide, right?" Armand asked, still holding his hands ready for battle.

"Yes, I am Kwando."

"Any relations to Dwar Kwando?"

"Yes, he was my ancestor. I am very much aware of his connection to you and the Nine, but we can compare stories later."

"Right," Armand replied. "How did you get in here?"

"I came through the floor," Kwando explained. "I would have thought you'd have security spells in place to prevent that."

"We do," Armand answered, a fierce look on his face. "The Coulder must have deactivated them while he was up here."

A Day at Georgie and Armand's Place

"Are you claiming the invader is your former master?" Kwando asked. "I understood all of the Nine had died."

"We believed that as well, until today."

"Right now he is down in the old areas of the Hotel, I guess where you attempted to make your first underwater wing."

"I'm an idiot at times," Armand mumbled. "Makes perfect sense and that means he's at the Vault as we speak."

Georgie was at the wheel setting it to the proper area.

"He almost had it set right," Georgie commented. "I guess we got lucky."

Standing at the portal both Georgie and Armand held their fists clenched with a crackle of energy coming from them.

"Ready?" Armand asked.

"There is little choice if I'm not," Georgie replied.

The two of them exchanged a kiss and together stepped towards the open portal.

Just inches before it they found themselves unable to move forwards.

"Why did you two stop?" Kwando asked.

"There's some fucking spell preventing us from entering the portal," Armand growled.

"Hmmm," Kwando floated forwards to find himself stopped by the same invisible barrier. "That's annoying." He tried to come at it from a different angle, only to find the spell seemed to stretch beyond the portal.

"I'll be right back," Kwando said as he went to phase through the balcony floor. He found himself unable to move down.

Georgie let loose his silver ribbons once again, this time with them attempting to find a way to exit the balcony into the Hotel. Their movements made it clear that the barrier spell covered the whole of the balcony and the suite.

Armand stood silently with his hands pressed against the invisible wall. After a few moments he backed away, closing his eyes and taking in a deep breath.

"Whatever spell he used, it's powerful and I have no idea how to counter it," Armand remarked.

"That... That...Conceited Bastard has trapped us in our own suite as he destroys our hotel," Georgie lashed out. "And all we can do is watch."

A Day at Georgie and Armand's Place

*****

A sliver of light cracked the cold pitch darkness of the Hotel room. White-Star cautiously crossed through the hole in reality, quickly followed by Gateway and a lumination orb.

"I thought they had spells in place to keep anyone from doing that portal thing into the Hotel," White-Star remarked.

"They do. Powerful ones that would give me a challenge, especially coming from that world, if I had ever desired to attempt to cross them," Gateway replied. "The fact that I had no resistance in bringing us here means the Hotel is falling apart."

"No way. The Dragons have this place overprotected with their magics."

"Anyone who could do this, is at a power level beyond mine. We need to be cautious."

"I'm all for that," White-Star agreed. "What do we do?"

"Find the individual behind this and stop them," Gateway replied.

"You just said whoever is behind this is more powerful than you."

"Yes, I did."

White-Star paused for a moment, making sure he was following the conversation correctly. "And somehow you think we're going to stop them?"

"Yes. We have no other choice. The Hotel is important and must be saved."

"What are you talking about?"

"I cannot explain it father, but trust me on this,' Gateway said with a hint of some greater understanding in his voice. "Now I must get to a more central point of the Hotel, or what is left of it, and reach out from there. I entered through your room figuring you would need to reload your weapons. Please do so quickly if it is needed. With the defenses down I will be able to use my powers at their fullest at least, that will be one advantage for us."

After a moment White-Star had a satchel full of equipment at his side.

"Let's do this, kid."

Gateway raised his hand and created a fresh rip in the darkness and the two of them walked through it.

A Day at Georgie and Armand's Place

"Hey, I know this place," White-Star remarked as he emerged into the abandoned shop. "Why are we in the Rebellious Soul?"

"The body modification shop is in a central area of the Hotel where the differing realms have the most overlap," Gateway explained. "It is the best place from which to get a full feel of what is taking place."

"Whatever you say. I'm betting Lee Ball's not going to be happy with us messing around in his shop though."

"Not my concern. Now let us see where everything stands."

Gateway leapt upon the reception counter, closed his eyes and held out his hands.

After a few moments, he said, "The Hotel is doing all it can to hold itself together, but it is struggling. A lot of high-powered spells have been cast throughout, with a good number of the wings made unstable through them. The damage is great, but if we can reverse it before there is too much more strain, it should be able to heal up once all is reset and back in place."

"You're making it sound like this place is alive," White-Star commented.

"In a truly unique manner it is. I am not sure if the Dragons themselves fully understand what they have created, but it is far more than just a hotel. And now it needs us."

There was a pause as Gateway focused his concentration.

"The Gatekeepers are active and doing what they can," Gateway stated after a few moments. "There seems to be an unusual lack of powerful mages outside of them. Our adversary must have done similar tricks as what they tried on me to clear out possible interference. That at least means they are concerned about my abilities.

"An odd place for Pendragon to be…"

"Where's he at?" White-Star asked.

"He seems to be in his own little pocket realm, just out of sync with the Hotel, stuck in the void. Not a place easy to access. It would take me some effort to portal there. Our adversary must have been concerned about him being a Child of the Nexus. That paints an interesting picture of what he is up to."

"I don't see it," White-Star remarked shaking his head lightly.

"Pendragon has more in common with the Hotel than most anyone else you have ever encountered," Gateway explained. "Removing him from the Hotel before disrupting things, but keeping him alive and in a place that I would guess some manner is set up to retrieve him from once needed… That suggests the plan is not to destroy the place, but to take control of it and rebuild it once that has been done."

"That's a good thing, right?"

"The methods are cruel and suspect," Gateway replied. "We also do not know the overall motives. If the goal is enslavement of the Hotel, that would be disastrous. With nothing more to go on, the chances of a change in control ending well… That is doubtful. Best that the Dragons retain their possession of it."

"I guess."

"But where are the Dragons?" Gateway said with a sense of worry creeping into his voice. "I cannot sense them, although there are blind spots in the Hotel, areas that are no longer connected or have spells hiding them. There is just too much to be able to properly search them all. But I can… Oh, that has to be our adversary."

"You found him?" White-Star asked, clearly ready for a fight.

"The powers emanating from this individual are… Massive and…Something new to me. And it would seem he is close to the Hotel vault."

"There's a hotel vault? What's in it?"

"I do not know," Gateway replied, lowering his arms and opening his eyes. "It was never a concern of mine before now. We should hurry though."

"What about finding the Dragons?"

"Our eavesdropper might be better able to search for them," Gateway commented. "As I am sure he understands the stakes right now. His feeling towards Georgie and Armand aside, he knows what best follows his sense of righteousness."

White-Star looked around in puzzlement. "What are you talking about?"

"Nothing."

Gateway leapt onto the floor and raised his hand to form a hole-in-reality for the two of them to walk through.

*****

A Day at Georgie and Armand's Place

The questionable one makes a good point. He is wise despite being the spawn of such a sinful being. It is regretful that he holds council with the sinful masses, as he has in him the essence of a savior. He is clearly powerful. If he had not been born by a sinner through such great sinfulness, he might have been worthy.

He is correct, we cannot know the motives of this newcomer. He has used all vile manner of corrupt magics to cause his chaos. There is the essence of madness in his actions.

It is time to get involved. But in truth, what can I do?

First I need to find the Dragons. As wicked as they are, it is odd they are not active in defending their place of sin. That is not a good sign.

May the Pure Ones of the All now guide me to where I need to be.

End of the Day Part 4

Alejandra and Stephan walked through the archway where the stone face of a young woman with a pleasant, but unique, smile looked down at them.

"This is all far more impressive than what I saw in those sketches," Stephan remarked. "I was surprised with the details in that book, but even then it didn't capture just how outstanding this all is."

"I believe we're walking through the remains of The Great Library of Dela CoErwine," Alejandra said. "The Dragons must have built their vault with those ruins. That would reinforce the stories that they were involved in whatever tragedy it was that brought the institution down."

A Day at Georgie and Armand's Place

"I keep feeling like I'm getting brought in on the tail end of a huge story around here," Stephan replied.

"There's a lot of history with two dragons who are thousands of years old..."

"Are you okay?" Stephan asked.

"It's Kwando,' Alejandra said with concern. "For some reason my connection with him is gone. That's a bad sign. I should be linked with him no matter how far apart we are. It would take a really powerful spell to break that link."

"This bad guy clearly has some power behind him. Are you going to be able to do anything to even slow him down?"

"Don't know, but I'm going to try,' Alejandra stated. "I know this isn't your world and this day has been overwhelming for you. I feel better having you at my side for this."

"I'm not about to let you go into this madness alone."

"I appreciate that. Just do me a favor, try not to die."

"I'll do what I can," Stephan promised.

An illuminated orb materialized in front of them, followed by two dark figures.

As Stephan moved to investigate, he found himself staring into the barrel of a pistol.

"He doesn't look like much for such a powerful being," came a smug voice.

"That is not our adversary," came the cold, formal reply. "There is nothing mystical about him. He could be a minion though."

"Okay, let's just settle down here," Stephan said as he raised his hands. "I'm no one's minion."

"The legendary Gateway I presume," Alejandra stated once she got a good look at the owners of the voices. "And this is your father I'm guessing. Fallingstar? I assure you, we are all on the same side."

"Fallingstar? At least it's close," White-Star remarked. "So now what?"

"My guess is you're here to stop whoever it is that has been messing with the Hotel," Alejandra replied. "We work together. Gateway, do you think you can stop this person?"

"His power is far greater than mine, but power itself does not make one invulnerable. When confronted, the hope is that a weakness will be shown."

A Day at Georgie and Armand's Place

"Okay blue and beautiful, lead the way," White-Star said, giving a slight bow.

"Not the time to be flirting, father," Gateway remarked.

"Yeah, what your… Son? Said," Stephan added, making sure to put himself in between White-Star and Alejandra.

Gateway's lumination orb floated into the darkness as the four of them followed.

"Let us discuss our plan once we encounter this individual," Gateway said. "I think we may need use of your spiritual abilities, Alejandra, if we are to defeat him."

"What do you have in mind?" Alejandra asked.

*****

"So this is their final barrier to the vaults," the figure said. He stood in a large dark chamber with no viable ceiling to it, before a simple looking stone door embedded in a fragment of a wall with various runes, markings from dozens of long dead languages, carved into it. "Clever, very clever. Anyone who was not familiar with the disciplines of the Nine would be stuck. And as it takes four masters to open…"

The figure removed his satchel of scrolls and placed it against the wall. He closed his eyes, raised his hands and spoke loudly in an ancient tongue. There was a flash of light with three new copies of himself standing next to him. Each identical except for the artifacts worn by the original.

The four of them took up spots in front of the door and each chanting, creating four different spells, one each of four rarely practiced, almost unknown, disciplines.

A crisp sizzle of energy filled the chamber.

The echoing pops of a series of bullets exiting a gun came as one of the copies found itself filled with four bullet holes. The other three stopped their chanting as they cringed in pain. The bullet ridden copy staggered forwards a few steps before turning to dust.

"Now what," the original said as he turned to see who had disrupted his work.

White-Star stood holding a smoking pistol. Gateway stood next to his father, his hands glowing with a ready spell. Alejandra stood on his

A Day at Georgie and Armand's Place

other side with her hands raised and her face in deep concentration. Stephan was slightly behind her with a look of shock on his face.

"Why do you creatures make things more difficult than they need to be," the original mumbled.

"Just step back from that door now and I won't have to shoot any more of you," White-Star stated.

"Now that's laughable." One of the copies waved its hand. A sharp green blast shot out, hitting White-Star's pistol. It quickly melted into a useless slag, becoming burning hot, causing White-Star to drop the formless clump. The leather glove he had worn was now mostly burned through and practically useless with noticeable burns left on his skin.

Gateway let loose his spell and the copy that had attacked his father was blasted to dust in a purple flash. The remaining two hunched over in pain.

"All you're doing is wasting your energy and slowing down the inevitable," the original stated as he straightened himself up.

"That would be your opinion." Gateway let loose another blast that took out the remaining copy.

As the original recovered from the loss of his last copy he remarked, "I had so hoped we'd be able to work together."

"I see no possibility of that."

"Agreed."

*****

Alejandra had remained in deep concentration during the conflict. The plan was for the men to keep the target occupied as she worked through his defenses on a spiritual level. The spells she found herself attempting were at the highest edge of her skills.

In the agony of losing each copy, the original left himself more open to her. She had gained a stronger hold into his spiritual center each time. The technique she was using normally would be used to cleanse someone's damaged spirit from possession of some other attack on the spirit. The method was not meant to be aggressive towards the owner's own soul, but she could think of no other way to bring him down.

A Day at Georgie and Armand's Place

"You are good," echoed a voice not her own in her head. "But did you really think I would not have protections in place for such an attack. Besides, my spirit was changed millennia ago in ways you are incapable of grasping."

Alejandra ignored the taunting and pushed on.

"I do admire your determination," the voice continued. "In fact, I think I might just let you experience my soul to see what happens."

A wave of spiritual energy flowed into Alejandra. She caught glimpses of a realm that, in her attempts to comprehend, actually resulted in her experiencing a new kind of pain that she had no words for. As she tried to back away and break the connections, the image of a dark, striped, four eyed being with two destructive looking tusks and a mighty trunk came rushing towards her.

"I did warn you," came the voice as Alejandra's mind started to shut down.

*****

"Alex!" Stephan rushed over to Alejandra, as her unconscious form fell to the floor.

Gateway was busy trying to maintain the beam of magic he was focusing from his staff on his adversary. The red beam seemed to make contact with the man's outstretched hand while having no appearance of causing any harm.

White-Star circled the adversary, firing at him every so often and finding his bullets vanishing before they made contact.

"Enough of this," the adversary proclaimed as he swiped his hand through the air. The resulting wave of energy threw Gateway and White-Star to the ground.

Stephan looked at the now unconscious forms and found himself being overwhelmed with panic.

"Now where was I?" The adversary turned back to the door, closed his eyes, raised his hands and began speaking loudly.

"Not so fast," Stephan said. He rose to his feet and picked up Gateway's staff.

As Stephan approached this being who was, for all purposes, a god compared to the lowly accountant, his mind was racing with the thought of, *"Oh shit. This is crazy. What the hell do you think you're doing?"*

A Day at Georgie and Armand's Place

*****

Georgie had reverted to his dragon form. Blasts of raw magical energy flew out around the balcony. They would reflect off the invisible barrier, fly back to strike various points around the suite, leaving scorch marks.

"I don't see that helping any," Kwando remarked.

"Let him vent," Armand replied. He was walking back from their sleep chamber with his arms crossed, his left hand to his chin, staring out past the balcony's railing. "The Forever Star has long since set, with the Dream of Realization now passing through the Infinite Harmony. Our day is coming to an end with all we hold dear under attack. Best for him to let it all out."

"This is not being productive."

"And what would be productive?" Armand asked, clearly agitated. "We do not possess the power to break the spells and have no way to call for outside help. Letting off a little steam seems reasonable to me."

"This is all just madness," Kwando stated. "How could you let this happen to your precious Hotel?"

"I would watch your tone if I were you," Armand replied coldly. "Spirit or not, there are ways to end you."

"Brutish threats are not…" Kwando noticed that Armand was now walking towards the portal. "See something?"

"Yes," Armand said as he looked through the portal. A short figure in worn brown coverings, wearing a metallic mask and tinted goggles, stood just on the other side examining the arch of the portal.

"Who's that?" Kwando asked.

"I think it's Fringe."

Georgie ended his barrage of spells and joined Armand, having returned to his human form.

"Yes, that's him," Georgie replied. He took in a deep breath to help him calm down from his exertions. "I hope he stays out there. He would be such a miserable creature to be trapped with. He has such a hurtful view of us."

"He seems to have no interest in joining us," Kwando remarked. "He might be seeing if he could close the portal to make our trap all the more secure."

A Day at Georgie and Armand's Place

"Do you think he's working with The Coulder?" Goergie asked

"No, that would go against his beliefs," Armand answered. "Most likely he's just taking advantage of our situation."

Fringe came to a point of almost touching the portal, holding his hand out. He looked over the full portal. His hand vanished back into the mess of his worn clothing. He turned and quickly vanished from sight.

"Such an odd little creature," Kwando remarked.

"He's up to something," Armand stated. "He's not one to engage in trivial acts."

"I'm not fooled," Georgie said. "He's just playing with us. He'll be of no help."

"I wouldn't be so quick to judge," Armand said, nodding his head towards the portal.

Fringe was returning to the portal. He carried a stack of panels taken from the walls of the long-abandoned lobby loaded on his back. He dropped the panels and quickly got to work assembling the panels into a doorway pattern.

"Very interesting," Armand mumbled. "I think I see what he's doing. It just might work."

"What?"

"He's going to make a tunnel for us through the barrier I believe."

"Oh...Yes, that should work," Georgie replied. "Why would he help us?"

"A question best saved for after we deal with The Coulder."

In short time Fringe built a full frame out of the panels. While it looked to be of questionable stability, he picked it up and moved it over to the portal where he slid it through, so that there was half of the makeshift tunnel on both sides.

Armand and Georgie exchanged questioning glances.

"I'll go first," Kwando said as he floated into the haphazardly constructed structure.

The two dragons watched as the spirit moved through the impoverished passage way. He moved into the old abandoned lobby with no resistance.

"I'm through, it worked," Kwando announced.

Georgie and Armand wasted no time in going through themselves. Armand gave Fringe a solemn nod of thanks as they rushed through the

A Day at Georgie and Armand's Place

large hole in the wall, entering the remains of The Great Library of Dela CoErwine.

*****

A twenty-foot staff with golden rings on both ends came flying through one of the cracks. Pods caught it with her left hand, threw it back into the crack it had come through, then caught the wrench she had tossed into the air to free up her hand and returned to work.

"Why is there so much junk floating in the void," Pods remarked. "People can be so careless with their belongings."

"Yeah, I can see that," Lonna said as he threw a metal box with a glass cover that had three lighted tubes that formed a 'Y' shape visible in it, into a pile of odds and ends that had been slowly accumulating as they worked. "It's killing our pace doing this clean up."

"Annoying, isn't it? But we will prevail. Now where is the… Do you hear that?

"I'm having a hard time separating all the noise coming through here."

"Somewhere in one of these cracks," Pods said with an odd smile. "Someone is singing."

"Are you saying someone is alive out there in the void?"

"All I can tell you is that I am hearing an actual voice," Pod explained. "And it's not any manner of recording, which would suggest that there is."

"How is that possible?" Lonna asked.

"No idea" Pods replied. "The workings of the void are far beyond my scope of knowledge. My curiosity however is getting the better of me. I believe this warrants investigation."

"Seriously? Don't we have enough to do without worrying about noise from the void?"

"Yes, but that's no excuse."

With acrobatic precision, Pods swung through the collection of gears and rods, pausing for a moment before one of the various cracks, then moving on to the next one, repeating the action. She finally stopped at a larger crack along one of the walls.

"Yes, it's definitely coming from this one," Pods stated before pushing her head into the crack. "Oh, now that is interesting."

"What?"

"There's a structure in here. Quick, throw me some rope. I'm going to climb over to it."

A Day at Georgie and Armand's Place

"This is crazy," Lonna said as he brought the rope over to Pods.

"I know," Pods replied as she took the rope. "Doing something crazy every-so-often helps keep life interesting." With that Pods kicked off with her feet, disappearing into the crack.

End of the Day Part 5

There was a sharp bite to the cold echoing laughter that filled the darkness.

Georgie and Armand rushed through the ruins, attack spells at the ready. It had been several centuries since they had had the need to venture to the original Vault of the Hotel, but they knew the passages well. They remained silent as they progressed. There was no doubt in their minds that their adversary was at the Vault and had spent more time there than they were comfortable with.

While the laughter was chilling, it also meant he was still down there, leaving a chance to confront and stop him.

A Day at Georgie and Armand's Place

Neither of the dragons were prepared for the scene they found.

The mage Gateway was unconscious on the ground, his skin red with burns, smoke drifting off his body. His father lay in the same state not too far from him. Alejandra's unconscious form rested farther away, but there were no signs of physical harm to her.

Despite all that, it was Alejandra's male friend, who stood between their adversary and the Vault door. He stood waving Gateway's staff in a reckless manner and screaming out incomprehensible threats that gave the dragons pause. This was clearly the cause of their adversary's fit of laughter.

"I really don't see that as being physically possible," the adversary remarked after Stephan claimed he would take a certain body part and place it within another body part in a forceful and rather extreme manner. "Best to just stand aside now, as you really present no threat to me."

"He may not, but we very much do," Armand said, his voice resonating through the chamber with a cold, determined tone. "Human, get away from there. We're not going to be gentle."

As the adversary turned to face the Dragons, Stephan dropped the staff and mumbled, "Oh thank you, thank you, thank you…" as he rushed back over to Alejandra's side.

As soon as Stephan was out of the way, neither Georgie nor Armand hesitated in releasing their prepared spells. The long, one sided, volley of magical energy blasts lit up the chamber with a cascading light show that under other circumstances might have been a beautiful display.

Finally the dragons had to pause.

As the smoke cleared there came a staggered coughing.

"Now that hurt," their adversary said. He had been pushed into the Vault door. As he pulled himself from the door, an outline of where he had been could be seen in the blast residue left on the door.

Their adversary stood there, making subtle movements throughout his body.

"No real harm done though."

"The Coulder?" Armand inquired with doubt in his voice. "You don't sound like my old master."

A Day at Georgie and Armand's Place

"Who me? Sorry Armand, he's dead. Georgie killed him. It was messy if you remember."

"Who are you?" Georgie asked.

"My dear, beautiful Georgie, do you really not remember me? Although this is not my true form. But you know all about changing form. Now let's see if I can remember my original form. I spent so long without a physical body, I barely remember what it was… I'm still not sure if I was trapped in Master Joh's world, or in Master Joh zirself. As ze was dead, ze couldn't tell me what was going on."

"Rodfire?" Georgie stated. "You survived…"

"That's who I am… Being, wherever I was for all that time, leaves me with some odd gaps in my mind," Rodfire replied. "Forgetting my form and my name. My whole sense of self was lost. But now that I remember my name, I can picture my form again."

The large human body quickly morphed into that of an even larger brown on white striped, four-legged creature with massive feline legs and claws. Its impressive head had four eyes, a powerful trunk and two intimidating tusks.

"Yes, that feels right," Rodfire said. "I have no idea how long it's been since I've been in my true body. For some reason I had it in my mind that there was something convenient and attractive to that human form."

"Rodfire, it's clear you've been through a lot," Armand said, his voice calm and controlled. "Why don't we all go to a meeting room and talk this out."

"No," Rodfire said, lifting his right front leg and stomping it down. A blast shot out and threw Armand through the air like a doll. "I have nothing to say to you. You stole him from me and for that you deserve to suffer like no other." As Armand tried to get back to his feet, Rodfire shot out another blast at him. "Just stay down for now. I'll destroy you properly when I'm done.

"Now, Georgie, can you help me open your vault so I can finish this all up?"

"This is madness," Georgie exclaimed, on the edge of hysterics. "You want me to help you destroy my hotel?"

"What? No, why would I… Oh, I see how you might think that," Rodfire replied, a sense of comprehension in his voice. "No, you misunderstand what's going on. I know you love

A Day at Georgie and Armand's Place

this hotel and how much it means to you. And once I properly cleanse Armand from your mind and all traces of him from the Hotel, we can rebuild it together, like it was supposed to be. If the Hearts had not been changed when Master Joh tried to destroy them, I would have already done it. Once they get repowered by your unaltered Hearts of the Gods, that will hopefully reset them to how they used to be."

"I'm sorry, I think I missed something," Georgie replied, shaking his head in confusion as he tried to grasp what he just heard.

Rodfire rushed and took Georgie by the shoulders, moving in so their faces were inches apart.

"Hax'georget'krestdawn, I have been in love with you since the moment I first met you," Rodfire stated. "Once I was free of wherever I had been for all those centuries, the one thing that I knew was that I was going to show you that I was the one you belonged with. Then I learned about this hotel and realized what I needed to do. My love for you was the one thing that remained with me, no matter what my mind went through."

"I... I... I never knew. I'm flattered I guess," Georige mumbled out. "But I love Armand."

"He was never right for you," Rodfire stated, with a cold gleam in his eyes. "That's why The Coulder made the deal with me. It would have been better for you to run off with me, where you would have been truly happy."

"Deal? What deal?"

Rodfire released Georgie and looked at him with a pleasant smile on his face.

"I killed Royal Chatwell and gave The Coulder his Heart of a God, with the promise he wouldn't kill you, but instead would let me take you away from it all."

"You did what?" Georgie exclaimed, unable to hide the horrified shock from his face.

"I know, the foolish things we do for love," Rodfire replied with a haunting smile. "If only you'd had gone with me then. And now we have a second chance."

Georgie backed away.

"You killed Chatwell..." Georgie said. "You've hurt so many people today, many of whom are my friends. How is any of that showing love?"

A Day at Georgie and Armand's Place

Rodfire looked at the scattered bodies around the chamber. Gateway was clearly beginning to wake as White-Star let out a soft, involuntary moan of pain. Stephan had been listening to it all as he cradled Alejandra in his arms. Her eyes had opened, but she didn't seem to be able to focus.

"The ones here, they are your friends?" Rodfire asked.

"Yes."

"I see why you might be upset."

"Good, so maybe we…"

"I'll fix this," Rodifre said with an odd passion. "I can destroy them fully. Then I can remove their memories from your mind and it will be as though they never existed."

"What? No!" Georgie replied in confusion and shock over the realization of what his old friend was preparing to do.

Rodfire lifted his full front half up and slammed his front claws down hard. A blast shot out heading in all directions.

"No," came Kwando's voice. His spirit form emerged from the ground and stretched itself out to take in the full blast before it could spread too far. There was an unearthly scream of pain as

the room lit up in a blinding blast and then fell
dark.

*****

"Now that was unexpected," Rodfire
casually stated.

"Kwando!" Alejandra yelled as she came
fully awake.

"His name was Kwando?" Rodfire asked.
"Was he related to Dwar Kwando? Now that
would make for an interesting coincidence."

"His spirit…" Alejandra said, her voice
filled with pain. "It's gone. Destroyed. No chance
to crossover."

"You will harm no one else in my hotel,"
Georgie said. He let loose a blast of purple
sparkling energy right into Rodfire's face.

Showing no sign of being affected by the
blast, Rodfire reached out with his trunk and
caught Georgie around the neck, throwing the
dragon roughly to the ground.

"Stop fighting me!" Rodfire yelled out. He
moved above Georgie, with one of his claws on
the dragon's chest, pinning him to the ground.
"Hold still and I will cleanse your mind of all this

A Day at Georgie and Armand's Place

nonsense, and you can be my partner. You'll be so much happier once you submit to me and love me."

"Remove your paw from my love's body," Armand demanded. He had gotten to his feet, reverted to his dragon form and was now rushing Rodfire.

Rodfire gave a push to Georgie's stunned form, sliding him across the floor. The beast stiffened up on his four powerful legs, leaned forward and prepared for impact.

The mighty black scaled dragon flew with purpose. As he neared the unflinching brown/white furred body, Rodfire raised and twisted his massive head. With a shifting of his weight his tusks made contact with Armand's body, slashing two great gashes into the dragon's flesh as the two creatures clashed.

Armand was attempting to twist around Rodfire's body to limit his movements. He dug his front claws into Rodifre's sides and bit down hard on his neck. With his back claws, Armand was reaching for the belt.

"I had forgotten what physical pain feels like," Rodfire remarked with an amused laugh. "As satisfying as ripping you apart with my tusks would be, I know what you're trying to do and I'm not about to let that happen."

The crackle of electricity filled the chamber. Armand screamed out in pain as the energy sizzled through his body, giving off a fluctuating blue glow to the chamber. He dug his claws even deeper into Rodfire's body.

"You are tough, I'll give you that," Rodfire said. "And while my Hearts are not what they used to be, they're still powerful enough."

A white-hot blast of heat shot out from Rodfire, blasting scales off of Armand's body. The dragon held on as long as he could, but the power of the blast was too much for him.

Armand's claws reluctantly slipped out of Rodfire's hide. The blast sent the dragon flying into the wall, where he slid to the floor, bloody and beaten.

Georgie had risen to his feet. He stood, his face contorting in anger.

"Enough!" Georgie yelled as he transformed into his dragon form. He took in a big breath and clenched his claws into fists. The sizzle of energy building up echoed through the chamber.

A Day at Georgie and Armand's Place

Armand let out a garbled, dry laugh as he said, "You upset Georgie. I've seen this before. So have you. Do you remember what happens next?"

"That I very much remember," Rodfire replied. "Now my love, don't make me have to hurt you."

A blinding blue blast of energy shot out from Georgie, striking Rodfire in the chest, sending him crashing once more into the Vault door.

*****

Gateway rose to his feet in time to clearly observe Georgie's transformation.

He took a moment to completely assess the situation and the condition of everyone in the chamber. He knew the only reason he was now standing was his personal magical defense spells that he activated when he returned to the Hotel. The remnants of Kwando's spirit still lingered in the air, and Gateway knew there was no way to bring it back. White-Star was beaten, a healing spell would be needed before he could be active again, but nothing life threatening at the moment. Alejandra was physically unharmed. Mentally however, she was going through a wild ride of instability.

He rushed over, kneeled down next to the hysterical Alejandra, who was fighting with Stephan to get to her feet and placed his hand on her head. Her face was covered in tears while her eyes were unable to focus, her mind clearly pushed too far.

He quietly said, "Sleep." He pulled his hand away as she closed her eyes.

"Keep her safe," Gateway said. "This is not over yet."

Stephan mindlessly nodded. Gateway knew there was nothing the young man could do if things went as bad as they might, but he also knew this was not the time to be honest about it.

Gateway looked to where Armand lay, his dragon body stretched limp across the floor. He was in bad shape and needed attention immediately. Blood was seeping out from his massive wounds as well as large patches of scales missing, revealing areas of burnt skin. Gateway cringed as he wondered if even his skills would be enough.

The charged air in the chamber made the climate of an on-going intense magical battle of

A Day at Georgie and Armand's Place

near god-like levels, inescapable for Gateway. Behind it all was the chaotic situation of the Vault trying to hold onto the countless strings of connections between it and the rest of the fragments of realities that made up the Hotel. The energies being released in their fight were working against the Vault.

"Oh Georgie, I'm sorry it has come to this," came Rodfire's voice as he raised up on his back legs and waved his front claws.

Gateway closed his eyes, allowing his senses to reach out in search of anything that might make a difference. His senses moved out, flowing through the Hotel, trying to touch every corner he could in hopes of finding something that could make a difference. A presence was calling to him from near-by; something both familiar and new. Realization swept over him as he was able to piece together what was needed. A familiar presence reentered an area of the Hotel that Gateway could still sense, there was a similarity between the two presences.

"That I can work with," Gateway said as he raised his hands up and began casting his spell.

*****

The world shook as Georgie pounded the defensive barrier Rodfire had conjured with spell after spell in a non-stop barrage. The energies being released washed through the chamber, throwing Stephan off of Alejandra and shuffling the unconscious bodies around, all caught in the tides of the battle.

"Okay Georgie, it's time to calm down," came the soothing voice of Armand from behind Georgie. "You've done it. He's finished."

"What?" Georgie mumbled as he shook his head. He stopped his assault and turned to look at where the voice had come from.

There was no one there. Armand's beaten form lay across the room, unable to do much more than breathe.

"What's going on" Georgie said, finding it hard to keep standing.

"I'm surprised," Rodfire replied as he shifted out of his defensive posture. "I wasn't sure if that would work. Voice projection is a novice trick after all."

"No..."

Rodfire leapt out and struck Georgie straight on in the jaw with his forehead.

A Day at Georgie and Armand's Place

Georgie fell to the floor. Rodfire raised his claws and struck Georgie with a series of harsh blows.

"I wish you hadn't made me do that," Rodfire said standing over the quivering form of Georgie. "Once this is over we'll erase all this violence from your memory and start things over. Once you realize you love me as much as I love you, there will never be the need for this again."

Rodfire let loose one more strike before turning and facing the Vault door.

"Now, where was I?"

As Rodfire raised his front paws and prepared to start chanting, a strong white beam of light flashed out from the cracks of the Vault door. It flew around him. He turned with it to see where it was headed.

Gateway and Pods stood there with intrigued looks on their faces as the white beam met up with the disoriented form of Conrad Pendragon.

"What now?" Rodfire asked.

"I do believe the Hotel wishes to involve itself in this altercation," Gateway answered.

End of the Day Part 6

Pods had been overly surprised to find herself pulling Conrad Pendragon out of a bleak cell and into her machine room.

Conrad was just glad to be back in the Hotel, even if it was a backroom left in shambles. He took the chance to stretch and was preparing to ask if either of the two workers he found himself with could tell him what was going on, when the portal opened before him.

A heavily tanned hand connected to an arm covered with leather straps and odd bobbles reached through and motioned for him to approach with a voice saying, "Pendragon, I need you."

A Day at Georgie and Armand's Place

"Whooa there, I've had a crazy day and am going to my room now for some rest," Conrad replied.

"I don't think he's asking," Pods said.

When Conrad made to turn away from the portal, Pods jump on his back, pushing him into the mysterious hand, which closed upon his shirt. With a quick movement Conrad and Pods were pulled through the portal.

Neither of them found time to take in their new surroundings as they witnessed Rodfire charge into Georgie and the unjustified brutal beating that followed.

Gateway took Conrad by the shoulders and positioned him in the middle of the chamber, lined up with the Vault doors.

"Hey, what are you doing?" Conrad protested.

"Hopefully saving the Hotel," Gateway answered.

Nothing was said as they stood waiting, watching as Rodfire began his spell.

"Is something supposed to be happening?" Pods asked.

"Trust in the Hotel," Gateway answered.

Before anything more could be said, the glowing white cloud seeped its way out of the Vault door and flowed over to Conrad. The singer's look of panic might have been amusing in other circumstances.

"What the hell?"

"Just calm down and let the connection happen."

Rodfire had turned and was now looking directly at Conrad.

"What now?" Rodfire asked

Gateway answered, "I do believe the Hotel wishes to involve itself in this altercation."

*****

Conrad stood, trying to turn to flee from the angry looking, giant, four eyed, tiger/elephant beast that was approaching, but unable to do so due to the white cloud that was surrounding him, holding him in place.

Staring at the nightmarish creature, Conrad felt a familiar sensation. He was syncing up with a reality, but there was something noticeably different this time. Whatever was going

A Day at Georgie and Armand's Place

on, it was far more intense than any sync he had experienced before.

Normally, there was a bit of a rush upon entering a new dimension as things synced up. Most of the time it was a mild sense of disorientation, then he was changed but rarely felt noticeably different and it was over quickly.

This syncing was a process. Time had slowed for him as Conrad could feel his body reacting to the sync, with his every cell pulsating with the changes. There was a conscious presence there attempting to calm him down as it altered him to its needs. It wasn't necessarily painful, but there was nothing pleasant about it either.

The tiger/elephant beast rose up on its hind legs and released a blast of energy towards Conrad. A sensation in his mind instructed him to raise his hands and project a shield to deflect the blast.

Without fully knowing what he was doing, Conrad conjured the shield in time.

The force of the blast still threw him back, despite the shield.

Conrad's mind cleared and time returned to normal.

As he realized he was in an actual battle with the tiger/elephant beast all he could say was, "Oh shit."

*****

The chamber was once more trembling as Rodfire let loose blast after blast at Conrad. The singer reacted to each attack, but clearly did not have the skills to do much more. His shields were holding with no signs of weakening.

Gateway turned to Pods and said, "I'll need your help; Conrad is not a mage and even with the help of the Hotel, I doubt he'll be able to end this. I'm going to need to do something rather risky, that I doubt has ever been done before."

"Sounds exciting," Pods replied, with a lopsided, playful grin on her face. "If it's going to save the Hotel, then I'm all in."

"Good, because I truly have no idea how to do what I am proposing, nor if it will work."

"Stop wasting time and get it done. I get the feeling mister Pop Star there would like to be done with all this."

"Right."

A Day at Georgie and Armand's Place

Gateway stood back, finding an empty spot far enough away from the fight to be safe. He raised up his right arm and held out his hand. He closed it into a fist and made a pulling motion towards himself. A tendril of the white cloud emerged from the mass surrounding Conrad and slowly stretched to Gateway's waiting, now opened, hand.

The Master Mage just stood there, opening himself to the Hotel. Soon the white glow was filling him as it had Conrad.

"Now for you," Gateway said looking at Pods. "Open yourself up and let it flow through you."

"Hit me big boy," Pods replied as she stood tall, with her arms spread out.

Gateway gestured towards her and a white tendril flew from his hand into her chest.

"Oh…" Pods let out. "This is… Oh my…"

"I know. But this is just the beginning. Brace yourself. We're going to need more connections throughout the Hotel."

"Right." Pods pulled out the earpiece Myts had given her and put it on. "Let's see if this thing is working."

*****

Myts was busy following Georgie's orders, trying to reactivate connections between areas of the Hotel, with his team, when he heard Pods' voice say, "Hey Metal Head, I need a favor of you."

"I am sorry Pods, but I do not believe this is the best time. It is good to know my equipment is working under these circumstances and..."

"No time for that boyo. We're trying to save the Hotel and I need you to be open to what's about to happen."

"What are you talking about?"

"There's going to be some white glowy, magic stuff coming to you through our connection, just let it do what it needs to do. Are there any other Gatekeepers around?"

"Yes, we were assigned to be in teams of five," Myts explained. "I am working with four others right now, each with their unique variety of skills and knowledge."

"Oh, now that is almost too perfect. Gonna need you to tell them what I just told you and to get them to let the white fluffiness do what it needs to do."

Myts was caught off guard when he realized his suit was now filled with a white smoke. He was prepared to activate his emergency protocols to deal with catastrophic malfunctions when he realized it must be what Pods had been talking about.

"I must say, this is truly unexpected," Myts replied as he opened himself up as he had been asked. "I have never imagined…"

"Yeah, stop the overthinking, buddy boy," Pods interrupted. "Get those others linked up and see if you can figure out any ways to connect to more Gatekeepers, or really anyone who is open to joining. The more the merrier."

*****

"Looks like the connection worked," Pods said as she turned towards Gateway.

"Good." White tendrils were stretching out from the mage in all directions. The five other individuals in the chamber were now joined in the connection. Dozens of other tendrils flowed out in all directions from the chambers, reaching to who knows where in the Hotel, hunting down beings willing to join in the fight.

In a manner that Pods could not explain, she was able to sense all the others. Even in their beaten states, they contributed as they could. She could also see that the connections were expanding; Gateway had found some means to reach out to others scattered around the Hotel and the Gatekeepers were continuing to spread the connection among them.

They were each aware that they were now connected and could sense each other. They formed a path through the hallways and lobbies of the Hotel, through the thousands and thousands of worlds that made up the Hotel. Each of them could feel the Hotel pulling itself back together.

The rush of seeing the Hotel becoming whole again gave those in the connection a stronger drive to find more beings to connect with to bring more of the Hotel in sync.

*****

A fresh rush overwhelmed Conrad. He stiffened up and let the shields drop as he adjusted to the new sensations.

A Day at Georgie and Armand's Place

Rodfire took advantage of the opening with a series of blasts that sent Conrad flying out of the chamber.

With an exhausted huff Rodfire proclaimed, "I am a god now. No mere mortal will be able to stop me."

"At this point you are not facing a mere mortal," Gateway replied as he approached Rodfire. "While the Hotel is not what you would consider a god, it is something far more complex and it is ready to end this."

Rodfire started to laugh, but trailed off when he realized the white glow was now coming from everyone in the room, white tendrils linking them all.

"You made a huge mistake," Alejandra said as she moved in next to Gateway.

"With all your planning, you failed to understand how the Hotel works," Georgie said as he joined the lineup.

"Although I must admit, even we didn't know this was possible," Armand remarked. He still looked beaten and worn, but he was walking to join the others.

"This place is an incredible, complex machine," Pods stated. "I can now see how it all fits together."

"There is so much diversity harmonising here," White-Star said.

"And with that there is such strength," Stephan added.

"Now it is time to finish things," Conrad said as he found himself flying back into the chamber. He hovered over the others, white tendrils criss-crossing in connecting them together.

"No wait…" Rodfire started to say as a blinding white light shot forth from Conrad, striking Rodfire.

As the chamber filled with an impenetrable whiteness, obscuring all visual details, the sound of the cling of a metal belt echoed with an eerie sense of finality as it fell to the floor.

A Day at Georgie and Armand's Place

End of the Day Part 7

The odd white clouds that had shot through the
Nona'He Mountain lobby, and seemed to have
entered several members of the gathered crowd,
had vanished just as mysteriously as they had
appeared. A few seconds later the normal lighting
of the lobby returned to life.

Nirron took in the condition of the lobby
with a sense of relief.

He had allowed the white smoke to
connect with him and remembered he had been
part of something great connected with the Hotel.
He knew there had been a conflict that was now
resolved. His memories of the full experience
were fragmented and fading away. He understood

that a single mortal mind would not be able to hold the full memory of just what had happened, but he would never forget what he had been a part of.

"Do you think the doors are working now?" Inquired a guest.

"Only one way to find out," another guest replied. The guest ran up to the closest doorway and took hold of its handle. She looked back at the crowd waiting with anticipation. She cautiously opened the door.

In the doorway a whirling, static filled passage was starting to form with a blurred city scene on its other side.

"Why don't we close that for now," Nirron remarked. "It would appear the Hotel is still in need of a little more time to fully reset itself."

*****

Kra let out a relieved chirp as he found himself standing on solid ground with the swirling, chaotic myst vanishing. Looking around the wing of the Hotel, he saw it had not suffered

A Day at Georgie and Armand's Place

much in actual damage. Most of the walls were cracked, but seemed intact and sturdy.

Disoriented guests were gazing around in confusion.

"I am not taking responsibility for this," Colliven remarked as he hobbled by. "Maybe you should go and do your job now. I need a repair team up here."

Kra was trying to hold onto the memories of being connected with the Hotel, but found it impossible.

"Huh… What did you say?" Kra asked when he realized Colliven had been talking to him.

"Clearly a professional of the highest order," Colliven replied. "As a hotel messenger, I need you to go and report my request for a repair team up here so they can begin repairs as soon as possible."

"I have the feeling that every section of the Hotel is going to be in need of repair. Just trust the Dragons for now. They have other priorities to focus on."

"I do not believe it is your job to ignore such a request, but to deliver them."

"Whatever," Kra said as he took flight. "I'm going to go check in now. You can deliver your own request."

"Humph," Colliven snorted.

*****

Liemen found himself joyously organizing the books. His eye stalks danced around to unheard music.

He had been weary when the white smoke came at him. Once he realized there was something more to it he let it connect with him. The experience was indescribable, but he knew it had been important.

He had always enjoyed his job before. Now he felt a greater sense of purpose. No matter how it may be perceived by others, he was doing his part to keep something far bigger than himself going.

Even the tedious nature of cleaning the mess of books was not enough to bring him down. He went about the chore with the tips of his legs happily tapping out a rhythm as he worked.

*****

A Day at Georgie and Armand's Place

"What just happened here?" The Man asked as the white tendrils faded and the lobby lit back up. "None of what I have seen here suggests this business is safe or being securely maintained."

Novick was still lost in a daze from being part of the connection. As he glanced around and saw that the lobby was recovering, he smiled.

"A stupid grin is not an answer to my questions," The Man remarked.

"Could you shut up for once?" Novick asked. "Something incredible just took place and you are so ruining the moment."

The Man gave an indignant huff and turned to see creatures opening various doors. There were fuzzy passageways appearing behind them now.

"Good, it looks like I can finally leave this mad house," The Man said as he headed off towards the door to his home reality.

Novick turned and saw the wavering passageways.

"Don't try it," Novick warned. "That's not how they're supposed to look."

"Nonsense, I can see the glorious buildings of Gad'den. I am returning home now."

The Man walked through the doorway and began screaming in horror. His body seemed to distort as it flowed into the twisting clouds that formed the tunnel to his world. It did not look as if he had made it through, vanishing from sight as he was violently pulled away by unseen forces.

"Ok, no one else is to go through the doorways until further notice," Novick announced loudly. There was a clear air of agreement from everyone.

Novick shook his head clear and rushed over to the crystal pool and was pleased to see that the water was once more flowing into the Aquarian Casa Lobby.

He waved to Jess'iah, who waved back. It was clear she was caught up in dealing with the chaos in her own lobby.

Jaya came up behind Novick and asked, "Uh... What do we do now boss?"

"We're winging it my friend," Novick replied. "With all the training, they never covered how to recover from the Hotel almost being torn apart. We should start by offering the guests a free meal for their troubles. We're going to need all the meal vouchers we can find."

A Day at Georgie and Armand's Place

*****

Ande blinked frantically bringing herself back to reality. She stumbled a bit and found herself resting on Groat, who was also coming out of the overwhelming sensation of the connection.

"What just happened?" Groat asked.

"Not really sure, but it was amazing," Ande replied.

The restaurant lights came alive in a sudden disorienting rush. That was followed by a round of thunderous applause which caught them off guard.

Ande realized they had been on the stage the whole time. The crowd at the Peachy Pegasus had been treated to a unique show that they seemed to have enjoyed.

Ande and Groat awkwardly waved to the crowd as they made their way off stage.

"With how intense that was to be a part of, I wonder what they saw," Groat remarked.

"I'm sure we'll be hearing all about it," Ande commented. "Just hope the reviews are positive. They'll just need to accept that there'll be no encore performance. Now you should be a good hostess and see what your customers need."

Ian Brazee-Cannon

*****

The static-filled moans of computers rebooting and coming back on-line woke Orr'koor'lon from the aftermath of being part of the connection. He looked around at the now flashing controls and lit up monitors. His world was returning to regular functioning status.

Once he was fully awake he started swimming around to the various controls to get the secondary walls fully raised and the filtration systems back up and running. The rush of fresh, clean water was revitalizing for him.

"All seems to once more be in order," Orr'koor'lon remarked to himself. "Now to get back to work."

*****

"Oh Rya'Je, thank you for that," Han'Gra said as the white tendrils left her body. "I did not think I was deserving."

The Nagetins were in shock, none of them seeming to be able to move. Han'Gra guessed that several of them had suffered heart attacks from the

A Day at Georgie and Armand's Place

stress. As they were not dead, that meant the magic that protected anyone in the Hotel had remained active, at least for the Peachy Pegasus. Chances were if they returned to their world right now, they would fall over dead in their first steps.

"You may end your panic now," Han'Gra stated. "The threat is over and the Balance has held strong."

The seven Nagetins once more ignored Han'Gra, huddling together in a tight ball of furry bodies.

"Those poor creatures," Han'Gra thought. *"If only they could have experienced the connection. Rya'Je has truly blessed me and shown me I was right about the Hotel. It is connected to the Balance. So much has faded already, but I shall always know I was able to do as Rye'Je bid of me and got to be part of something so much greater than myself."*

*****

It is done. The dragons are victorious.

I do not feel dirty for being part of the connection. It is not the place itself that is evil but those who fill it and use it for the foul purposes.

There is something grander to this Hotel than I had suspected. It has a destiny far greater than what one can imagine. If only the unworthy who fill it with their corruption understood this and showed it the reverence it deserved.

Time to pray that I had made the right choice.

Despite it all, they will continue in their evil ways and this place will host all manner of disgusting sinners.

I will continue my task of cleansing, for I knew when I began that it would be never ending. I shall go to my death knowing that I fought with all of my being to make all of reality a more holy place, worthy of the grace of the true gods.

*****

Blossk sat at zirs desk, zirs head was still clearing up. Zir mind was going through the whole experience. Ze had been connected to... so many others.

"We were connected, but there was no mind reading in it," Blossk thought. *"No one slipped in while we were all linked? No, it wasn't that kind of connection. There's nothing for me to*

A Day at Georgie and Armand's Place

worry about. My telepathic blocks are still up and strong. I'd know if someone got through them."

As ze came to, ze saw that everyone else in the room was staring at zir in puzzlement.

"What are you looking at?" Blossk snapped. "We got work to do. Looks like the Hotel is pulling itself back together. I want our people out there looking for opportunities."

"Uh...Honored One, what just happened?" Colby asked.

"Nothing. Now we have work to do."

"But there was glowing white smoke all over you. Was this some kind of attack?"

"It is none of your concern. The Hotel is injured and we are in a position to be of aid in its recovery."

"Injured? Odd word choice," Colby noted.

"Enough fooling around," Blossk replied, giving the quiet Prags a gentle, comforting scratch. "This is the perfect chance to create some goodwill between us and the Dragons, helping out as we can. Let's not waste our time discussing something you need not know about."

*****

Lonna stood alone among the collection of fallen gears, pistons, rods and springs. He watched the last of the white smoke fade away from around him. The tears in reality had sealed themselves, although the junk that had fallen out of them was still there.

Despite the work that he knew was needed, Lonna had a huge smile on his face.

Lonna picked up a few of the gears and looked at them. He was surprised to realize he saw just how it all fit together absent any diagrams or explanations. He glanced over the mess and was picturing in his mind just how it all should be arranged in order to work. There was a clearer than ever understanding of how it all functioned and achieved its purpose.

"Damn," Lonna mumbled.

"So is this me understanding the Hotel itself better, or did Pods sneak in while we were all connected and implant some of her thinking style in there? Or is her training finally taking effect?" He thought. *"Doesn't matter I guess. When she gets back, I'm admitting nothing."*

"Now to get back to work," Lonna said as he picked up a wrench. Without pause, he knew

A Day at Georgie and Armand's Place

just where he needed to go to get everything back together properly.

*****

The chamber was silent as the white mist seeped back through the cracks into the Vault. The Vault door and the wall around it were covered in scorch marks. Chips of the ancient stone structure littered the floor. Many of the engravings had been damaged beyond recognition.

The door itself had held with minimal cosmetic damage.

The belt of silver frames rested on the ground in a pile of ash in front of the Vault.

One last tendril of white was still connected to Conrad.

Once her mind cleared Alejandra fell to her knees and let loose a river of tears. Stephan took to his knees behind her and pulled her into his arms.

"Kwando is gone," Alejandra let out between sobs.

"I know. I'm so sorry," Stephan replied softly.

"His sacrifice helped us save the Hotel," Gateway said. "He will not be forgotten."

"No he won't," Armand added. He was still in his dragon form. He held Georgie, who had collapsed once the connection ended. After stroking Georgie's scales for a bit, he gently placed the red dragon on the ground. As soon as his arms we free, they went straight to clutching his side. His body was covered in massive scars, with his insides still in need of healing.

"Not sure why the Hotel couldn't have fully healed me while connected," Armand mumbled as he reverted to human form. He smoothed out his suit and let out a relieved breath "At least clothed I look functional."

"Hey, why am I not disconnected?" Conrad asked.

"As you are a Child of the Nexus, I do believe the Hotel will need to stay connected to you for a little longer while it realigns and repairs itself," Gateway answered, his eyebrows raised in thought. "You are right now the pivotal force holding everything together."

"Wouldn't be my first choice for the salvation of my Hotel," Armand stated.

A Day at Georgie and Armand's Place

"You be nice to him," came Georgie's weak voice as he stirred.

"So now what?" White-Star asked.

"Now we get to work putting everything back together," Pods answered. "Lots to do. Best we get moving. So big, bad mage, you think you can port me back to where you snagged me from?"

"With Armand's permission," Gateway said, glancing at the dragon.

"Of course."

Gateway waved his hand, tearing a gap in reality. Pods enthusiastically jumped through.

"Still not big on the magic stuff, but that was something," White-Star said, putting his hand on Gateway's shoulder. "We don't make a half bad team, boy. Maybe we can work together more in the future."

"That does not sound like a bad idea, father. I do not believe it would hurt my destiny to include you in my missions more often."

The two of them hugged.

Armand had opened a portal of his own. Sna and Mmm'ddeliommm had come through it and were now taking in the aftermath of the battle.

"As touching as all that is, and as much as we are truly grateful for your aid here today, I must ask everyone except Gateway and Conrad to take their leave of this place," Armand stated. "As you leave, understand that as far as the rest of all reality is concerned, this place does not exist. There is no vault in the Hotel containing mystic relics of unimaginable power. When we release an official announcement as to what took place today, you will each defend it as being an accurate account of events."

Heads nodded in agreement as White-Star, Alejandra and Stephan headed through the portal.

Once the portal closed Gateway turned towards Armand and asked, "What was that? That display I witnessed from Georgie was unlike anything I have ever seen in all my journeys."

"I truly wish I had an answer for you," Armand replied quietly. "While it has been some time, I have seen him enter that state four times before. Not once was I able to discern its true nature. It seems to be some manner of connecting with magical abilities in the most pure and direct way. I have been looking for these answers since we first met."

"We all believed you to be the more powerful mage of the two, but when it comes

A Day at Georgie and Armand's Place

down to it, Georgie in that state… It is something to be admired and feared."

Armand looked protectively at Georgie, who was still reorienting himself. "On that, I fully agree. Best not to question Georgie about it though. He retains no memory while in that state."

"I understand."

"Now we have work to do down here," Armand announced loudly. "First off I do believe it is time to entrust another who has earned our trust in the secrets of the Hotel."

The three other mages gave their signs of agreement.

"Let us open the Vault and get that contraption safely put away," Armand said, gesturing towards the belt of Hearts of the Gods. "We have a lot to discuss. The Hotel is going to need a massive upgrade of spells now."

"And what of these?" Gateway asked holding up Rodfire's satchel filled with scrolls.

"Those will go in the Vault as well until we have a chance to go over them and determine just what they contain."

Georgie had reverted to his human form and was now standing in front of the Vault door. Armand, Sna and Mmm'ddeliommm took up their places in a line next to him. They went into casting spells they knew by heart, although they had rarely used them in the last thousand years.

The Vault door vanished to reveal a blinding glow beyond it.

"Oh, this is going to be so intense," Conrad said.

"Sorry, but you will be staying out here," Armand replied. "I do not believe you are ready to experience the contents of our vault. Chances are it would destroy your mind."

"Uh...Okay... I'm good with that," Conrad said. "Now how long is this going to take?"

"No idea," Armand answered. "Too many variables to consider. Hours, days, centuries. The Hotel needs time to heal and you are the functioning bandage for it."

"Ha ha, yeah. I get it. I never thought of you as having a sense of humor before. Seriously though, how long you think?"

There came no reply as the five mages vanished into the majestic light of the Vault.

"So... you're just going to leave me alone out here then," Conrad yelled after them. In a more subtle voice he said to himself, "Just great. I

A Day at Georgie and Armand's Place

save them all and this is the thanks I get. A living legend in music across countless realities, now trapped as a medical aid for a hotel... There's a song in that."

Conclusion of the Day

Armand had never seen his employees work more efficiently or with greater purpose. The events of the day had stirred a new sense of comradery in them. Even the employees who showed up in the aftermath seemed to feel it.

The Gatekeepers had already organized their people before Armand and the others had emerged from the vaults. While there was a lot of work to do, they were off to a good start. It had taken centuries to create the Hotel, Armand hoped it would not take that long to repair.

Despite the pain throughout his body, Armand was determined to be active in getting everything back in working order.

A Day at Georgie and Armand's Place

"Seriously though, would it have been too much to ask to be fully healed when we were connected?" Armand asked the Hotel as he looked up to the ceiling of the Nona'He Mountain lobby.

"I see you cringing with every movement," Georgie said as he came up behind his lover. He was now wearing a simple, undecorative blouse and faded jeans. His face was covered in bruises, with small cuts around his lips. He gently put his arms around Armand, making sure to not weigh him down. "You need to come back to our suite and get some rest. I will not have you falling dead doing managerial work when we have others, who did not almost die today, that can handle it."

"Yes, yes, yes," Armand replied. "I can keep myself alive for a little while down here. I have a few things I need to attend to, then I promise a long rest. Might take a day or two off even, well at least at a reduced work load."

"If you're going to be stubborn, I am going to be right by your side the whole time."

"Of course you are. And I wouldn't have it any other way."

"What important tasks are we working on now?" Georgie asked.

"First off we need to talk to him," Armand said, as he turned and looked at the diminutive form of Fringe, who had been standing quietly in a corner of the lobby, not trying to hide. "You will come with us to my office."

Fringe nodded his head and followed behind the dragons.

*****

Georgie made sure Armand took a seat in his desk chair before he was allowed to address Fringe. The glass container with the captured spell sat alone on the desk.

"I know you hate working from a desk, but for the next few weeks I do believe this will be the best place for you to manage from," Georgie said.

"That might not be a bad idea," Armand replied, upon realizing just how much relief he was getting by sitting down and being off his feet. "We can talk about that later. Let us first talk with our visitor here."

Fringe stood quietly just inside the door. His fingers were intertwined in front of his chest. The cold lenses of his mask gave no insight into

A Day at Georgie and Armand's Place

his emotional state. Despite his size and scruffy appearance, there were no signs of him being anything but confident.

"We owe you a great thanks for freeing us and allowing us to save this Hotel," Armand said. "I am aware of your dislike for us, so I am puzzled by your actions. Would it have not better served your beliefs to just let someone else take control or even just let it all fall apart and be destroyed?"

There was silence in the long moments as the Dragons waited for a reply.

"You are great sinners, of that there is no doubt," Fringe finally said, in a clearly artificial voice. "And it is truly horrific the amount of vile activity you allow to happen in this unique place. You two are an evil I know and can trust to sin in your ways. It was clear this new evil was something worse, with methods that showed him to be far more dangerous. And this place itself is innocent. You may allow sins to take place in it and commit countless ones yourself, but the Hotel is not guilty of that.

"The nature of reality and destiny are ever in change, and we must commit our actions based on the ebb and flow of those changes. Today your release was the needed solution. In other events I would feel no guilt in leaving you trapped. Don't mistake my actions for anything other than what was needed for the greater good."

"Understood," Armand replied.

"Now if I may go. I have no wish to spend any more time than I have to in such close proximity to undesirables, such as yourselves."

"Sure. And thank you again."

The cloaked humanoid quietly opened the door and quickly vanished from sight once he passed through it.

*****

The office fell silent as Armand closed his eyes.

"For all we went through today, somehow we were not done with being hit with surprises," Armand remarked with a weak laugh. "I seriously wondered at times if he was even capable of speech beyond his religious ranting."

"He's still such an unpleasant creature. The less contact we have with him the better."

"At least with him, we know where we stand and always will. He doesn't play games, always honest in his intentions. There is much to

A Day at Georgie and Armand's Place

admire there, if he wasn't so focused on the idea
that we need to be destroyed."

"That unpleasantness is done, what are the
other tasks that are keeping you from getting your
needed rest?"

Armand looked up at the ceiling then back
down to his desk.

"Hand me that binder behind you,"
Armand said.

Georgie turned to find the requested item.
He took it and handed it to Armand.

"Why are you looking through the lobby
listings?"

"I'm just double checking something."

Armand shuffled through the pages until
he found what he was looking for.

"Good, I never did like that name,"
Armand mumbled. "I think we picked it during a
period of heavy expansion and were just naming
the lobbies somewhat randomly."

"What are you talking about?"

"The Equitable Lobby. It houses the
doorway to Alejandra's home world," Armand
explained. "I believe we should rename it the
Kwando Memorial Lobby."

"Oh that is a perfect idea. Alejandra will love it. Although, she needs her rest as well. We can wait to tell her and make the change official on another day."

"Right. Rest is needed, and time to personally mourn."

Armand picked up the glass container with the black goo in it. He produced a pen and began inscribing various symbols on it. The markings glowed as he wrote.

"Protective runes? Do you believe that to be a threat still?"

Armand let out another laugh, "No. The magic has gone from it. Now it's just a blob of goo and trash. But it will serve as a reminder to not underestimate the simple things."

Armand slowly rose from his chair, clearly suffering pain with every movement he made. He placed the glass container on the bookshelf.

"Now I am finished. Things should survive without my supervision for a little bit," Armand said, letting out another laugh, which clearly hurt.

"You should stop laughing until you're healed up."

A Day at Georgie and Armand's Place

"I thought you wanted me to show more of a sense of humor."

"Not if it's causing you pain."

"Interesting that being near death loosens me up," Armand remarked. "I think I prefer being serious and focused, while being in good health."

"I think I prefer you that way myself,' Georgie replied. "All I know is I love you and that I will feel much better once I get you naked and curled up in our pillow nest."

"I have no doubt that will help me feel better as well."

Acknowledgements

The creation of this first book about Georgie and Armand's Place was a long process that took well over a decade to do. While I get credit for writing it, there is no doubt it was built on a great deal of work by others who helped me along the way.

Gotta start with my parents. Patricia, Howard and Dale. They always were there to encourage me in my creative endeavors. No matter how badly I failed to live up to expectations and potential, they still supported me and my dreams.

And I'll throw in a shout out to my girlfriend Lorelei and my boys Quinn and Hayden, who are the ones who have to put up with my madness and mood swings when I'm suffering from writer's block.

This all came about because of one Bryan Hineser, who as Game Master for a Rifts

A Day at Georgie and Armand's Place

campaign, decided to lead our characters into a cavern where we first got to meet Georgie and Armand. White-Star was my character in that campaign (His name is a reference to the Rangers in Babylon 5) and Bryan did make him pregnant after he had a one night stand with a six-breasted woman there. We also had a side-plot about him being cursed with hair that never stopped growing, unless he got a magical pink ribbon that Georgie for some reason had on display, that when tied in his hair would halt the curse. Gateway's story however never got played out until now. Bryan also created the world Conrad Pendragon is from. I do believe that is the extent of the elements influenced by him. He was excited when I told him I was wanting to do this project and graciously gave his blessing.

Writing this story has taken me a long time, as I had several false starts, often not really knowing what the big story was here. I had help from a writers group (No Name Heroes) in shaping the beginning of it. David Boop, Josh Vogt, Travis Heermann, Sam Knight, Holly Roberts were the ones who critiqued it I believe. The group had a good deal of members come and go, but I do not believe any of the others read my early drafts of this. Stant, Dana, Peter, if any of you actually did critique, feel free to take some credit. I do remember that it was Holly who pointed out that Georgie would not pick out his outfit to work in before he had chosen where he was going to start the day at. When writing, it is interesting to realize you overlooked something so basic that you wonder just where your mind was. Writer's groups are great at helping you fix your stupid slips like that.

Then there were my test readers. Josh Wash Whitby, gave me some good feedback, thank you. Michael Dryburgh went above and beyond as he often does for me, having put up with me since grade school, finding a lot of little 'opps' that made me feel really stupid at times (I promise I do know the difference between your and you're).

Lou Berger, who at one point I was thinking about hiring to edit. He did a really good edit of the opening story for me that helped me see a few of my flaws, one being the over use of 'started'. Was able to go through and cut a lot of them out with some simple editing that I feel improved the flow.

A Day at Georgie and Armand's Place

I finally settled on Virginalee Berger (No relation to Lou as far as I know) to edit it. Outside of the thousands of missing commas I had, the most common caught error seemed to have been sentence fragments. That happens. Had to fix it. But I do think in the end her suggestions helped a great deal. If this little story feels polished and smooth, Virginalee helped it get to that point.

Of course we have the beautiful cover by Chaz Kemp. He was nice and easy to work with. My original concept was a little crowded, which is what I suspected it to be when I first presented it to him. We settled on a much simpler design, giving the first visual representation of Georgie and Armand. In getting out and promoting this little book, there was no doubt people were drawn to the cover and liked it.

We also have Shawn 'Mac' Smith and MadCat, who did work on character images I used on the Facebook page I created to promote the book. Got a lot of beautiful rendering of these characters that had been only seen in my head before this. Some of the artwork did make me go in and make changes to character description, as what they came up with visually worked too well and needed to get included in there.

Ian Brazee-Cannon

So as with any undertaking it is not just one person who creates it all, it is a group undertaking and I had a great group that helped me get this thing together. What I have put out here would not be what it is without such a great deal of diverse influences in my life.

About the Author

Time for Ian Brazee-Cannon to write in the third person about Ian Brazee-Cannon and figure out how to make it all sound interesting.

Ian Brazee-Cannon has been called the 'greatest writing voice of a generation' by characters in his head. They call him a lot of other things as well, most of which are not suitable for polite company. He rarely associates with polite company though, so this is not something he normally worries about. If you do find yourself talking with one of these characters, they somehow having escaped from Ian's head, best not to believe a thing they say, as they cannot be trusted.

On the creative side, Ian keeps himself busy with writing, podcasting, film making, game designing and other creative endeavors. Over two dozen of his short stories have seen publication. 'Divided States of America,' 'The Fifth Di...', 'Wondrous Web Worlds', 'Forgotten Worlds', 'Tales of the Talisman' and various anthologies have featured his works. He has worked on supplements for the Ephemeris RPG. He is a founder and regular co-hosts on the Amateur Skeptics podcast. Dangling Carrot Films, Running Riot Productions and Ijin Studios have made use of him as a writer, director, producer and editor on their projects.

Ian has no need for pets, as he lives with his two teenage boys, Quinn and Hayden, who are incredibly bratty and difficult and he loves them more than anything. He also lives with his girlfriend Lorelei, who is herself a creative type as a musician and writer. The four of them live a highly geeky life and are active in many geeky activities in the Colorado geek communities.

Made in the USA
Las Vegas, NV
25 November 2022

60266371R10273